THE M1

EROTIC TALES of PLEASURE, PENETRATION & TRANSFORMATION

By A. Delight

7 Tantalizing Tales pleasure packed and graphic, full of juicy language and strangely amazing happy endings ranging in era from Victorian to contemporary and including alien abduction, mythical creatures, a mad scientist, virgins, a mugger, a terrorist, strange viruses, frequent penetration of all kinds, and of course, world peace.

Plus: Bonus Tales for even more pleasure......

THE MILKMAID

EROTIC TALES of PLEASURE, PENETRATION, AND TRANSFORMATION

Copyright © 2015 A. Delight All rights reserved.

ISBN: 1503050807
ISBN-13: 978-1503050808

The Milkmaid:
Erotic Tales of Pleasure, Penetration, & Transformation

Dedicated To:

Dear Friends & Delightful Orgasms

Table of Contents:

ABU'S BRIDE
(or How Abu Must Have Lost His Head in the Matter of Zina's Hymen)..Pg. 10

PENNY AND THE PILOT PROGRAM
(or Sizzling Sex for the Skilled Nursing Set) Pg.14

THE MILKMAID
(or How an ingénue from the country ends up the subject of some rare experiments, makes some shocking discoveries and finds herself rather transformed by them)
Part I..Pg. 23
Part II...Pg. 44

TAMALAINE'S IMPLEMENTATION OF THE NEW POLICY
(or An "Ace in the Hole" as Teen Temptations go Untempered)..Pg. 56

TIFFANY AND THE TROJAN TWINS
(or Out of the Monkey and Into a Menage a Trois)...Pg. 61

LORD FORTINROD'S CASTLE
(Or How Two Young Virgins receive a Proper Education and, As It Turns Out, a New Life)................................Pg. 70

LOVE NOT WAR
(or The Alien Elixir is Quite a Fixer)....................Pg. 93

Bonus Tales:

SISSY IN SEXXTASY
Part I..Pg. 125
Part II...Pg. 136

THE TAMING & TRAINING OF JULIA....................Pg. 153

SEXING IT UP ABOARD THE AQUADELIGHT
(or Love and Lust in a Submarine)......................Pg. 166

THE HOUSE IN THE THICKET
(or Miranda's Cherry for a Faery King)..............Pg. 198

BRAD & THE SEXTIFICENT GENIE
(or Strange Cure for a Dead Bedroom)...............Pg. 216

FORWARD

I offer up this body of work with one sole purpose: the promotion of personal pleasure. Be informed; however, that there are occurrences in these stories that are not for real life application. These stories are given with the assumption that most individuals are well equipped to determine for themselves what to try at home versus what to relegate purely to the world of fantasy.

In case of any confusion on the matter, however, I will state my firm belief that in real life, non-consensual sex is never okay. Nor would I condone or in any way recommend bestiality or the promotion of rampant sexual expression in institutions. In real life, I heartily encourage the use of safe sex. Nonetheless, this is a warning: In my stories, things that would be abhorrent or unwise in real life do occur on a rather frequent basis for your titillation.

That is because in my fantasy life, of which these stories are a mere outgrowth, I do not worry much about real life. There are things that turn me on in fantasy, that I would actually find revolting, disturbing, or upsetting in real life. That is the fact of it. In fantasy, one can eliminate all harmful consequences through creatively engineering entirely different outcomes than would otherwise naturally occur. As some of my stories actually illustrate, a different outcome re-shapes perception of the entire experience.

In real life; for example, an author would never encourage someone they love to go jump off a cliff without protective gear. That same author; however, would readily send a beloved character careening unprotected off a sky scraper or even the moon because the author trusts implicitly in their own ability to cause the character to sprout wings and land on a fluffy magic mushroom.
Similarly, whereas a person subject to non-consensual sex in reality, risks ending up with emotional scars, post traumatic stress and a sexually transmitted disease; someone who has had non-consensual sex in fantasy can instead end up ecstatically turning into a pink unicorn. In real life, the latter does not happen. I have no illusions about that and neither should you.

The way I see it, fantasy is a wonderful outlet for all the things you would not do in real life, but which still turn you on and can thus supply some pleasurable release when you are on your own.

Despite my generally liberal view on the subject, there are still some internal parameters in my work even so. My own sexual awakening was in full force at age 16 with many great memories which play into my stories. Nonetheless, I generally agree with the effort to safeguard girls at that vulnerable age by having a protective age of consent. Accordingly, I have carefully made everyone in my stories officially 18 years old or over.

Also of note, is the fact that I am passionate about happy endings and find suffering to be a major turn off. So, all my characters are lovingly cared for and anything odd or unusual they might go through is but a step on their journeys to be blissfully repaid in full. Ideally readers should know themselves well enough to know what they could best manage for their benefit.

To support readers in that endeavor, I will supply a rating and footnote for each story with clues as to content, which could be of particular concern to some readers. A little asterisk with footnote down below will specify questionable content nature. That said, we are all unique and I cannot anticipate everything that might be of particular interest to a specific individual. If anything is disturbing to you, it is fundamentally up to you to stop reading and engage self-care.

Basic rating system:

1*: within basic cultural norms, would have been publish-able as mainstream erotica. Accordingly, no footnote provided.

2**: Some outside-the-norm content

3***: May have some form of non-consensual sex, involvement of animals, (never at their expense), or other occurrence worthy of a trigger alert, (will be specified).

Additional notes: I have left out much in the way of specific descriptions of personal appearance. This includes body types except for special fantasy driven endowments. I have especially left out most cues as to color or race. The exception may be names and some pink nipples here and there as I have a penchant for pink. Generally, folks should feel free to imagine the characters as they see fit. The disclaimer being that I grew up enraptured by all white fairy tales and musicals, which inevitably shaped my erotic sensibilities. I suspect we are wired very young for what excites us most but also that we continue to evolve and adapt as we go through life.

At any rate, I make no assumption that what turns me on, will be appealing or even inoffensive to everyone. Perhaps, you will need to sift for what works for you and skim the rest. Go for it! I don't mind. At any rate, my sole aim is to provide something penetrating and pleasure packed; distinctive, and useful. If any of it thrills you, it has served its purpose. Enjoy!

Lastly: This is a work of pure fiction and any resemblance of characters or names to actual individuals is completely coincidental.

In a letter from a friend after she had read contents in full:

"The only thing I might add, but I don't know how to say this, is that you have an underlying philosophy that is deeper than just "the promotion of personal pleasure." You see personal pleasure as something that ripples out into the world and creates more love and ease and peace. You see personal pleasure as more important than cutting down forests to develop housing, or damming up rivers for electricity.

One of the things I have most enjoyed about reading your work (pure physical pleasure aside), is getting to see your view of a world in which love reigns. So maybe you don't want to write it here, but you have a manifesto in you, Angelica, that is about love and spirit and body and what is good for the world - and the pure and innocent goodness of the human mind and body and imagination - and someday I want to read it. I feel I have been given clues to it as I have read your stories. You are a blessing, and your view of the world has blessed me."—-H

ABU'S BRIDE (1)

(Or How Abu Must Have Lost His Head in the Matter of Zina's Hymen)

Abu Zomar had been given a young bride for his 21st birthday. Although she was already 18, she looked very young and was certifiably a virgin having been quite thoroughly overprotected from a tender age. Still, her figure was ample and ripe. The bump of her sweet nipples indelibly and gently popped through and the curves told true despite layers of modest draping fabric. Her hips gently swished when she walked. The promise of what was hidden inside that walk was like a tantalizing scent. Men could sense it and wanted to be near her, without even having seen her face.

When Abu Zomar got her home that first night, he was not sure what to do with her. His desire for her was so intense. He could have ripped off all that fabric and had her brutally quickly and been spent. But he did not want to do it that way.

Married men had already talked his ears off about having to beg or beat their wives to get their manly needs met at home. He himself rather suspected such things were entirely preventable with more careful handling. As a young merchant, the law of reciprocity was not lost on Abu. He knew full well how a transaction begun with kindness and courtesy would save much grief later. He was not so wealthy that he could afford more than one wife. Nor was he at all sure he would want the extra complexity in his life anyway. He knew he had best do it all right the first time.

But there was yet another, compelling reason that Abu wanted to get off on the right footing in the bedding with his brand new wife, as it were. Abu had heard and perhaps read in a few illicit books that even women themselves could have desire. They could come to yearn and want a man in their nethermost regions. Not just to please a man so that he would treat them well—no, it was something more. Women were said to have their own womb fire extending into their privates that could be teased out so that passion would have its way with them. In still other places he had read that they would become like purring sensual kittens, responding like sea anemones to your touch. If you seduced and caressed them, they would open up like flowers. They would sweetly and willingly yield their entire contents to your member and manhood. Then you could possess them entirely. Abu wanted all that.

Her name was Zina and she knew nothing of sex. She had had strange moments of hearing a bit of gossip and feeling flush, or a kind of pressure down *there*. But, she tended to pay little attention to such sensations., Beyond seeing at times knowing smiles and mysterious allusions to danger and taboo, she had no name or context for feelings of that kind.

On her wedding night, her mother had merely told her to just do whatever Abu wanted her to do, even if it seemed strange. But then on her wedding night, Abu had done nothing except watch her get undressed. Well that *was* a bit strange. He watched with such intensity. Had he never seen his mother or sisters outside of their modest dress? It was as if he had never seen a woman before the way he looked at her; as if he could consume every part of her with just his eyes. Then he had kissed her hand and left her.

Abu was supposed to have supplied to his family a cloth with virgin blood on it; proof of her pierced cherry. That would satisfy everyone of successful consummation. But, he had resisted saying that that was an old and unnecessary tradition. Zina was well known to be a virgin! He refused to rush her. They would get their cloth, but they would have to wait for it. Old men and women rolled their eyes. How difficult could it be? But Abu had always had a mind of his own. Apparently it was no surprise that his other head would be similarly wayward.

Meanwhile, Abu went out of his way to be kind to Zina. He bought her pretty trinkets and told her what an excellent job she was doing as she took on her responsibilities as a goodly wife in the household. He would even come up and work some beside her; helping her with a heavy load of wash or the water for mopping. He would come so close to her at times like these. She could smell the sweet musky scent of his sweat. He was such a rugged man but he somehow still managed to have clean fingernails and gentle hands. She could also see how strong he was. Sometimes he would brush up against her. Was it an accident?

Zina grew very curious. She begged her married female relatives and friends to tell her what she was waiting for or what was to happen. They were embarrassed and not even sure of the words.

They would only make hints about swans joining to make baby swans or about men and women being made differently but fitting together like a key and lock. Zina tried to imagine this fitting together but with difficulty. She also began to wonder about the waiting. Was it her? Had she done anything wrong?

Then Abu began to come to her when she undressed. He would just gently lay her down so that he could look at her like that. Every inch of her was like a luxurious delight to savor and drink in. After many nights like that, he began to ever so gently stroke her. He would drape her arms upwards so her hands were relaxed above her head. Then he would stroke her, starting with her flurry of long silky hair, her fresh rosy face, and, sweet tickles of nuzzling into her armpits to smell her. He stroked from top to bottom, everywhere except between her legs.

At first, she had tended to stay very still trying to figure this special treatment out. She wondered anxiously what would be next. But after night after night of this, she began to have more difficulty thinking her way through it. Instead, she began to have very pleasurable feelings reminding her of swimming in the ocean as a child or of that first delightful taste of ice cream. The sensations started to have their own brand new thrilling and inexplicable connections. Now, when Abu touched her hair, her nipples became erect. When he stroked around her breasts, she could feel it in between her legs; even though he was not touching there. With repetition, it was impossible for her to brush off these connections. Like her body connecting the dots, her body began to know things. Now, when she smelled his sweet musky scent, she could feel it in her breasts *and* between her legs, and he had not even touched her at all!

Abu could sense these changes in her and they were only intensifying his own feelings. One night, he slowly eased her legs apart, exposing the tender pouting flesh of her pussy. It was indeed like a sweet flower bud, closed up together so tenderly. He began to kiss her there, to her great surprise, finding the sweet little button of her clit which made her cry out in wonder. When the bud opened, and a little cream showed on her pussy lips, he knew it was time. He rolled on top of her, and with one hand, pulled those lips a little apart and slid his ample member into the tight vestibule. He lingered there for a moment with the head at the door, allowing her wetness to catch up, and then he pushed slowly but firmly into her. Zina moaned and cried out a little. She felt quite a stretch there where never before had there even been a finger or a tampon, so untampered and new it was. He was pushing, and filling her and pulling her quite apart to make room for his substantial member; full of pent up seed and bursting with desire. Abu could barely contain it now, he plunged and plunged in mounting speed until he veritably exploded and filled her with seeming months worth of jism; cascading into her in undulating ripples. He lay in her still while soft. Their bodies were like one body awash on an ocean of post orgasmic aftershocks and tingles. Then he was already hard again and could not get enough. He was insatiable that night, taking her again and again, this way and that---from behind and many positions. Amid it all, he kept reveling in feeling her beautiful breasts and kissing her sweet lips above and below.

Zina liked this new discovery, and made herself ready for Abu at every opportunity. She even sought to enhance his pleasure as he had hers, in ways she had never imagined. She surprised him too by slipping his member fully into her mouth and sucking until he came into her that way and she swallowed it all. They copulated everywhere and at any time of day. They were so eager not to lose time. Zina would be bending over washing the floor, and Abu would come up behind her and slide his member into her before she knew what had happened. Holding her hips fast, he would plow into her until he had gushed his copious wad in deep. She had so much semen coming into her from all directions now. The fluid kept filling and swimming in her and soon new life had started in her womb.

Oh—and Abu did eventually give the deflowering commemorative cloth to the family. It was hardly a proper one. Actually, it was more of a pink creamy mess rather than a blood blot. Abu was clearly so ecstatically happy with his new wife and she was going to have his baby. Really, what could they say?

PENNY AND THE PILOT PROGRAM***(2)
(Or Sizzling Sex for the Skilled Nursing Set)

Bernard Dowlinger was reading a newspaper in the nursing home lounge next to his friend Pete Frank.

"Hey Pete, you see they're implementing that cool thing we voted for. You remember?"

"Remember? That was the first time I'd gotten out to vote in 30 years. Can't believe we get to have sex."

The state of California had elected to have sexual services included in their MediCal program for folks in nursing homes or otherwise incapacitated with reduced access. What had begun with the Baby Boomers and further evolved by the liberal millennials had progressed. The healing effects of sexual activity were now fully recognized. Sex work had long since been decriminalized. It was now regulated purely by the health and safety department.

"But, Bernard, when do we get to fill out the papers?"

"I think they got 'em in the nursing station now."

Bernard and Pete slowly pushed their way out of the armchairs and leaned doggedly into their walkers. They made their slow way up to the nursing station just a few feet away.

The nurse looked a bit distracted but still responded kindly to their approach:

"Good morning, Mr. Dowlinger and Mr. Frank."

"Good morning, Nurse Connie," They both said respectfully. Then Frank came out with it:

"Hey—-we wanted to ask you: when do we get to fill out our sex papers?"

"Mr. Frank, they are hot off the press. You may have yours now, if you like. I guess you must have seen it in the newspaper. This is going to really be something else. But we've sure had enough meetings to prepare for it. I would hope."

Connie kept talking as she flipped through folders trying to find the bureaucratic wonder.

"Ah! Here it is."

---

* (Penny) Hired sexual services for institutionalized elders, medical experiments

* (Milkmaid) This Victorian Style fantasy epic contains non-consensual sex, medical

She handed them each the brand new hot-off-the-press papers and also pens to fill them out. They did as best they could to get all these materials back to their chairs while still keeping both hands on their walkers.

Once seated,

"Holy Mackerel, Pete. This is going to be good!"

Pete, smiling, did not really want to look away from his paper to speak.

"Yep, Bernard, it sure will, it sure will."

They perused what was actually a comprehensive questionnaire about their preferences. Pete cackled,

"Did you mark small, medium, or large titties, Bernard?"

"Actually, Pete, I kinda like those tiny pert ones with the big nipples"

"Bernard, you are something else. What did you put for activities?"

"Pete! a guy gets to keep some things private, don't he?"

Just filling out their forms made for a lot of laughs.

"You know, Bernard, I feel younger already."

Penny was new on the team having only recently passed her certification as a MediCal reimbursable sex worker. You had to have some other credentials in a healing profession in order to move forward with the process. It could be low level, but even so, you had to already be like a massage therapist, certified nurses aid, (that's what Penny had been), or an EMT, etc. Then you had to get all your shots. Boy that was a lot of vaccinations. Thank heavens they had vaccinations for STDs here in 2050 so you didn't have to worry about all that any more. Then you had to take CPR, universal precautions, and the special elderly handling class. Oh—you didn't want to be the one to break any osteoporotic bones or polish someone off with a heart attack. Might be a nice way to die, to go while in the act, but you didn't want to be the poor girl to see it happen! No sirree.

Penny was excited she had been picked and had her first couple of clients. She had dressed up really special with her pert little boobs pressed up in a push up bra and sporting a G-string and heels. Then, she got to wear over everything a white medical practitioner robe with her badge on the front, so the skilled nursing center would know she belonged.

Penny strutted briskly down the halls until she reached the proper room. Stepping in, she drew the skimpy privacy curtain, and said cheerfully,

"Hello, Mr. Dowlinger"

Bernard's body had been aching all over that day, but seeing this ray of sunshine just made him glow. She had already let her robe slide open so he got an immediate rush looking at her young, succulent, and supple body. It was all toned in smoothly round lines. He could see the curve of her nipple through the push up bra, how her tummy faded into her hidden pubes, and how tender and soft her bikini line looked. All that was down below. Up above, She had such an open and inviting face, with soft rosy lips and caring eyes. It took Bernard awhile to find words. Then, he tried to lean toward her. Squinting at her badge, he said:

"Hello, Penny"

"So, what can I do for you, Mr. Dowlinger?"

"I don't know what to say...."

"Well I read your paper and it said you might like this."

So saying, she slowly took off her push up bra for him, and leaned forward and put her nipple in his mouth. Bernard looked like he had gone to seventh heaven as he suckled that pert nipple. Penny noted with her eyes that he had already popped a tent. Seeing her eyes go that direction, Bernard commented,

"Yah—it is about the only part of me that still works."

Penny slid her hand down his chest and tummy until it landed skillfully on his cock and began stroking it.

"Oooh" Bernard moaned.

She leaned over and licked at the tip, teasing with her tongue. She pressed into the little indentation, rubbing circles with her tongue, and then popping the whole member into her mouth to begin to suck it whole. To get in a better position, she turned around and straddled him, so he was facing her pussy. Bernard took a finger and gingerly lifted the G-string aside to get a better peek and saw her pouting pink pussy lips in a soft little nest of hair. "Wow," was all Bernard could say and then he came. It was the first orgasm he had had in a very long time. He had forgotten how good they were!

Penny let him plunge his member in and out of her lips in orgasmic thrusts and spurt fully into her mouth. She swallowed his jism and then smiling, snuggled up to him like a kitten, pressing her tits up against him, and then turned and kissed his cheek. "Okay, Mr. Dowlinger, I think you're good. I'll see you next week."

Penny walked across the room to Pete; who had of course heard everything. You might get sex, but privacy was another matter. Of course who needs privacy, if you can get sex? Penny brightly greeted him with:

"Hello Mr. Frank"

Pete was ready.

"Helloooo, Penny. Boy am I ready for you. I am so excited I am just afraid I will end things before I've begun."

Sure enough, Pete's peter was already really hard and standing full erect.

"Well, Mr. Frank, let's take things a little slow then——you want to talk about something boring like physical therapy?"

"Please, no"

"Or, something interesting but off topic like sports?"

"No—thanks for trying, but all I want to talk or think about is you. Do what you will. If I come early, I'll get another chance next week, right?"

Penny reassured him in the affirmative.

"I saw from your paper, Pete, that you're a pretty kinky guy."

"It's true. I can't help it."

Penny slipped her bra down to expose her tits over the top and then she climbed onto the bed and squatted over him.

"Where do you want it to go, Pete?"

"You know where I want it, Penny. Can you really do that for me?"

Penny took both hands and parted her butt cheeks, and eased herself down the length of his erect member, working him into her tight ass slowly until he was in all the way. She squeezed and pumped up and down just a few times. As he had predicted, he came quick in a wave of ecstasy so intense, he was gasping and sputtering like a fish. He shot his wad into her in one gooey thrust. Penny slid off and then took wipes and ever so sweetly wiped him off.

"You bad boy," she said with a smile.

"Thank you, Penny. That just means so much to me. Now, I get to think about that all week instead of all the less pleasant stuff around here."

Penny reported for weekly health checks to make sure everything stayed in order; that she was healthy for them and they were healthy for her. Like software updates, there were often vaccine updates. It was at one of those health checks, that Penny was invited to participate in a pilot program. The pay was excellent. Really, it was about 3 times what she was already making and would be on top of her regular pay. The program would be for 6 months and with that kind of funding, Penny realized, she would be able to purchase one of those sweet little micro-condos for her very own in the heart of downtown instead of having to share housing with other working girls on the fringes of the city and commute; like she did now. Not that commuting was so bad but she did not want to have to do it her whole life. Anyway, this opportunity would give her a big boost and a safety cushion.

Penny did not ask for much in the way of information about the pilot program but it was just as well. They were not giving much out. It would require a brief in hospital procedure and then some follow up injections. Really, that did not seem like that big a deal; given the amount of vaccines she got on a regular basis. Penny signed the paperwork and made her appointment.

Penny showed up for the hospital procedure right on time; having followed the instructions and fasted. She got into the hospital gown and lay on the gurney as instructed. They put in an IV and began the anesthesia. They needed to identify what level of the serum they would be using, and how much her particular system could tolerate. It was easier to do all that under these controlled conditions.

They also needed to try different modes of entry to measure absorption rates. They tried under the tongue, in her cheek, up her rectum, up her vaginal canal, by injection in her gluteus muscle as well as in her arm. They also tried flooding her system by infusion and then measuring her body's resistance and what it would take to shut that down. Part of the pilot program plan was that bodies like hers would serve to naturally change the virus under designable means that other bodies would then be less resistant to. When they had found the particular pathway that worked best for her, they allowed her to become conscious again and gave her, her instruction package. She would have a series of just 3 high intensity injections in her butt. 'I can do that—no problem,' thought Penny.

After that first exposure to the serum, Penny did not notice a whole lot. One exception was that a mole she had had for years just disappeared. Also, sometimes at night all her skin would get tingly and she would feel flushed. But that was it and really, that was nothing.

Penny went to visit Pete and Bernard again.
"Mr. Dowlinger, how have you been?"
"As good as I can be without you, Penny."
"Well, let's see what we can do. You want that other, more traditional thing today?"
"Oh Penny, that would be so nice…"
Penny lifted Bernard's hands up to her bra to stroke her breasts through it, so he could squeeze them. Penny then pulled aside her G-string panties, so he could see her furry clit and lips. Then straddling him, she slowly rubbed her creamy pussy up and down the length of his cock and then expertly tilted her hips to the right angle to scoot back and push him in. Bernard moaned, as she leaned over him on her elbows, tits brushing his chest, and slid her hips up and down with a little gentle thump; her pussy squeezing tightly. She put his hands on her ass, so he could feel her that way as she worked him. Bernard felt the rumble of pleasure bubbling over. Then, there were waves and waves of it tumbling through him, such that he could not help yelling, "Uhhhh!".

A nurse came running, and yanked open the curtain and then said:
"Oh—right. Sorry!"
And closed it again. Bernard just laughed.
"I think it will be awhile for them to get used to the new program, Penny. They have had to think of us as sex-less for so long…"
"Well, there's no stopping you being sexed now, Mr. Dowlinger"

"Penny, by all rights, I really think you should call me 'Bernard' from now on"

Then per new norm, Penny stepped over to Pete, who was straining with anticipation.

"Are you having trouble waiting your turn, Mr. Frank?"

"This should make you behave"

Penny straddled Pete's face, sticking her perky clit right into his mouth.

"Lick me, Pete."

Pete dutifully started to lick her, while she patently ignored his already sizable erection for the moment. She toyed with her nipples in front of him, moaned and responded to his licking. Then she flipped over, so she could suck him at the same time, taking his cock back deep into her throat, exerting pressure with her lips and tongue, she expertly began to blow him while his face was buried in her pussy and covered with her cream. It was too much, and Pete came in chugging jolts, shooting wads of cum into her throat. Contrary to professional intent, Penny came this time too, writhing with pleasure, while his cock was in her mouth. He really had done such a good job with her clit. It was just a side benefit of the job.

Penny showed up for her health and pilot program check and they wanted to know of any changes. She told them about the mole. "Ah, good," the doctor said and then they gave her, her mongo shot in the butt. Later that evening, she thought she had a cold, but it only lasted a few hours. 'Must have been an allergy attack,' thought Penny.

The next week, when Penny went to see Pete and Bernard, they looked more energetic and like they were hornier than ever. In fact, they each wanted two rounds. A little tuckered from so much work at once, Penny strutted up to the nurse's station and asked the nurse:

"Hello. I was wondering if there have been any changes in Mr. Dowlinger and Mr. Frank's conditions. They seem particularly feisty today"

Nurse Connie looked up from her paperwork and said,

"Actually, now that you have mentioned it, we have noticed significant changes. Neither needs physical therapy anymore, and their medical conditions have been somehow diminishing. Mr.

Frank's chronic obstructive pulmonary disease seems to no longer obstruct! Mr. Dowlinger no longer shows signs of a very established cancer he formerly had. The changes are so extreme; we really don't know what to think, Penny. It is as if someone just came in and gave them each a magic pill. One thing for sure, though, they keep this up and they will no longer meet medical necessity…"

When Penny came in the next week, Pete was not in his room. She found him down the hall in Mrs. Jennings' room—actually up to the hilt in her ass.

"Mr. Frank! My goodness--"

"Just a moment, Penny, I'm kind of in the middle of something here. She said I could do it, Penny, and she is such a sweet thing. Oooooh um."

Mrs. Jennings did look sweet, like one of those very soft elderly ladies who had just stayed pretty her whole life.

"Are you okay, Mrs. Jennings?" Penny asked as Mr. Frank kept thrusting pleasurably away.

"Oh, yes, thank you, Penny—it's really rather nice—somebody wanting to do something with this old body—besides taking my vitals…and me and Pete go way back."

Penny then went in search of Bernard, only to find him similarly occupied, spooning and fully engaged in a carnal way with a Mrs. Feynmore. She had such a big smile on her face; Penny did not bother asking her anything. They looked really cute together, Bernard's arms clasped lovingly around her breasts, languidly pumping in and out of her.

With little work left to do, Penny reported back to the agency and let them know she could use more clients.

The pilot program would go on to be a great success. The genetically engineered virus that Penny had helped spread, would prove quite effective at eliminating or greatly diminishing the most prevalent diseases of old age. Between the great help via the new law and the boost the virus also gave to the libido, its spread would be expedited exponentially across the country. It would greatly reduce the need for skilled nursing facilities and enhance the sex lives of the elderly everywhere.

As for Penny, when she found out what she had been a part of—well; she was just tickled pink. Watching all that happy news while lounging in her cozy micro condo living room with the stunning view, she would think about Pete and Bernard; her very first clients. Penny smiled. No need to wonder what they would be doing now…

THE MILKMAID (3) ***

(Or how an ingénue from the country ends up the subject of some rare experiments, makes some shocking discoveries and finds herself rather transformed by them)*

PART I

A New Position

Lizzie was a frolicsome country girl, robust, and hardy. She had rosy cheeks and was amply endowed with a bosom hard to contain in laces such that it often overflowed. She was never one to work steady because she was easily distracted by such things as a beautiful sunset or the squeals of pigs mating in the pen.

Lizzie lived alone with her mother, a kindly widow, and they had fallen on some hard times. So, when the scout came to the house looking for work talent for the great Sir Rodney estate, Lizzie was excited to try for a position there. Being that her reputation for dawdling was already well established, everyone else was quite surprised when the scout made his announcement. Lizzie was apparently just what the Grand Estate had been looking for. Lizzie was to show up at such and such a time and bring nothing with her; even though she would be staying there for some months at least. All would be provided.

Lizzie arrived with only butterflies in her stomach and was invited into the servants' quarters and fed a delectable spread of food. Then she was promptly stripped of her clothing and given an array of garments to wear. The new bodice seemed a little small to her, so much did her bosom bulge at the top. Stranger still, the bloomers were of the crotch less variety; usually reserved for married women. Still, they would be most convenient. While busy working, she would not need to undo so much clothing in order to go pee. The best parts; however, were the petticoats and skirts. They were of such a softer and higher quality of fabric than she was used

---

* (Milkmaid) This Victorian Style fantasy epic contains non-consensual sex, medical experiments, bestiality, abduction, forced impregnation.

to, it was difficult not to simply linger and luxuriate, flouncing around and feeling them against her legs.

But, too soon after she had changed into her new clothes, a serious and severe butler hurried her into a grand library. There, she was surrounded by large well polished and ornately carved wooden furniture and over-sized upholstered chairs and couches. He told her to sit and wait. Once left there alone, Lizzie was unsure where to sit until she set upon the most normal looking chair in the room. She was in a nervous flutter by the time Sir Rodney came in.

Despite being well groomed, he had a rakish air. Sir Rodney told Lizzie in no uncertain terms that she had not actually been hired to be the milkmaid---although she should invariably continue in that official capacity for the sake of appearances. He had actually hired her to satiate his *peculiar tastes*. Should she consent to the real position, he could assure her that he would neither impregnate her nor besmirch her reputation, and anything that happened would only at most hurt a little. Furthermore, he would make it well worth her while. For all her time in his service, he would put her mother up in lush circumstance and grant every little thing she might need or desire. If Lizzie completed the entire term, a sizable nest egg would await her on the other side. But, she would need to cooperate with his every whim.

Cream and Milk

Lizzie was a little afraid but it was clearly too good a deal in her situation to turn down. She agreed and signed her name to a special private ledger Sir Rodney kept for that purpose. He then told her with a glint in his eye that she should go get a good rest because milkmaids have to get up early in the morning and one of the cows is quite ornery.

Early in the morning while doing battle with that cow, Lizzie thought, 'ornery is putting it lightly.' Lizzie was earnestly perched on the little stool; clutching and pulling down on those cow teats. It was no time at all before the cow gave a sudden kick and both Lizzie and the bucket of milk were upended on the ground. Milk spilled everywhere. At just that moment, Sir Rodney walked in. Lizzie was mortified.

"What have we here? You do not seem to have done a very good job! But remember, Lizzie, that is not what you are really here for."

Instead of helping her up, sir Rodney used his riding whip to push her down further so she was lying face down in the milk. He used the whip to lift up her skirts to expose her bloomers, where the round rise of her buttocks could be seen through the muslin. Prying yet further with the end of the whip, he toyed with the folds of the crotch-less bloomers.

Almost as soon as he had come, he was gone. As if on cue, a maid entered the room and began fussing over Lizzie---what had she done, and was she all right, and "we'll get you all cleaned up in a jiffy".

It was with an understandable bit of dread that Lizzie returned the next morning to her milking task with the ornery cow. But this time the cow just mooed pleasantly. Lizzie was able to successfully squeeze her teats in rhythm; squirting loads of milk and cream into the bucket. So occupied with this task, she was, that she did not even hear Sir Rodney come in. He crept down and hugged her from behind, raising her up, smelling her neck, and holding her bosom. Then he tugged up her skirts and parted her bloomer folds. With the other hand, he scooped some cream off the top of the milk bucket, and before Lizzie knew what was happening, he had slid his creamy fingers in between her legs, feeling and getting intimate knowledge of every crevice and cranny while holding her fast, until he ended by sticking his finger slowly up her ass. Lizzie let out a gasp and instinctively tried to wriggle free, but he held her tight with his finger still there. He whispered he had to go now, but would have that more fully later. Then, he released her. Lizzie turned around just in time to see Sir Rodney walking out of the room with a flushed face and a very large barely contained bulge in his pants, that seemed to make walking a bit difficult.

As Lizzie was straightening her things, a maid peeked her head in and loudly announced,

"The master says you are not to clean off any cream."

"What?" Lizzie exclaimed.

"You heard. The master says to leave the cream *on*."

So Lizzie went about her affairs the rest of the day with a lot of cream between her legs and on her backside. As the day wore on, the cream became a pastier and pastier consistency and seemed to sensitize everything in the region. She was now acutely aware of her pussy lips when she walked and they seemed to be lusciously rubbing a special spot at the top as she moved. Lizzie was so distracted by this condition; she could hardly focus on anything at all. By evening, Lizzie was wondering how she could have ever ignored such a sensuous part of her body before. So sweetly and insistently did her nether regions call to her at every moment; sending little tendrils of pleasure up her womb and even up her butt. Lizzie had never heard of anything like this before and wondered if perhaps Sir Rodney had put some strange spell on her with his "peculiar tastes."

Lizzie was fully undressed and about to put on her nightgown when her musings were cut short by an entourage of maids bursting into her room. They bodily picked her up, bundled her up in her bedding and proceeded to carry her up to a special room in the master's quarters where they placed her on a very fluffy bed. All disheveled and unnerved, Lizzie tried to keep the sheet about her breasts as she met the gaze of Sir Rodney. He had a big expectant smile on his face. He made a gesture to the maids and they set about pulling up metal loops in the bed to which, She could see they intended to tie her up. Lizzie exclaimed that she did not need to be done this way. Had she not agreed to serve his every whim? Why then would he do that? Sir Rodney said that he liked to see her so and it would help her stay still for what was to come.

After unwrapping her like a present and raising her knees, the maids began to tie her ankles and wrists and even clasp a little strap over her waist to keep her immobile so that she was quite vulnerable and her downy pussy with the cream still on it was there in the open for all to see. Lizzie was blushing up to her roots but there was nothing for it. Sir Rodney told the maids, "Go get them now." Lizzie waited what seemed an interminably long time under Sir Rodney's interested gaze, to see what "*they*" were.

In walked the maids all a giggle with a large basket of very young mewing puppies. They were gently placed on the bed underneath her raised legs, close enough to her tender parts that they could smell and start pawing their way toward her. For good measure, and under Sir Rodney's approving eye, the maids periodically added a bit more cream. Puppies and cream were added to her breasts as well. The sensations were so intense it was at times impossible for her to not cry out, moan and writhe. Amid the busy action of so many tiny tongues, she was alternately tickled, aroused, and ever so slightly discomfited. The hungry puppies were quite unpredictable and she could not see where they would turn up and what they might lick next. One could be suckling her breast, while another was lapping and had gotten a tiny tongue under the hood of her clit and yet another had slid its tongue right up her butt. Lizzie gave up trying to track what was happening as waves of sensations rocked her frame, making her breasts jiggle and quiver and her back involuntarily arch under the amused gaze of so many maids and Sir Rodney.

He had pulled up a bit closer to see her all the more clearly. The bulge in his crotch was very large now, and there was a little split starting in his fine pants. He pulled a maid onto his lap as he watched and toyed with her breasts. At last, Sir Rodney made a gesture and the puppies were gathered up, the ties unfastened, and a very exhausted and pinkly tenderized and cleaned of all cream Lizzie, slowly sat up.

A Cup of Chamomile Tea

Lizzie was led to a large warm pool covered in rose petals and invited to bathe. The water was so relaxing and soothing after all the recent excitement. From there, she was given a brew of chamomile tea, bundled off to her comfy bed, and told to sleep well.

In fact, she slept so heavily that she did not even hear when Sir Rodney came quietly into the room. The tea must have been very strong indeed because she felt so groggy, she could barely move. After slipping his hands into her nightgown and caressing her breasts, Sir Rodney rolled her onto her tummy and raised her hips, lodging a little lacy pillow under her loins. He eased up her nighty and began to stroke the soft fluffy down between her legs but then put his finger on the tight little hole at the top. He smoothed a rose scented balm into it with his finger. Lizzie could vaguely hear his belt buckle coming undone and the sound of breeches unbuttoning.

Then, she could feel this hot and fleshy tool right up against her buttocks. It was so large. Where indeed had he been hiding it? He could not mean to fit all that in that tiny space meant for other purposes.... But, in her present condition, it even seemed mildly amusing and she could hardly be anxious. He began to rub into her there, pulling apart her butt cheeks with his hands, his strong member standing firm and exercising its own right of way.

Lizzie was so relaxed from the strong chamomile that she could not have resisted if she tried. Sir Rodney would move into her just a little, and ease up against the tightness, then press on harder still. In this way, he gradually made way until his huge member was stuffed fully in up to the hilt. She was veritably pinned by it, having such hardness lodged so deep up such a sensitive and private part. Then he began to pump faster and faster, moaning to himself with pleasure as he did so. At one point he reached around to touch her clit---expertly rolling it gently like a little gelatin jelly bean under a tender fleshy blanket. All the sensations of the day seemed to build for Lizzie and she began to have what turned out to be her first ever orgasm which meant she involuntarily clenched her buttocks, making the pressure even tighter for him. In spasms of churning plunges, he could hold out no longer and came also, spewing gooey hot semen deep into her ass. Sir Rodney then slipped sumptuously out and just left her there. She was too tired even to move. Buttocks in the air and semen dribbling at her crack, she fell into a deep sleep, full of very sex-filled dreams like she had never had before.

If Lizzie was a bit distracted before, she was doubly so now. It was difficult for her to think of anything that did not now remind her of her private parts or Sir Rodney's substantial tool and what he might do with her or it next. Sir Rodney had given her a day off to go visit her mother, but in a state of confusion, she realized she was not sure she even wanted to go. Dutifully; however, she went. Her mother was per agreement living very well and delighted with the great help of Lizzie's salary and new position. She was eager to know how well Lizzie was obeying her new master and how she liked the work there.

Mr. Boss

Lizzie returned to the estate in a craving state she had never experienced before. How had she been awoken thus that she wanted and wanted and knew not what?

Meanwhile, Sir Rodney had left a note for her. She was to meet him in his menagerie where he had captive all manner of exotic creatures from near and far that he wanted her to see. A maid showed her the way so she would not get lost but then giggled and left her there. It was a vast space with large glass cages encasing not only rare animals of every kind but also impressive habitats including lush plants and deep pools. There was no other sound except the rustling of animals. Presently, Sir Rodney showed up and asked if she liked it. Lizzie said it was all quite amazing.

Sir Rodney led her into a little tiny room off to the side with all manner of equipment and a busy round scientist in a lab coat, named Dr. Mm. They were doing some experiments of interest on the copulatory habits of high level animals; only the most special specimens in the entire menagerie. She would be their human subject, but first, he would need to examine her. Lizzie obliged by getting into the patient apparel granted her, which like all such, barely really covered anything. She got up on the exam table and Dr. Mm pulled down his magnifying goggles and with little fanfare, split her legs and stuck a newfangled speculum right up her vaginal canal, prying her a little open. Lizzie had never had such a thing happen before. They did not have such gadgets where she was from. Peering in, Dr. Mm told Sir Rodney:

"She will do very well." He then took a little bottle and squirted a little goo on her pussy. Then he gestured that she was all done.

"What was that?" Lizzie asked.

"Oh, just a little animal attractant scented lubricant," Dr. Mm mysteriously answered.

Dr. Mm explained that they had an alpha albino male chimpanzee, by the name of "Mr. Boss" who was exceedingly frustrated these days and getting increasingly aggressive. They had a theory that if he could just successfully copulate, he would become more docile and manageable again. Adding to the value of the experiment was the titillating question as to whether they could get the animal to mate with a human female. Although, the way the chimp had lately been behaving with female animal keepers, it seemed as if such activity would be quite agreeable to him. Nonetheless, for scientific purposes, Dr. Mm assured Lizzie, they needed to see the act actually take place. Absorbed with processing all this new theoretical information, it took Lizzie a moment to realize that they were talking about using her! She thought of trying to flee, or backing out of the deal. But, how could she when all was going so well?

Dr. Mm could see Lizzie was getting a bit stressed, and he whispered something in Sir Rodney's ear. Sir Rodney gave the affirmative, and a cloth was moistened with some substance and put promptly to Lizzie's face.

When she later awoke, she was naked and on the other side of an enclosure. She could see nothing through the one way glass but could well guess that Sir Rodney and Dr. Mm were avidly watching. 'Oh my goodness,' thought Lizzie with some indignation. 'Don't they realize I'm a virgin?' She had assumed Sir Rodney would have taken that pleasure for himself. Although, now that she thought about it, he did seem more interested in other things. Still, how could he leave her to have her cherry picked by a chimp? Lizzie looked around the habitat to get her bearings. There were a couple trees, shrubbery, a nest of leaves and various climbing apparatus. Lizzie knew better than to try to run anywhere, even if she could think of where to go. Whenever she ran as a child, it just made boys, dogs or anything else chase harder.

Lizzie's musings were cut short when suddenly, out of the bushes came Mr. Boss in all his glory and in full display. He came her way thrashing, waving branches, and grunting loudly. When he actually saw her; however—or rather, caught a *whiff* of her, he stopped in his tracks. He seemed momentarily uncertain of his good fortune. Coming over and smelled her, grunting, preening at pieces of her hair. Then he summarily picked her up, and tossed her lightly over his broad shoulder. He carted her off and dropped her neatly into his nest.

Lizzie was in a state of shock as she lay on her back in the nest. She could immediately tell that this grunting animal knew exactly what he planned to do with her. She tried helplessly to cover her privates with her hands, but Mr. Boss tossed her hands easily aside and honing in on the prime spot informed by a formidable instinct, rooted with his boner toward her tight virginal opening and found purchase. With the help of Dr. Mm's lube, one firm push and just a little cry from Lizzie, he achieved full penetration. Holding her in an extremely strong but still gentle grip, Mr. Boss drove his primate member into her with a kind of fevered urgency; his white fir rubbing against her skin. As he pumped and pumped with growing gusto and speed, Lizzie was just starting to think that this was actually not so bad when she noticed with some chagrin that it really felt quite good and kept getting better. Almost against her will, her lips parted and she started making noises she had never heard herself make. It was almost as if she were receiving an intensely sumptuous whole body massage but from the inside out. All at once, Mr. Boss ejaculated inside of her, loads of Chimp goo. Then he stroked her hair and fed her a banana until Dr. Mm came and let her out.

Sir Rodney and the doctor were delighted with their experiment and announced it roundly a success. Back to the exam room she went. They took a sample of the monkey jism from her pussy and then allowed her to take a much-appreciated bath.

Lizzie was beginning to wonder how she could ever return to normal life after these adventures. She would never be able to tell anyone that she had been deflowered by a chimpanzee! Even more confusing to her sense of reality was that, well, she had enjoyed it. She felt marked as a sexual plaything now. It seemed her primary existence would simply be to continue to do the bidding of Sir Rodney.

Sir Rodney, knowing the enormity of her most recent project, gave Lizzie some time off to recover. Lizzie had another day off to go visit her mother. While she was there, she found herself unbearably randy which was such a new sensation yet. What was more, it was as if the village boys could tell. They would smile at her and she would find herself smiling back and getting creamily wet. They would then smile at her again and it seemed as if it would never end. One of them, named Dick, came up to her and said,

"It seems like you've changed, Lizzie, what have you been doing up at that there estate?"

Lizzie blushed and said,

"Only what I'm told to do, Dick. You know that."

But the banter and teasing went on until finally it was time to head back to the estate.

Of Piggy Pillows and Ponds

Lizzie arrived refreshed but in such a state; her bosom heaving, her pussy perpetually wet. What had Sir Rodney done to her? Sir Rodney arrived at her room and asked how she was liking her assignments and whether she had learned anything in the course of them. He had a small smirk but also seemed genuinely interested.

"I'm changed, Sir Rodney and I don't know what to do. I think about the things you have had me do night and day and seem always to be in the midst of unrequited arousal."

"Poor Lizzie, I will send you someone to help you."

Later on in the day, as Lizzie was changing her clothes, a maid entered her room and bade Lizzie sit on her lap. Lizzie found this a bit odd but profoundly comforting; the soft mound of the maids breasts behind her and her hair falling on hers. Lizzie breathed deep and relaxed as if returning to her very own mother as a newborn. The maid's name was Amelia. Amelia took hold of Lizzie's hand in hers and showed her how to stroke her own parts in a soothing motion, something that Lizzie had somehow never dared to do. Then she had Lizzie get up and lie down next to her. She showed her how with her legs up, she could use one hand to penetrate her fingers in from the side while the other hand rubbed juicy circles on the flesh above her clit. Amelia gave Lizzie names for these things; the names she liked: "clit," "pussy," and "pussy lips." Amid some delicious giggles, she had her say the words slowly as they rubbed and frigged themselves rather silly. It took awhile and some work, but then the build came and Lizzie could feel powerful pulses throughout her body and even into her toes as she arched and contracted in a massive orgasm.

Amelia smiled sweetly and then nodded toward a side wall, where it turned out the eye of Sir Rodney was there peeping. Amelia tucked a much more relaxed Lizzie in, and turned to go, but Lizzie asked, couldn't she stay awhile and sleep there? So they spooned and slept the night.

The next morning, Amelia was gone, and Lizzie was rudely awakened by the butler. He said,

"You are neglecting your duties. The cows *still* must be milked. Sir Rodney said I can give you a little spank, if you misbehave."

With that, he peremptorily pushed her over the side of the bed and lifted her nightgown. He proceeded to slap her smartly on her bare dimpled cheeks until they were red. It was only the briefest of moments but it made a big impression. Shocked and a bit indignant, Lizzie dressed hurriedly and rushed off to the barn. She set to work immediately and was so preoccupied with what had happened, she again did not notice Sir Rodney come in.

He asked what had happened, and she told him the frightful story. He asked if he could see the damage, so she pulled up her skirts and down her bloomers for him. He tenderly cradled her rosy ass, and bent down close to look at it and kiss it. Then he led her over to a large sleeping pig. He pushed her implacably into position so she was on her knees but her bosom and arms were nesting on the strange fir of the pig. He then snagged some cream. Hoisting up her petticoats, he creamed in between her cheeks and eased himself in. He got in much quicker this time, it no longer being virgin territory. He slid right up her ass, making her moan. To her surprise and embarrassment, she was actually starting to like this. The penetration was so hard, deep, and thorough. Being entered thus consumed her whole focus. The motion increased in speed and intensity such that he was really starting to ram her. Again he reached in front to touch her pussy. Her clit was now so much more trained, it responded immediately. Choking back the cry bursting from her throat, Lizzie had a huge orgasm. Clutching her buttocks uncontrollably, she milked Sir Rodney into his own frenzied state until he had again inserted loads of cum into her bottom.

The pig was beginning to stir at this point, and so Sir Rodney picked Lizzie up and carried her out of the pen. He told her what a good job she was doing—but that he may have a more difficult assignment for her yet. She should meet him at half past Three at the menagerie.

It was morning yet and so the appointed time was still a ways off. Lizzie tried to keep her mind off of it because whenever she thought of the anticipated appointment, apprehension would seep in. She would even again contemplate running away. As if her mental state were known, Amelia showed up at lunchtime and suggested they go swimming in the pond. This was the perfect distraction for Lizzie.

Like two children, they ran off down the path. As they ran, they unlaced their bodices and their breasts tumbled out. Eager to be unfettered, they slipped out of their petticoats and bloomers. Jumping into the water, they were like mermaids together. Amelia commented that Lizzie sure was a strong swimmer. Indeed she was. She propelled herself with ease, making graceful ripples in the water. They played together until they were tired. Once on dry land, they cuddled together on the warm flower filled grass and basked in the sun.

Amelia asked Lizzie if she knew any special ways to pleasure a woman? Lizzie exclaimed,

"It is all so new! But I really would like to pleasure you."

And so Amelia pulled Lizzie down, and guided her face so that her lips were nestled neatly into Amelia's pussy mound. Then she drew Lizzie's hips over her own face, so planting Lizzie's pussy onto Amelia's waiting tongue. Lying on top of each other opposite like this, Amelia began to show Lizzie the kinds of licks and touches that would feel especially good to her and Lizzie could begin to emulate them. Lizzie also tasted, for the first time, the tangy taste of pussy juice and felt that softness of those more private lips on her own. Lizzie became fully immersed in the pleasure of scents, tastes and textures. Simultaneously, she was thrilled by the sensations aroused in her own tingling tender parts, as perfectly stimulated by Amelia's skillful kissing and licking action.

They were so well and happily occupied, that at first they hardly noticed the change in weather. Clouds passed above them and converged, letting loose a warm spring rain. What began as a light sprinkling, soon grew heavy like a gushing waterfall. The spring showers made their naked bodies a new kind of fresh and slippery. Lizzie and Amelia continued their watery lovemaking with abandon amid the soft grass and wildflowers.

They could have gone on luxuriating like this for awhile, but the butler arrived all wet and bothered. Seeing them naked and so carnally engaged, he looked a bit shocked. But, he still found words to remind Lizzie that she had an appointment. She must not be late or he would have to spank her again.

Peculiar Preparations

Lizzie had lost all track of time! Trying to dry herself briskly and hop into what were now very damp clothes, she rushed off to the menagerie. She arrived all out of breath. Dr. Mm was there in his lab coat and seemed quite pleased as he led her into the exam room, helped her easily back out of the damp clothing, all the while mumbling how this would be the most exciting copulatory experiment of all. He asked her hurriedly, had she eaten anything since breakfast? Actually, she realized, she had missed lunch. Lizzie thought with longing for a moment of what luscious things she had been doing instead.

"Excellent! You are fasting; perfectly per plan," Dr. Mm exclaimed.

This time, when Lizzie lay down on the exam table, Dr. Mm had her turn over. Taking out a hypodermic needle, he swabbed her butt with alcohol and gave her an injection.

"Ouch," Lizzie said. "What was that for?"

He told her that it would help her with temperature regulation and other functions for a prolonged stay under water. Lizzie asked if she could turn back over, but Dr Mm said, "Not yet." Out of the corner of her eye, she saw that he was holding a large green bumpy and slimy thing that looked like a very large pickle only it moved slightly and she thought she saw eyes. Dr. Mm said that Sir Rodney had reassured him she could handle this without an anesthetic. Lizzie gasped as without more ado, he parted her cheeks and shoved the slimy bumpy creature decisively up her butt. It seemed to stick and would not come out, even though she could not help but try for a moment to bear down and squeeze it out.

"What was *that* for, Dr. Mm?"
"That is a sea cucumber, which will funnel food to you from the water and consume and process your waste in return. Don't worry, we'll get it out when all this is over."

Then back on her back, he fitted her with a special mask that adhered tightly to her face and mouth, including a tube part that went deep into her mouth so she could not now speak. He explained that this mask was specially designed to filter oxygen out of the water so she would be able to breath under water. They had already observed that she was a good swimmer so now she would have everything she needed to be fine when they put her in the tank. Sir Rodney came in then to see how things were going. Seeing Lizzie in her new get up, he looked well satisfied that all was in order.

Sir Rodney then paused and said,

"Lizzie, I have been thinking. I know we have a deal, but how about if we change a little part? Would it be all right to impregnate you? If I may, I will keep you and your children permanently in good condition. They will have all they need in education and material comforts. Your mother too, will be extremely well cared for, and the nest egg we spoke of will be quadrupled. What do you say, Lizzie? Nod yes or no."

At this point, Lizzie could not imagine ever going back to normal life. As nerve wracking as all this was at times, it was also so titillating and interesting. She hated to admit it, but she was also starting to have feelings for Sir Rodney. She was flattered that he was interested in getting her pregnant and keeping her around. Without much more thought, and knowing that it was a little difficult to think with that mask in her mouth and a sea cucumber up her butt anyway, she nodded, "Yes." Sir Rodney clapped his hands in delight. Nodding to the doctor, Dr. Mm then prepared another hypodermic needle and gave Lizzie another shot, only this one was a much bigger one. "Ouch," Lizzie tried to say. "I thought those were all done." but it only came out "Wahwahwah."

Then they helped Lizzie up and led her to a very large tank habitat. It was so large, it was difficult to see the end of it. The part she could see was brimming with plants, algae, fish and other creatures. It was deep, mysterious water but quite beautiful as well, with rainbows of color and bubbles of oxygen being pumped in and the undulating of plants and micro flora that shimmered in the filtered light. It seemed to be calling to her.

Sir Rodney and Dr. Mm helped push her up the steep ladder and unlocked the lock at the top. They dropped her into the large pool and locked the tank back above. Lizzie found that, to her relief, there were some floating seaweed covered fish homes like mini coral reefs that she could rest on; although there was no way to be fully out of the water. The temperature injection worked well because she felt the perfect temperature and the sea cucumber must be working also, because despite having missed both lunch and dinner, she was not in the slightest bit hungry. She did feel very sleepy though. What had been in that last big shot that they did not tell her? She wondered in sleepy fragments as she drifted off to sleep.

Castlemar

Lizzie awoke as she was being dragged fiercely downward to the very bottom of the tank by her feet. Once there, she saw an amazing creature. He looked man-like in some respects, with long hair floating in every direction, but he had gills in the sides of his neck, webbing between his fingers and toes, and a dorsal fin on his back. His coloring was also like none she had ever seen. His skin was pale in parts but alternately purple, pink, and green in others. He also looked exceedingly powerful. Lizzie could sense how predominantly curious he was about her at that moment. He touched the mask on her face. Holding her down, he ran his webbed fingers over her body and felt her nipple as if examining how supple it was. Unlike with the chimp, Lizzie could feel the intelligence of this merman. He might even be smarter than her, so piercing and knowing was his gaze.

He reached out and caught a fish with one hand and swallowed it in front of her, studying her while he ate. Then he scooped her up to him, holding her in a tight embrace, as he spun in circles, swam energetically around the tank. She was dizzy by the time he stopped. She did not even attempt to resist as he he stroked her hair and fondled her breasts. She noticed that there was a fold at his groin, and watched amazed as out of it popped a huge fleshy member. It looked meaty, throbbing, and a deep purple. The mer man lodged her against a mossy rock on the side of the tank for leverage. Holding her firmly, he pushed this alien seeming rod into her little plush pussy. It was so large, that she could feel herself having to stretch to accommodate it, so tightly around. It felt so heavy and hard, like he was shoving a flesh covered weighted piston into her. Lizzie tried to cry out but nothing came out of her masked face. The sea cucumber was likely only enhancing the tightness of the fit.

Once he hit all the way home, a strange thing happened and she felt a slight pain, as if the opening to her womb was being pierced and something else was sliding even further into her. Simultaneously, waves of a kind of euphoria started to pour through her as the mer man began to plunge and plunge, and there was that strange other even deeper plunge happening. It began to feel better than anything she had ever felt before and she would have never wanted it to stop except that at one point it was so intensely good that in her excitement, she had begun to hyperventilate and even start to pass out. She revived just as the orgasm hit. It rocked her body like none before and seemed to be sucking in the merman's juices like a whirlpool with each orgasmic shudder, as if none of it could escape into the water, but must get sucked all the way in to her womanhood. Riding faintly above those waves of pleasure was that strange slight sting but then when the dense copious semen flowed in like hot marshmallow topping and stopping her up in every way, it made her forget and all she felt was amazed relief and sudden blissful fatigue. The mer man grabbed some strong seaweed and fastened her legs together, then tied up her wrists so she would not untie them. He swam carrying her to a soft nest of seaweed, and left her there for a time.

Lizzie wondered, as she lay there drifting off: would Sir Rodney and Dr. Mm ever really get her out? Or would they just leave her here as the mer man's plaything and part of the exhibit? But she became so very sleepy; it was difficult to keep up those trains of thought.

In Like Fin

When Lizzie awoke, her breasts were a bit fuller and the areolas had darkened. There was also a little bulge at her lower belly. The ties were off her wrists and legs and she was free to swim around. Strange sore spots were etched in her neck like striped cuts and her back ached. Then there were the little areas between her toes and fingers. They itched. Not sure what all this meant but determined to keep her own spirits up, she had just thought to go look about the tank when she began to notice still more: the spots on her neck opened and closed and she suddenly realized that they were fledgling gills, like the mer man's. That must be why she was able to breath without her mask, which she noted, was now gone. There seemed to be some fold keeping her from inadvertently breathing in through her nose. She put her hand on her back and felt a bump there, like something would be popping through the skin soon.

"Well, you were the one saying you were not ready to go back to normal life!" Lizzie sighed to herself.

Lizzie began gradually to adjust. One morning she woke up to feel and hear strange vibrations wafting against her ears---they were strange sounds like she had never heard before and slowly, they began to string together and form messages that made sense, as if her mind were learning how to interpret them. She heard Castlemar, as the mer man was called, telling her all manner of things; including how the humans thought they were experimenting on him. But, actually his people were experimenting on the humans. The mer people's gene pool had become too small and inbred and so they had to find a way to expand. The serum Dr. Mm thought he had discovered had actually been carefully planted for his discovery. That was the serum that had been injected into Lizzie, so she would pop a bunch of good eggs out of her ovaries in optimal rhythm for the Mer Man to harvest them with his seed. In the course of coitus, when she had felt that sting, his special other member had punctured into her cervix and entered her womb. There it claimed the very best eggs and sent powerful swimming sperm into two of them, making sure they implanted. Every pregnancy was a sure thing for the mer people.

"Why two eggs?" Lizzie wondered and heard the response:

"Because you only have two breasts"

Castlemar then informed her in no uncertain terms that she was his woman now and it was time to meet the others. Others? Lizzie had had no idea there was any other sentient being in this exhibit and she was both extremely curious and a little frightened at a group of these magnificent powerful creatures.

She soon saw there were no children among them but a bunch of elder mer men and women, all eyeing her meaningfully. Since their privates were hidden internally behind a slit, much like a dolphin's, her pouting soft pussy lips, now even plumper and spongier from pregnancy, were subjects of substantial fascination. Everyone wanted to touch them and she gave up trying to fend them off. Lizzie could see also that the elder Mer women had 4-6 breasts.

A Time to Eat Fish

Castlemar proclaimed to her that it was time she start eating fish, as it would be good for her babies. The sea cucumber could not provide high enough density nutrition to support her pregnancy. The idea of eating raw fish revolted Lizzie and she got severe morning sickness at the thought. The elders chatted together and came up with another way, but the sea cucumber would have to come out. Lizzie cried "no!" She did not want her sea cucumber to come out. She was terrified of embarrassing herself and soiling the water. They reassured her not to worry about it:

"Around here, we have a fish for everything."

Supporting her body with her legs held up high, they put a special fish near her bottom. This seemed to lure the sea cucumber toward the opening. It poked out enough that they could then catch it and pull. Lizzie shuddered as the bumpy, slimy animal slid out of her butt.

It turned out that their plan was to feed her a raw fish stew they made, up her ass. The elder women thought any activity with her interesting human body was quite fun. It was nothing to them to pull her cheeks apart and insert fish stew into her butt and then pinch her cheeks and wait for her to absorb the nutrition.

For Lizzie; however, this activity got old very quickly. She decided she had to learn to eat fish. She decided to try to eat it the way the Mer folk did: By just swallowing them whole. Castlemar reassured her that her digestive tract should now be able to handle it. Lizzie opened her mouth and closed her eyes and tried to suck the fish down her throat whole. With practice, she was able to do it and it was a great relief to dispense with such unpleasantness so quickly. She began to feel stronger and clearer for the quality food. It was also true what they had said. The moment in agony when she could not hold it any longer and had to go to the bathroom, there was a fish already nibbling at her ass. As soon as she lifted her legs and parted her cheeks to go, this little fish shot in and out her butt, rapidly eating all she would have left behind.

"She's Ready"

By now she had a beautiful dorsal fin, her gills were well formed and no longer sore and the webbing was complete between all her digits. It all really did help her move around, especially now when her breasts had become so swollen and full, and her belly so large and round. Castlemar explained that the humans had not planned for her to turn partially mer. They were unaware of the powerful properties of mer semen and its impact on a cellular level. Her body was still changing from the repeated applications.

Apply, Castlemar did. Lizzie at first resisted. She had not thought it appropriate to have intercourse while pregnant. But, Castlemar insisted and would not take "no" for an answer. He told her it was essential to a healthy pregnancy and that he was talking through his rod to his progeny and she must not interrupt the special messages he was sending. Castlemar would pull Lizzie onto his member and carry her around while he swam like that. With her on his lap, large member lodged securely in her yoni, she would cling to him like riding a sea horse on a carousel. Only, it was she who was mounted on a pole. Periodically, Castlemar would start to move his hips and member inside of her until he came, much more gently now, but soaking her insides with his substance.

As time passed and her belly had swelled to yet enormous proportions with flutters of quickening kicks within, Castlemar said it was time for her to spend time with the elder mer women, as they would have some special work to do to help prepare her. They were delighted to have her at their disposal and held her aloft with her legs parted, as they began one preparation they deemed especially important. She would need her pussy stretched to the point of being able to fit the largest fist among them. Rubbing jelly from sea snails on her tissues and massaging, then stretching and sticking their hands in, they worked on her despite all protestations. They were all really into it and had no trouble holding her still for their administrations, being as strong as they were. When she would stop struggling, they would tell her stories and helpful information about labor and how to breastfeed and what it meant to be a mer-man's woman. Lizzie listened avidly to all this. She was so hungry for knowledge about what would be happening to her and what was expected.

After days of this, they could successfully fit a full fist into her opening. They delivered her proudly to Castlemar with a seaweed garland around her hair and a painted flower on her belly.

"She's ready," they said.

Castlemar said he wanted to see, and parted her legs. He tried to put his fist in but his was of course larger than the elders'. One of them came forward and pushed her fist slowly into Lizzie's privates under his watchful gaze, and he said,

"Very good!"

After they left, he seemed particularly aroused and caught Lizzie in his arms and jammed his hard member into her more aggressively than he had since that first time. He kissed her and suckled her nipples, then held her head to his muscled chest as he pounded into her. He hit some amazing angle with the knobby purple head of his member such that she felt this yummy pressure build in a certain spot in her pussy, making it contract tightly and feel engorged with blood. Lizzie moaned and cried out and as she began to have an orgasm, she felt some other kind of powerful contractions kick in, rolling through her body like tidal waves. Castlemar held her tight and kept pounding into her. The contractions began to intensify such that she began to feel like she was being pried open from the inside. Just as the pain of the contractions started to mount, she felt that familiar sting and then waves of euphoria as Castlemar shot his wad deep within her, soothing every part within reach, blanketing it all with soothing gooey jism. Lizzie was then able to relax as Castlemar's member slid out.

Suddenly she felt a new kind of pressure, as the first twin began to crown. With the elder mers chanting in delight, Lizzie bore down and pushed. Soon she felt the marvelous ripple of a baby sliding down her birth canal. As the infant emerged, the elder mers, immediately affixed it to Lizzie's breast where the baby rooted, latched on and began to suck. That powerful sensation intensified her contractions such that the other one was then crowning. Just one push sent it sliding heavily out of her pussy also. That baby too was promptly put to her other breast, where it latched on and sucked, making Lizzie's womb contract still harder and expel the after birth.

After the pulsing in the umbilical cords stopped, the mer women neatly nipped the cords with their teeth.

New Motherhood

Lizzie looked down at her babies and they seemed to her to be the most exquisite creatures she had ever seen. They were so beautiful to her, that she could hardly bear to look at anything else at all. She felt herself falling into an entirely new kind of love as she felt her breasts letting down and squirting, giving them vital nectar as she gazed into their cosmic eyes and at their sweet tiny features and felt their gills blowing bubbles on her skin. So immersed in this rapture, she did not argue when the mer women insisted she eat her after births for the nutrition. She knew it was no use resisting anything they were so adamant about and she wanted as little distraction as possible, so dutifully she opened her mouth and like she had learned with the fish, sucked the whole bloody things down.

Lizzie had thought she would be left alone now that she had her newborns but Castlemar seemed insatiable for her as always. He did not at all think her parts might be too sore or that after labor a reprieve was indicated. It was true, she later learned, that his special semen seemed to expedite her healing.

While she was nursing her babes, as she spent most of her time, he would just flip her over so he could take her from behind, shoving his great purple mer manhood into her pussy up to the hilt and holding her buttocks with his fingers, maybe even sliding his webbed thumbs up her ass. Holding her thus, he could pull her back and forth in rocking motion on his great member, the water being an excellent aid for such maneuvers. By the time Castlemar came in shooting spurts which made Lizzie's womb contract tighter and that special spot (new discovery!) get all plump and delicious again, the babies would have been rocked sound asleep at the breast and Lizzie's nipples would slide out of their satiated little mouths. Castlemar then scooped up his new family and carried them around nestled in his arms, using his legs and fin to propel himself through.

The elders were so happy to have all this new life about. A baby girl and boy: Such an auspicious start for their species.

As for Lizzie, there was nowhere in the world she would rather be.

PART II

Experimental Results

Sir Rodney and Dr. Mm really could not help but be delighted at the turn their experiment had taken. Through key peek-holes and hidden cameras in the exhibit, they had been able to see all. They were amazed and thrilled at Lizzie's transformation and how fully she had been claimed by the tribe. They really had not anticipated that she would become a merwoman and at various points had been seriously tempted to pull her out in order to better examine and interview her. Fortunately they realized; however, that not only might that mean interfering in regrettable ways with yet unfolding recent developments, but also that Lizzie was already so altered, that to do that to her, would be like taking a fish out of water. It might no longer be feasible for her to return to land without great discomfort and certain risk. With the enormity of this knowledge, of there being no return, Sir Rodney faithfully honored his obligations to her mother. He even sent a note, that due to the high level of responsibilities and commitments required of her in her new position, that Lizzie would be unable to visit any time soon.

Now, Sir Rodney had conflicting impulses. His driving desire was to add to his Mer collection as one would add to a fish tank---breeding these exotic intelligent creatures was affording many hours of fascinating entertainment! On the other hand, he now knew that he was no longer inviting someone to engage in an activity that any form of informed consent could remotely cover. If a subject had any idea what was in store for them with this experiment, they would certainly never agree to it. At the same time, Sir Rodney could readily observe that Lizzie looked absolutely ecstatic with her new life. She really seemed happier than he had ever seen her previously.

Receptive

It was true, Lizzie was very happy. Her sweet cherubs were now newly weaned and at the toddler stage but seemed to be hardly any trouble at all to parent in this watery milieu. This was in part because the elder mers took such extreme delight in playing with and caring for them. Additionally, the little ones were already more independent than human babes at this stage, with strong instincts helping them avoid the few perils in the exhibit and enabling them to even catch and eat their own fish.

Since the babes were weaned, Lizzie was receptively fertile again, and Castlemar wasted no time in taking her much like the first time, in a frenzy of lovemaking, plowing hard into her little pussy with his huge purple member and at a certain peak, connecting into her firmly and so deep so she felt that sting as he penetrated her other still smaller opening still deeper inside and then the rush of euphoria as all his copious cum flooded her insides. He tied up her legs to help them stay closed as she slept but he did not tie her wrists---as she knew better than to try and untie them this time. He carried her and gently placed her in their softest sea plant nest and she fell into a deep timeless sleep as before. When she woke up, she was of course once again newly pregnant. She understood all the signs more easily this time---the full tender breasts, darkened areolas, and bulge in her lower belly-- and pregnancy was a fine state of being for her now—the weightlessness of the water and healthy lifestyle meant that even pregnant, Lizzie felt better than ever before.

Lizzie had also grown attached to Castlemar. Seeing how well he led his people, how attentive and caring he was, in addition to being so courageous, had given her new appreciation for him beyond his profound penetrating capacity.

Perhaps it was these budding feelings within her that had led her to spontaneously attempt to kiss him. The Mer folk had never heard of such at thing and so when Lizzie at first tried to put her lips on Castlemar's lips and slide her tongue into his mouth, he stayed absolutely still; actually a little shocked. Knowing this might be new for him, Lizzie just kept at it—-tickling, nibbling, tasting him in this way. It turned out to be easier; she realized, than kissing on land, because she did not need to breath through her mouth and nose, all that being handled by the gills. She became very absorbed in this new experience of kissing Castlemar underwater, sampling him thoroughly and feeling all the sensual slippery-ness of it all. She was now exploring him and entering him. Suddenly, Castlemar emerged from his surprise and thinking he had the hang of it, joined in. His tongue was quite large; however, and before she knew it, he had slid it deep down her throat. This aroused him so intensely, he had very soon parted her legs, and plowed into her pussy so he was penetrating her both above and below. The meme of "tongue swallowing" as kissing translated in Mer-speak, would spread far and wide.

Meanwhile, with the kids so well and happily tended and occupied, Lizzie was left with plenty of time free to both satiate Castlemar's ever hungry manhood and still have some time to learn some new arts and skills that might come in handy---like how to weave a seaweed net and communicate with the more intelligent species of fish. The only thing she lacked and sometimes missed, was a woman friend of her own ilk---someone from her world to share discoveries with, who might fully understand her as only someone from one's own culture can.

An Old Friend and a New Subject

As luck would have it, Sir Rodney had decided to put aside any residual compunctions, reservations, or doubts. He would instead focus on identifying potential subjects who would not have anyone come looking for them and who would hopefully be able to transition successfully to be as happy as Lizzie in their new life. Such optimal candidates were few and far between, so he and Dr. Mm strategized that in case they found someone suitable, they would move very quickly.

Sir Rodney settled on Amelia. Amelia was one of his most loyal and capable maids, gracious, nicely formed, and easy going. She had been the one he had sent to help with Lizzie in the early stages.

Amelia had originally shown up on his doorstep, one step away from the poor house with some shameful past such that she really had no one and no place to turn to. In all her time working at the Sir Rodney estate, she had had no visitors of any kind. She was easy to get along with and all the girls and guys in Sir Rodney's employ liked her. But, importantly, no one could claim an especially close relationship such that they would question her having rushed off to a more favorable position elsewhere.

Amelia really mostly focused on serving Sir Rodney. Perhaps out of profound gratitude or it could have been that she may have been secretly enamored of him. He had not taken advantage of her in his way. He just had not gotten around to it, having others more specifically for that purpose. She was useful to him in so many other ways. He saw now, it was almost as if he had been saving her for this most special assignment.

Sir Rodney had her fetched to the menagerie. This was a place she had actually never seen before in all her years of service. He let the grandeur of high ceilings and magnificent exhibits lush with wildlife, pools and other wonders impress themselves fully upon her senses. While she was looking around slack-jawed in wonder, Dr. Mm came up behind her and put a sedative moistened cloth on her face; at which she struggled a little and then fainted into his arms. They then carried Amelia to the lab, where they undressed her beautiful unknowing body, gave her, her injections in one of her dimpled cheeks, parted them to insert the sea cucumber gently but firmly up her behind, and affixed the underwater breathing mask to her face, making sure that the breathing tube was positioned correctly deep in her mouth. They then used a harness and pulley system to lift her up and drop her into the Mer peoples epic sized water tank.

Under Lizzie's Fin

Lizzie heard the splash and along with Castlemar, went to go see what it was. She was delighted to see Amelia and with Castlemar's help, brought her gently down to the deeper quarters where they liked to spend their time. Soon, Amelia awoke and was understandably in a bit of a surprised panic. There was no way Lizzie could really say words to Amelia that she could hear. Sound just did not carry in that way. She gave herself to trying to convey in every other way possible, that Amelia would be safe and in good hands. Lizzie held her, soothed and rocked her, stroked her face and hair, until Amelia calmed down and realized that she was okay and not drowning and that although Lizzie looked really different, she was still Lizzie after all and seemed to mean her well.

Castlemar was respectful of Lizzie's efforts, knowing Amelia was her friend, and this despite his strong desire to get this newcomer pregnant as soon as possible. He knew that the serum injection for her well-timed ovulation would only last so long and it would take many applications of mer semen to make her mer enough for it to happen naturally. Then pressingly and personally, on top of that, his meat was aching intently for her. He had recent compelling associations with human flesh. As if magnetized, his rod had already bulged and popped out of its slit fully erect, and now the weighty head was following her every move---yet he restrained himself and waited for the right moment.

That moment came when Amelia's body visibly relaxed and her sense of humor and curiosity returned such that she smiled and began to look around. Castlemar showed himself then. Amelia was immediately entranced by this beautiful and fully exotic merman. She gazed, intrigued by him in all his grandeur. She also could not help but notice the huge purple phallus, evidently for her.

Lizzie was happy to share and help. She embraced Amelia from behind with her arms across her luscious bosom while bracing herself against the same mossy rock they often used. Castlemar came so close, his gills blew bubbles against her skin, and he began to stare deep into her eyes, and caress her with his webbed hands. He could not wait much longer though; she could feel it.

As the telling moment for entry drew near, Amelia was momentarily a little frightened, feeling his hefty member now straining against her belly, and wondering how it would fit anywhere else. She might have even tried to resist but really, where could she go? She was so disoriented by this unexpected environment and Lizzie's arms were holding her quite firm. On top of all that, her fascination was much stronger than her fear. Anticipation seemed only to heighten it as her body became increasingly acutely aroused by the mere presence of Castlemar and his formidable equipment. Her nipples, belly, and clit all began to tingle, and she could feel blood rushing to her privates such that the whole region felt oddly hot and heavy. In the end, resistance was clearly futile. Lizzie could sense that moment of total submission, and she reached down between Amelia's legs and slid her lips apart for Castlemar's member.

Holding Amelia for this intimate moment, brought all of that first time back to Lizzie as Castlemar penetrated the tender folds of

Amelia's pussy, pulling her wide as the tightness of the fit was enhanced still more by the sea cucumber up her butt, the intensity of that stretching and fullness, immense hardness as he slid heavily and dynamically in and out. Then Lizzie could feel Amelia start as she got momentarily stung by Castlemar's telescoping other member, piercing and entering her womb, and then how she began to move involuntarily in a kind of rapture as the flood of hot marshmallow topping like semen pulsed and flooded her inside and the euphoria kicked in. Lizzie knew how good that felt, like you would never want it to end.

Castlemar tied Amelia up per custom, legs fastened together and wrists tied too, and carried her to deposit her in their soft nest. Lizzie went to lay with her and comfort her for when she would wake up. It was neat for Lizzie to be able to observe the changes unfolding that she had herself experienced. She watched as in a deep sleep, changes began to occur in Amelia's body. When Castlemar could see her gills forming and easily opening and closing, he came and removed the cumbersome mask from her face. Lizzie got to see how this process that felt like only a few hours, actually took a few days. First the little bump formed on Amelia's back and her lower belly began to protrude ever so slightly. Then her areolas turned a darker shade of pink. By this time, Castlemar had removed the ties.

Amelia awoke looking even more beautiful than before and quite well rested and radiant. She seemed also to be starting to be able to interpret some mer messages, as she looked significantly less confused. Castlemar came to aid this process; made clear his intention to promptly insert himself into her again, to pump some more of his mer elixir into her. Amelia obediently obliged by spreading her legs to expose that sweet pussy again and Castlemar entered her fast and hard. He gave her a quickie with some rapid strokes, shot his wad, and then he was off.

Lizzie was so delighted to have Amelia under her fin, so to speak. It was such a joy to be able to explain to her everything she would have liked explained, show her things, and just have her most excellent company. Amelia proved very adaptable and liked a lot of what Lizzie herself enjoyed about life down underwater. Castlemar had plenty of erections and semen to go around. He seemed to have a hard on practically all the time, and Lizzie was perfectly happy sharing. As extremely good as it was, it was also a little tiresome being penetrated *all* the time. As their pregnancies progressed, Lizzie showed Amelia how to swallow fish whole, coaching Amelia on how to open wide her mouth and throat, and just suck the whole thing down. Now that she knew how to do it, she also helped get Amelia's sea cucumber out. Of course Amelia was a bit shocked: she had not even known that thing was in there!

Rite of Passage for A New Member

As if things were not exciting enough, something still more unusual had happened. Sir Rodney had found another ideal subject. This time it was a young man named Arthur. Arthur was a particularly handsome and charming youth whose parents had died in a flying machine accident. He and his brothers were not on speaking terms. He had lost their respect through some scandalous involvement with a gypsy girl. Being of the disinherited upper class variety, he would hence have to make his own way. Sir Rodney had taken pity on him and hired him as a footman; something for which Arthur had proven entirely unsuited. He was far too randy to the peril of all females in reach, and also given to reckless adventuring. Inevitably, Sir Rodney would have eventually had to let the well built chap go. Instead of firing him; however, it had occurred to him that perhaps some change of assignment would be more worthwhile. Sir Rodney did his little internal calculations in consultation with Dr. Mm and they both agreed that Arthur would be an optimal subject and with his evident hankering for excitement in life, he might well flourish. Dr. Mm was especially intrigued by the potential experimental value of a male subject. What indeed would the merfolk do with him?

So Arthur too was called to the Menagerie and handled similarly to Amelia, except for the part where Dr. Mm took a moment to measure Arthur's penis and testes, and seemed to overly enjoy handling them—"Purely for professional purposes," he assured Sir Rodney

When the Mer folk discovered Arthur, it was true, they were not initially sure what to do with him. Unless they could get enough of their powerful semen into him to transform him into mer folk, he would not be useful to them at all for expanding their gene pool, as his sperm would remain too human and overly subject to human limitations. To their minds, he would be condemned to stay in a sort of limbo, living forever with a mask on his face and a sea cucumber up his butt. Castlemar and the elder merfolk consulted about the situation and decided to take drastic measures. Lizzie was aware of the plan, and knowing it might be disturbing to Amelia, who was still so new, was given the task of keeping her distracted.

The merfolk brought the sleeping Arthur down below. He was nicely muscled with a beautifully shaped body—broad chest with tapered torso, and tight, round buttocks. As a kindness, thinking it best to prolong his sleep for what was to come, they caught a sea viper and had it bite and inject some venom into his arm. They knew this would give them a few days in which Arthur would be nicely sedated.

First they removed the sea cucumber, saving it for later. Then They turned Arthur over and different elder Mer men took turns alternately holding him, while others entered his thankfully now sea cucumber pre-stretched butt hole, and began ejaculating loads of cum into his behind. Although the elder mer men's semen was no longer reliable for impregnation, it could still transform other being's tissues and organs on a cellular level and so they knew that the more of it and the more repetitions of applications, the better. They tried to be as gentle as possible, but they were large, and it could not help but feel good, which invariable made them unintentionally thrust at times intensely into this tight young man's ass, as it exerted its natural squeeze on their members. They did the best they could and after they had all spent themselves in orgasm after orgasm and unloaded as much copious sticky Mer infusion up his rear as possible, they inserted a little sea sponge, and then strapped his cheeks together to hold it all in for some hours. The procedure then fully complete, they untied him to remove the sponge and replaced the sea cucumber, as if nothing had really happened.

When Arthur came to, he did not have a mask on. Of course, he had never known he had ever had a mask. His butt felt a little sore and full as if something was in it and even stranger, he was under water and seemed to be able to breath. But, by far the most compelling and absorbing change for him was his penis. It was actually really difficult for him to focus on anything else. His dick had entirely changed size. Along with his balls, it all looked huge, and was this purple color. Upon touching his newly fortified member, it became instantly erect, which of course only enlarged it further. 'Wow,' Arthur thought. The corresponding sensations seemed measurably that much larger also. In fact, the urge to have sex was so intense, he felt like an animal in heat and could now relate to the plight of the poor scandalous canine who rubs frenetically on a guests leg; such a frantic state of rutting—so consumed with urgent yearning!

At that moment of need, a female with webs and fins floated over to him. Wait a moment. Did she really have four breasts? But even if he could, Arthur had little time to think too deeply about any of this because her lips closed around his huge phallus and it felt like fireworks were shooting bolts of pleasure through his body. She sucked him rapidly into climax and he reeled and thrust uncontrollably as he came. The mer woman happily swallowed his cum and then smiled at him as she swam away. She was one of the youngest of the older Mer women, and was quite beautiful. He was now in post orgasmic bliss. Everything inexplicable would surely make some new sort of sense without any need for reason at all.

As if the merfolk were not busy enough with all these newcomers, one more was dropped in the next morning. Although; this one was actually already one of them. Unbeknownst to much of the group, Castlemar had been trying desperately to send signals to his people beyond the exhibit, small group that they be, to let them know that they had a newly prepared male now, and it would be really nice to have a young mer female to couple with him to aid their mission of survival through expanding the gene pool. One of his signals had apparently gotten through and mer folk were able to send one of their few remaining young females into easy capture for Sir Rodney's contacts, who scoured certain waterways for specimens to add to his menagerie. Sir Rodney had been absolutely delighted---things in that exhibit were just going swimmingly!

Castlemar had examined Arthur while he slept. At first, to Castlemar's amusement, Arthur looked quite blissed out as he apparently had a number of juicy wet dreams punctuated by powerful emissions. The curling and streaming ribbons of semen in the water as he came provided much entertainment for multitudes of fish. Of course, Castlemar knew this was just an excellent sign that Arthur's body was purging all the remaining human sperm and soon his testes would swell and get heavy laden with new powerful mer sperm production. Then later on, toward the end of Arthur's transformation, (which had been greatly expedited by the elder mermen's abundant semen application), Castlemar checked and was relieved to see that Arthur's member was now fully functional in merman fashion. It was large enough to meet the mark and equipped with the additional mini member that would pop out at the proper time to pierce the center of a female cervix, reaching right into the womb to assure proper egg claiming, fertilization, and implantation. So when the new female mer maiden was dropped in, Castlemar was full of expectation and confident in his plan.

Bianca

Her name was Bianca, and she knew that by embracing this young human turned mer, she could help save her species. Bianca was fully prepared to receive Arthur, had already heard all about him. She swam down and touched his cheek and then smiled. Hapless Arthur was just as immediately smitten. Perhaps the hormones pulsing through his body and the fact that his attention consuming and reborn phallus knew exactly who she was and what she was there for, made it easy for him to not even wonder but rather be glad about her six jiggling tits, and the exotic colors of her skin and fins....It was almost as if his dick had not only grown on the outside, but also in how much space it now occupied in his brain.

At any rate, Arthur gave himself up easily to it and rushed at the beautiful creature, pressing himself against all those succulent nipples and eagerly parting her legs. He found a tight little slit that seemed to encase everything. This was Bianca's first time, so the slit needed a bit of pressure to open. Arthur hit the right angle and jammed his new mammoth cock through the opening and into the warm, tight squeeze of her pussy. He started thrusting vigorously, hardly able to contain himself or even control the movements. It was as if they were propelling themselves through pure instinct. As for Bianca, her clit was situated strategically on the inside and so it got immediately intensely stimulated, as she had never known before. She trembled in stunned rapture as he thrust deeper and deeper.

Waves of pleasure were coursing through both of them with mounting intensity and it seemed to only go up and up a notch. Suddenly, he felt this wild new sensation of another erection on top of the first and as if a deliciously sensitive other part of him were now penetrating yet another tight space and then he came, in what seemed like wave after wave of spurting and gushing, as Bianca clung to him, quivering with floods of primal chemistry, the effects of the deep semen injection, and waves of pleasure as she was swept up in the intensity until she passed out.

    Afterward, the Mer elders reassured him she was quite okay, and directed him in the practice of tying up her legs and carrying her to a Mer nest, explaining she had just fallen into a deep sleep. Arthur realized that both he understood what they were trying to tell him and that he really did not understand anything at all. This was a brand new world and he had better just go with the flow and do what they said. Besides, what had just happened had felt really, really good. So in love, he saw everything through that golden mist now anyway. Arthur snuggled close and looked at Bianca as she slept, in utter delight. It was as if his huge member were intricately connected to his heart and they were fully in sync, such that Bianca was now the center of his universe. She had relieved him so fully; he felt his desire finally satiated for the moment so he could relax. Arthur was a bit tired himself from all this excitement, so he soon fell asleep spooning her.

    They awoke at the same time, and when Bianca saw his instant erection, she eased him into her opening gently, and pumped her hips slowly until he came. It was a more gentle orgasm, but enough to relieve him and empty his balls again of yet another load of jism, so he could once again think more clearly. Brimming with gratitude, he looked at her and then noticed that she looked a little different. Her tummy was a bit bulgy below her belly button and her breasts, were now sporting brighter pink tips. Well anyway, she looked delicious and he hugged and kissed her.

Afterward:

    As things would go, between Sir Rodney and Castlemar's compatible interests, the Menagerie Mer group would grow to robust proportions. They would go on to outgrow their habitat, become strong as a people again, and large numbers of them, including our key mer persons, would be ultimately released to the wild to continue their lives in the larger natural environment. Sir Rodney's menagerie would become famous all over the world as an example of exotic species conservation. Highly edited and censored papers of Dr. Mm would be studied avidly in universities. And as for Lizzie, Amelia, and Bianca, they would all became very close and go on to bear, suckle, and help raise loads and loads of babies who would flourish joyfully amid the many delights of the sea.

TAMALAINE'S IMPLEMENTATION OF THE NEW POLICY (2) **

(Or "An Ace in the Hole" as Teen Temptations go Untempered)

All of the state sponsored youth boarding schools of the Republic of Huzro where all youth[*] went upon turning 18, had received the same urgent mandate: Due to plummeting fertility and genetic viability rates in persons over 21 years of age, there would be a new policy requiring immediate implementation:

"All facilities are now required to produce a 90% pregnancy rate in their female resident population within one year of admission. Once pregnant, young women will be transferred to appropriate mothering institutions aimed at meeting the state need for a viable work force.

These results are to be achieved without informing the youth and without any resort to violence or force. Rather, the general approach should be to give play and license to formerly restricted and/or limited activities so as to further enable and promote the natural instincts and tendencies of young people to procreate."

*Strategies for implementation and action planning should include but not be limited to the following:

1. Elimination of all access to sexual education and birth control information or resources
2. Provision of frequent late-running parties without supervision
3. Black-outs at opportune times
4. Empty easily found rooms and other supplied private refuges (they should appear secret and unplanned)
5. Doors kept unlocked between male and female quarters at night
6. 24 hour access to the spa and gym facilities.
7. A general decrease in academic requirements to allow plenty of unstructured time

---

[*] (Tamalaine's) : Dubious consent, Institutionalized set-up for youth.

Lindsey arrived at Tamalaine Boarding school in the Republic of Huzro on her appointed day, or rather her eighteenth birthday. Her short cotton summer dress was clinging to her legs as she held her state regulation size suitcase. She was so excited. She had been going stir crazy at home where there had simply not been enough guys. Lindsey was quite healthy, both limber and lithe, with a perky nose and just as perky breasts. Her mother had told her to keep her mind on her studies and she really intended to try.......

The class load seemed really light compared to what she had heard and they let out early for a romp in the pool. She dawned her bikini and played in the water like a child. At one point she dived down and did a somersault. On her way back up, one of her breasts slipped right out of her bikini top. One of the boys clearly saw, and gave her a wink as she hurriedly stuffed it back in. She found out later his name was Ryan. He came up to her a little later and asked her,

"So, are you new to Tamalaine? I don't think I've seen you around"

Lindsey tried to speak but only blushed.

"Well hey, let me introduce you to some folks."

He took her by the hand and led her to a little cluster of guys sitting at a table drinking juice. They all looked up at her unabashedly; taking in her beautiful body and shy but eager interest.

"*Welcome* to Tamalaine!" They roundly exclaimed.

Lindsey's roommate, Natasha, turned out to be a ready friend, and they chatted and giggled about the boys they had met. Lindsey told her about what had happened with her bikini and Natasha was very empathetic but suggested,

"Don't be embarrassed. Ryan was just lucky is all."

They changed into cute little flattering outfits and got ready for the party that was happening later on that night. Boy, boarding school was way more fun than she had thought it would be.

After eating bonbons and dancing for a while, Lindsey and Natasha ended up embroiled in a game of truth or dare. A really handsome and fit young man by the name of Johnson was there as well as a wild, lawless longhaired guy named Ace. They made the game super exciting with their antics and goaded the girls on to expose their most intimate secrets. Before she knew it, to avoid telling still more, Lindsey had been dared to kiss Ace. She had actually never kissed before and this sure felt like a high-pressure way to begin. Giddy with adrenalin, she sure was not going to back out. Before any further thought, Ace had swept her up. Suddenly, his mouth was on hers, kissing her lips, and then sure enough, he was sliding his tongue into her mouth. He tasted warm, musky, and sweet and led the way around that deep kiss in quite sophisticated fashion. They got so carried away, that a little crowd had gathered to watch.

"Hot damn, Ace!" Johnson exclaimed.

Next it was Natasha and Johnson's turn. Johnson followed Ace's cue and took Natasha in his arms very assertively and proceeded to kiss her amorously. At this point, little alarms were going off for Lindsey and Natasha. They knew they needed a way out unless more was going to happen in one night than they might be ready for. With no staff in sight and the party showing no sign of ending, they grabbed their purses and said they were tired and needed to go check in for the night.

As they were heading back to their room; however, there was a blackout. Ace and Johnson caught up with the girls, and told them they would help them find their rooms, which they did. But then it seemed they were in no hurry to leave. They all chatted together in the dark while they cuddled. Ace whispered in Lindsey's ear,

"I would love to try that kiss again, can I?"

And Lindsey said, "yes."

Ace took her lips in his and kissed and kissed, again sliding his tongue past her soft lips into her mouth, only this time as he did it, he let his hands begin to wander and stroke and feel her breasts and thighs and even raise her dress. With his tongue in her mouth and occupied in such fervent French kissing, Lindsey was at first rather distracted. Besides, everything he did felt really good. She had been fantasizing about all this for a long time; she had just never done it before. 'Why not now?' a little voice said. So, she let him slide his hands all over her and eventually between her legs, which gave her an electric jolt sensation.

"Oh!" she cried out.

Natasha, similarly occupied, asked,

"Lindsey, are you okay?"

Lindsey reassured her she was, just as Ace's mouth closed on hers again.

Something new was happening down below but the kissing was so intense, it was hard to tell what it was. It turned out to be Ace's rather large dick rubbing between her silky thighs. It was really hard, and kind of pulling at the skin, so Lindsey very naturally shifted her legs a little. This inadvertently opened them more and made it easy for Ace to deftly begin to slip his dick on its way in to exactly where it had always wanted to be until it got a little stuck at the entrance of her virginal vestibule. During that momentary pause, Lindsey had a little trepidation, like she might just change her mind. Sensing this, Ace thrust his tongue into her mouth deeper and then Lindsey gasped as, taking hold of her hips and with his fingers, pulling her apart from underneath ever so slightly, Ace pushed right through and drove his large member home. "uhh, uhh, uhh" Lindsey involuntarily sounded as he kept sliding tightly in and out and with each plunge, hitting her cervix squarely with the head of his dick. She could feel the penetration all the way up to her tits, making her nipples erect and giving her goosebumps. With mounting momentum, he began to climax, and spurted his wad in multiple substantial squirts deep into her pussy, where he then lingered with his rod still inside her for a long time until...

Surprise! The lights came back on. Ace and Johnson, in similar predicament rushed to get their clothes on, and with quick parting kisses, hightailed it out of the female quarters. Lindsey and Natasha looked at each other a bit bemused, clutching sheets to their by now naked bodies, and feeling all that sticky semen in their pussies. "Natasha, I don't think we're virgins anymore."

Ace and Johnson found the girls everywhere now. They pulled them into little side rooms for a quickie on the way to class. They even snuck in at night and entered the girls while they were still asleep. The girls would wake to find big dicks in their pussies, and the young men kissing them with big smiles on their faces.

Ace and Johnson would compare notes and agree on new things to try, like taking the girls from behind. It all felt really good to Lindsey and Natasha and they were also enjoying all the attention and passion that came along with these interesting activities. They just had to be careful that they did not always smell of sex, so often were they sticky with their men's juices.

This went on for an entire month but then one day they were not feeling so well. Lindsey was frequently nauseous and Natasha actually threw up. They went and saw the Tamalaine nurse, who took a urine sample and then smiled at them and said they would feel better soon. The next day, to their surprise, they each got cards in their morning mail saying that due to their exemplary school performances, they had been granted scholarships to a different, more prestigious school. It was made very clear, that this was far too great an honor to turn down. Very soon thereafter, with tears and last kisses, they said goodbye to Ace and Johnson.

Ace and Johnson, incidentally, had been observed by school administers to be especially effective studs and so they were put in charge of orienting new female students at Tamalaine.

TIFFANY AND THE TROJAN TWINS (1)

(Or Out of the Monkey and Into a Ménage a Trios')

Tiffany was a sweet natured dancing girl at "the Golden Monkey" and although she loved men and sharing her ample charms and endowments, she detested the slow times as well as the high-pressured ones when she would be besieged by strangers. She was also, it turns out, not much enjoying her home life. She felt trapped living with her parents with whom she had sadly never been close and who had no idea what she did for a living. Tiffany felt quite oppressed by the little deceptions and impositions inherent in this situation. At times, she really wished she could just get a brand new life; one that would be a bit more straightforward.

The Trojan twins were Tiffany's regulars. They were so fond of her that they knew her schedule. In fact, if they arrived at the Golden Monkey and she was not there, they would often just turn around and leave.

Jake and Tom Trojan were independently wealthy from a substantial inheritance but they were also unusually service minded and preferred an exciting life. Consequently, they had managed to get themselves into med school to become doctors. They hoped to someday travel the world with a service like Doctors Beyond Borders, an organization to which they had donated substantial funds.

Amid the demands of med school, they had found they lacked the time necessary to manage or maintain a real romance. Instead, they relished temporary escape from the academic world of high pressure and sick bodies. They would go immerse themselves in the nightclub experience of beautiful and robustly healthy female flesh. That was the ultimate study break.

Tiffany was their favorite. She was so sincere and sensitive. Like an affectionate kitten, she would easily and naturally smooth her particular balm anywhere, as required, on their bruised psyches. She was also exceedingly responsive and flexible, in more ways than one. To see her on a pole, was to see a true artist at work. She could propel herself all the way up it, around it, and then hang off of it in amazing feats of daring finesse. But she had a limber mind and personality as well. She was well able to adapt herself to whatever was needed or desired, no matter how unspoken.

One day at the Golden Monkey, Jake and Tom were enjoying her so much, they were just loath to leave her. Part jokingly, Tom asked Tiffany if they couldn't just take her home? Tiffany surprised them all, including herself, by saying, "Yes!" and so began an interesting arrangement. They excitedly chatted up the terms and details in the car so that things were at least as clear as possible from the start. Being doctors, Jake and Tom required a health check, but being wealthy, they were able to get a pronto house call for any labs and tests.

Once satisfied in that regard, they gave Tiffany her own room in the epic ten star apartment on the 15th floor with a luxurious balcony. They offered her whatever food she liked, installed a pole in the apartment, instituted a very generous allowance for lessons or anything else she desired, and got her a cell phone.

On top of these amenities, when Tiffany woke up in the morning, she was surprised to discover a steaming hot breakfast served up by an enthusiastic cook and fresh warm towels handed to her by a kindly maid.

In return for all these benefits, Tom and Jake required of Tiffany that she quit the Golden Monkey, be monogamous for sexual activity with them alone, and either be at home or consider herself on call at all times of day or night unless she took time off by prior arrangement. They wanted her to be receptive to entry at any point.

Foreplay for Jake, involved pampering and grooming Tiffany to a comprehensive degree. It was soon clear that he wanted a monopoly on all such activities---he loved to wax her bikini line, trim her pubes, shave her, and paint her nails. He also delighted in dressing her in fine lingerie and fixing her hair. Tiffany found it quite luxurious to be able to just lay back and allow him to lavish all this attention on her and she discovered in the process that he was actually quite good at all these things. He had a masterful touch and was thorough and attentive. Plus, his pleasure in it all was so palpable. It was quite novel.

Once he had her all dolled up, he liked to slide the silky lingerie aside and go down on her super sweet pussy. He kissed and he nuzzled with the same expertise with which he did everything else. Jake would use his lips and tongue to work her pussy lips and clit into paroxysms of thrills and pleasure until Tiffany would orgasm uncontrollably.

Then, feeling he had earned it, he would roll her placid pleasured body over so she was on her tummy, and then dipping his well hung cock a little into the wetness of her now very juicy pussy, he would then poke it into the little opening in her ass, and pressing slowly but firmly, he would slide his member all the way in. It always ached the slightest bit at the beginning at the initial pressing stretch, but then it was like her ass would acclimate and relax to accommodate that large expanse of firm meat, and it would start to feel really kind of good, in a kinky way, all that heat, pressure, and silky sliding right up her butt. Lying on top of her, he would then take her thoroughly that way, buggering into a kind of oblivion, he would be so swept up in the rapture of it, he would yell when he came, victory spurts of semen pulsing and injecting deep into her ass. Then it was time for Jake to get ready to head back to his residency. He would kiss her on the butt and run off to get ready.

Tom, on the other hand, had a very different approach. He had no idea of foreplay and would usually arrive home with a huge boner, having thought of Tiffany all the way home. Bursting in the door, he would say "Hi Tiffany" and all she had to do was hear that and see his large erection, and she would be instantly creamy herself. He would then promptly pick her up with her legs apart and mid air, while rushing to unzip his pants to free his cock, manage to hold her against the wall while he rammed his cock into her. While holding her, he would move her hips up and down with his hands increasing the leverage for better slamming. Since Tom worked out regularly with weights, this was all quite easy and just oh so satisfying for him.

Other times, Tiffany would be on her poll when Tom got home. She could easily propel herself so the poll was down the length of her back and between her buttocks and she could stay perched there, open her legs wide for him, and he could just go right up to her, pull her little G-string aside or any other bit of lingerie she hung out in around the house, and push his member plumb in. Usually moaning in relief his customary, "Honey, I'm home."

When Tiffany elected to go out, to see a friend, for example, she would take her cell phone. Getting a call from Tom or Jake, they would use GPS to go to her wherever she was. Her friends did not mind if she needed to spread her legs for a quickie at their house. Likewise, in a restaurant or department store, she and the Trojan twins could always find some place. Perhaps it would just be the car. There was always somewhere for her fulfill her special duties and for some quick focused insertion to relieve their pent up needs.

Some days at med school, were particularly rough. Tom and Jake would end up strung out on too much caffeine, picked on by supervisors, or blamed for errors that were not theirs. At such times, they had a little code they would sidle up to each other and whisper: "Tiffany." She was their sustaining emblem and focal point and they were very sure, as superstitious as it might seem, that she was giving them good luck. Everything difficult was much easier with an underlying reminder that all that was wonderful was waiting for them ready to flood their senses with pleasure. Juicy fruits were hanging low for the picking, and such a lovely girl was theirs for the taking at any point.

As for Tiffany, she really did make most excellent use of the time and resources afforded her by her new position. With the luxurious aid of private lessons, she took up electric violin and French and learned with startling speed, being a bit hungry for more intensive learning after years of mostly just working and reading novels. If Jake or Tom needed her services in the middle of a lesson, there was enough money to work with to simply have her teachers return a little later. Tiffany would also work out hard on her dancing pole—keeping herself quite limber. She had the time to develop even more impressive aerial tricks to allure and excite. Some sunny days, she would just go onto the balcony naked and sunbathe, enjoying the extravagant view.

Jake and Tom had different schedules and sometimes were home separately and other times together. The brothers were very close and enjoyed the idea of having sex with the same girl between them. One time, they did both happen to be home, and Tom said to Tiffany "Come here, babe, and hop on pop." She cheerfully obliged, and straddling his lap, mounted herself onto his hefty rod, easing herself with her plush tight pussy down the shaft until she felt the head of his dick hit her womb with an intensely pleasurable little thump. Tom then began to hug and kiss her, her hair tickling his face, he slid his tongue into her mouth, savoring her taste, her soft lips and cheeks. She was so beautiful in every way. Then he slid his hands onto her ass, and pulling her cheeks a little apart, beckoned Jake to join in. Tiffany, said,

"But Tom, I don't think it will fit." But Tom shushed her gently, "it'll fit, Tif, just relax your tush." As soon as Tiffany nodded, 'okay,' the head of Jake's dick began pressing on her butt hole. His pre-cum moistened the way, as he slowly pushed all the way in. Now Jake and Tom moved in sync together in and out and when they both arrived all the way in, Tiffany felt like her eyes were going to bulge out. The fullness of the pressure, was so intense, but it felt really good at the same time. It felt good to be so fully sandwiched between these two beautiful men.

When they came, it was like so much energy and movement forcibly contained within the tight squeeze of her pussy and ass together---there was nowhere for their orgasmic spasms to go except to thrust in and out deeper. Densely pleasure packed with the added complexity of feeling strangely vulnerable, being so fully penetrated, Tiffany began trembling and hyperventilating in a state of acute arousal. The trembling intensified as she began having her own involuntary thrusts, force-ably squeezing her pussy and ass. For the first time ever, she had her own orgasm during actual intercourse amid the already crazy constellation of shuddering climaxes.

Ah yes. It was always so good. Between them, Jake and Tom took Tiffany multiple times a day. Whether they were rushing home from their shifts, upon waking, upon crashing---they had huge hard ons for her all the time.

After a few days, Tiffany was a bit sore---her pussy and butt hole had never seen this much action. Seeing her plight, Jake and Tom had an idea of another way she could oblige them. Laying her on her back, Tom got on top of her and straddled her face, with one hand holding her mouth, and the other holding his erection, he guided his dick into her parted lips. He did it in such a way that he was sliding his large dick along the top and back, so it slid down the roof of her mouth and deep into her throat. That angle made it possible to completely bypass her gag reflex, so she could actually just relax and find herself deeply swallowing his substantial member. Meanwhile, Jake was gently putting a healing salve on her pussy and asshole. His administrations felt so soothing and delicious at the same time, although of course she was in no position to say so. Tom began to thrust in her mouth just as he would in her other parts, sliding in and out of her lips and it was very clear that this felt super good because his movements became more urgent and intense. Then in a burst of heaves and trembling, Tom came and hot semen slid down Tiffany's throat.

    No sooner was Tom done; Jake wanted to give it a try. Tiffany nodded it was fine. She really did not mind this oral penetration at all. It was actually much easier than the usual way of giving a blowjob. The sucking and provision of pressure came easily in this position. All she had to do was lay back and relax, and let them push their dicks deep into her mouth and down her throat. She could feel a stretch in her soft palate, and smell the delicious smell of their manhood. Only a man has that distinctive scent; smelling like sweet animal musk and fluffy sea foam all at once. Aside from tickling her nose with their pubes, it was all good.

    Jake climbed on and slid his rod into her parted lips, angling up like he had seen Tom do, and sliding his meat all the way down into her throat. He then began to hump her face. Tiffany gently slid her fingers into her own pussy with the wet salve on it. After a little while of stimulating herself with soft yummy circles, and thinking Jake might get a kick out of it, she surprised him by then sticking one of these wet fingers up his ass. Jake cried out in ecstasy as that propelled him into a powerful orgasm, sending copious cum pulsing down her throat. Afterwards, Tom teased about having given Tiffany some nice hefty doses of zinc by squirting all that jism down her throat, "it's really good for your immune system, you know."

    After a day or two, her pussy was all in top shape again--- seemed actually more resilient, like it had added new layers, ready now for the bouts of friction multiple times a day that need be teased out of it. Her butt too, was just fine, all tight and toned. It was like the first time, so excited were the guys to enter their most favorite spots again.

    They decided they would all take a break during her period also. They would completely abstain from all sexual activity by special agreement. It was very hard. Rather, they were very hard. Sometimes they would be erect for so long that they would consider the medical advice they had learned about how you should go to the hospital if you have a hard on too long……. But, it would not be quite that long. The agony of longing and anticipation; however, would sometimes be quite consuming. At the end of their self-imposed 5 day chastity period, Jake would bathe Tiffany and massage her with oil and then the Trojan twins would ravage her insatiably, reveling newly in every curve and entry point of her body, and in short, fucking her brains out.

One pleasantly warm day, Jake and Tom both received happy scores on some brutal exams they had taken. Eager to celebrate and with big smiles on their faces, they elected to tie Tiffany to the bed with silky straps they had purchased some time ago in case of such a special occasion. Since they had never tied her up before, she realized pretty quickly that this was going to be something new. "What are you two up to?" By this time, she really trusted them and was not worried so much as really curious. She had noticed the ice cream and other goodies they had brought home. Of course, Tiffany had no idea they were planning to make her into an ice cream Sunday.

Tom and Jake put dollops of gourmet vanilla ice cream on her breasts, sending chills down her spine and making her nipples erect but then they poured loads of warm hot fudge all over her and dipped their dicks in and fed it to her that way. They had her lick and suck all the ice cream fudge off. What a blast they had, spraying her everywhere with cans of whipped cream, sticking cherries and sliced strawberries up her pussy and then trying to get them out with their tongues and lips, licking her clit in the gooey chocolate fudge. Then in a sweet messy way, they made love to her together in full consummation.

Afterwards, they all went into the mammoth luxury tub and while Tom held her in his lap, Jake used the spray nozzle, teasing her how messy she was. She really needed cleaning! He sprayed Tiffany all over but with special attention to her tits and pussy. Jake worked the nozzle expertly. The water droplets cascading onto her softer sensitive parts began to work their wonders sending electric signals throughout her whole body and she began to tremble, arching her back and moving her pelvis in little jolts as she came. Then they all soaked together in the tub until bedtime.

Another day, Tiffany happened to be on her pole, when Tom came home, and he plucked her right off of it, lay her on the fake fur rug, and pulling off her panties, plunged into her pussy missionary style. They kissed and he slid his tongue deep into her mouth as he thrust into her, feeling every sumptuous inch of her and the squeeze of her tight juicy pussy, reveling in her wonderfully smelling silky hair, then looking deep into her stunning eyes. He thrust and thrust, staring deep into her eyes in between passionate kisses, like he could enter her womb direct, even her belly, even her brain. He wanted to enter every part of her being with his massive member; wanted to penetrate and possess all that beauty. When he came, this time it was like free falling down a powerful waterfall, he was so delirious with it as he shot his wad into her core.

Jake was similarly in rapture. 'Really, I think I am in love with her.' She had completely fulfilled her part of the bargain and beyond. During the high stress of his residency, Tiffany had been like an oasis in the desert, quenching his greatest thirsts.

He came in to find her sound asleep on her stomach, looking like an angel in a little pink nightgown. Jake eased the soft fabric up, and felt the little fir between her legs. His hard on was almost unbearable, so hard and eager. He bent down and licked her little pink butt hole and then as she lightly stirred, he pulled her apart to make way for his dick and holding her hips, pushed it inexorably the full length in. Tiffany woke with a start to find herself pinned down, his dick sliding tightly in and out. Of course she knew immediately whose it was.

"Oh, hi, Jake."

Jake responded with more thrusts and grunted affectionately, "Hi, Tiffany."

Jake came in a smoking volcanic way, shaking and sputtering as he pounded into her and then spent himself in spurts of hot semen.

Thankfully, in the rare leisure moments when they were not spending all their time bonking with abandon, they discovered that whether it was chatting and giggling over sushi, being moved by a world situation, or taking in an action flick; they actually really enjoyed each other's company. With relief and delight, they noticed how when they were together, it all felt cheerful and easy like they had entered some special convivial comfort zone.

As the Trojan twins began to see themselves actually making it through their program, they could begin to imagine life after med school. With that came the realization of how deeply they wanted Tiffany to be there with them; really for forever. They shared their inspiration with Tiffany and they all chatted about their future plans together. A decision was made to put Tiffany through a part time nursing program, which would coincide with their completion of their residency. That way, when the time came to travel and serve in the world, she would be their natural companion on paper as well as in the home. Jake and Tom were prepared to sacrifice a little current availability in favor of future security. Of course, Tiffany was someone who did not mind her own study breaks punctuated with quickies. It was also decided they should marry. To be fair, Tiffany married Jake in a church and Tom in city hall.

Down the road, they would travel the world, saving lives by day, and continuing their luscious activities by night. Even further down the road, Jake and Tom would vie with each other, tackling her during her fertile times and trying to pump as much of their semen into her pussy as possible. She would end up having twins, and DNA would later show that one sperm had come from Jake and the other from Tom. Their little family would grow. To outward appearances, she was married to one brother and a good sister-in-law to the other. Strangely, different groups would have different ideas of which brother was her husband. They all grew to a ripe old age together, and had lots and lots of sex up until the very end.

LORD FORTINROD'S CASTLE (3) ****

(Or How Two Young Virgins receive a Proper Education and, As It Turns Out, a New Life)

Genevieve was on a train with her sister, Kate. She really wished she had asked Kate not to pull her corset so tight in the morning before they left. It was a little difficult to breath and the ribs were digging in. Aside from that, she was very excited about the trip, despite the sad occasion.

Their parents had recently passed. They had been so bereft at first and so it had been a huge comfort to get the letter from their distant relative, offering them assistance and a place to go. Now they were on their way to his actual castle. They had never before met or even heard of Lord Fortinrod of Candlebury. So, they had been especially surprised not only by his letter but that he had offered to put them up in his regal estate, see to it that they had a proper education, and provide them with a new life.

Genevieve and Kate's minds were in a tumult of questions. They wondered especially, amid ample excitement,

"What would Lord Fortinrod himself be like?" and

"What would life at a palace entail?" But mostly, they were just so thankful.

"Really, Kate, after something so awful, it seems like the best possible thing that could happen. What a relief to just get away from everything we know and get on to someplace entirely new."

They were as free of all attachments as two young ladies could be. Though both of marriageable age, neither had been allowed to have suitors before their family had suddenly become so poor that it was too late to make a good match. Without help, their prospects would have been rather dim. Now, with an air of expectation, they felt as if anything could happen.

The train had been a little nerve wracking. During the whole trip, all manner of men took visual liberties staring at them. The two girls were very beautiful, it was true, and they did feel flattered by

---

* (Lord Fortinrod) Another Victorian Style fairy tale, but containing dubious consent, mild bestiality-stroking a horse.

all the attention. It seemed fairly harmless as well, as if the men really just could not help themselves. The men simply kept forgetting to look away. Nonetheless, Kate and Genevieve felt a bit vulnerable without protection and so they cast down their eyes and sat closer together. They did not get much sleep on the journey.

By the time they arrived at the castle by carriage, they were absolutely exhausted. A little entourage of servants were there to greet them and maids scurried to attend them.

"You must be so tired and worn from your travels, poor dears," said the mother hen of the servant group. She bustled them out of their clothes and into bathtubs. Then she coordinated the servants in tending to their things, brushing their long hair, and getting them into nightgowns and bed after a quick dinner of meat and bread.

Genevieve was so grateful to get into the big comfy bed with soft sheets and fluffy pillows, that she barely landed before she was fast asleep. Even in the depths of sleep; however, there were times in her dreams where she felt like someone was watching her. Even that someone had carefully peeled down all the covers to look at her the better in the candlelight through her thin nightgown, and then just as carefully put the bedding back in place. In the morning, she shared this with Kate.

"What a scandalous dream!" Kate replied. "It must be from all that ogling on the train."

That morning, servants helped them dress and once in their bloomers and corsets, they were surprised to be gifted with brand new elegant petticoats and dresses, already exquisitely matched to their coloring in anticipation of their stay. All Genevieve and Kate could do was gush,

"Oh, they are so beautiful!"

They were also fed extravagantly well-prepared meals—everything tasted delicious. They had to be especially mindful not to overindulge. Over just a few days, they both put on a little weight, but thankfully it all went mostly to their rear ends and bust and so did not affect their waistlines in a way contrary to fashion. Generally there was just such comfort, beauty, and abundance in every facet of life at the castle.

So it was, with hearts already brimming with gratitude, that they finally met the Lord Fortinrod. He cut a dashing and powerful figure. They were quite impressed as he paced in front of them in the study, tapping a riding whip in his hand with little thought as he told them about the grounds, their studies, and other sundry.

"Within reason, you shall have the run of the place, my dears. Feel free to explore. I shall only expect that you will be obedient to your professors as well as myself. And, that you will learn our ways. Other than that, I expect you are grown enough to keep out of trouble. Lady Lucy will be coming to stay and so can tend to any matters in regard to you two that require a woman's touch."
Then turning to look at them squarely, he said with a grand smile:
"I really do plan to take very good care of you both."

Kate was to have vocal as well as horseback riding lessons and Genevieve would study art and gardening, as they had expressed those interests in their letters. They would also be expected, of course, to keep up their language and general lady skills.

The first day was amazing. Kate was surprised to meet such a handsome vocal instructor and then learn that he would be teaching her horseback riding as well. He ran her through various vocal exercises, complemented her voice, and then came up behind her, placing his hands under her bust, to teach her about her breath. She could feel and smell the sweet scent of his breath on her cheek as he explained various things to her, and begged her release and relax, release and relax. He was also strict, and challenged and worked her hard. Kate was certain she had learned and improved much the first day.

Then, they went horseback riding. Kate had thought to get on the horse sidesaddle as she had been taught, but Sir Maxwell, set her straight right away and said that at this castle, ladies ride astride and bareback. Kate was little prepared for such a thing, and tried to object. Quite oblivious, Sir Maxwell picked her neatly and bodily up, and planted her on the horse just as he had instructed. She was at least in a riding habit. Lord Fortinrod had kindly bestowed it upon her. She did not know how she would have managed if she had had all the bunching of petticoats to contend with. She had never had something like this pressing between her legs. It seemed a bit embarrassing and discomfiting at first, until she had gotten used to it.

With time, she realized how much easier it was to ride, and also to feel the fine steed beneath her and let it know her wishes. The horses name was Longhorn, and he was indeed an impressive stallion. Lustrous white, and majestic, he towered a bit over her when she stood beside him. They soon struck up a marvelous understanding. Similar to vocal training, Sir Maxwell tasked her hard with riding, such that she ended up riding until she was quite chafed and almost ready to drop. A sweet servant kindly put salve on her tender regions. Thankfully they did heal up in time for the next session.

Meanwhile, it was Lady Lucy who would be instructing Genevieve in art as well as gardening. Lady Lucy seemed quite radical in her approach and eschewed the idea of an easel, but had Genevieve get down on her hands and knees to work with the paints and other mediums. Instead of trying to keep tidy, Lady Lucy said that at the end of the session, Genevieve should look like she had been painting. She encouraged her to touch the texture of the paints and examine the slightest differences in shades of color and she constantly invited and encouraged her to paint everything she saw. At one point, Genevieve looked up, and was surprised to see that lady Lucy had given her something new to paint, having scandalously undone her corset and stays, and removed her blouse, so that Genevieve could paint her beautiful and ample naked bosom. Lady Lucy encouraged Genevieve to pay attention to light and shadow, line and flow. She also pressed Genevieve to not just see, but smell and feel everything deeply, take it all in, to be alive to every moment. This approach to life and art continued when it was time for gardening lessons as well. Lady Lucy made Genevieve remove her shoes to go in the garden.

"But what if my hem gets muddy?"

"No matter, Genevieve, there are more where that came from."

So, off to the garden they went; Lady Lucy inviting Genevieve to acknowledge and talk to each plant and learn their names and even the differences between individuals of the same species.

"Growing things like to be seen and felt and appreciated, Genevieve."

Genevieve and Kate met up that night and although again exhausted, they were so exhilarated by their experiences; they could not wait to tell everything to each other. They each had their own grand quarters but because of Genevieve's strange dream, they decided to both sleep in one room, and chose Genevieve's because it had the beautiful large French doors leading out to the garden.

That night, right after they were all ready for bed, a knock came on the door. Opening the door, in came Dr. Bold.

"Lord Fortinrod sent me to give you two girls your nightly constitutional and see to your care."

"But we are not sick, Dr. Bold," the girls demurred.

"No matter, we will make sure you don't become so." And with that, he took out his black bag and ushered a couple maids around making provisions. The first thing he had them both do, was lie on their tummies, and lift up their nightgowns to expose their buttocks, so he could take their temperature.

"Is this really necessary, Dr. Bold?" Kate tentatively asked but he answered without missing a beat:

"Absolutely!"

He promptly put a little grease on the thermometers and stuck them simultaneously in. The little glass rods felt very cold as they slid up their bottoms. The girls were highly embarrassed to be thus exposed as they waited for what seemed an interminable time. Dr. Bold bade them stay put as he pulled the thermometers out and read them leisurely but with care, then noted down the temperature in a little black book.

"Is everything alright?" asked Genevieve.

"Oh, yes" Dr. Bold said absently.

He then took out an impressively sized cobalt blue bottle, and a large spoon.

"You can sit up now and open up, girls."

"What is this, doctor?"

"Just your constitutional, per Lord Fortinrod's instructions. We need you in tip top shape, we do."

Obediently, the girls swallowed the substantial drought of who knows what. The liquid itself was a deep green hue and in all its immense bitterness and strangeness, did not seem made for human consumption at all. To chase the flavor away, he followed up the constitutional by giving them some cherry flavored syrup.

Kate and Genevieve had thought they would then be alone and have more time to chat, but they soon discovered it was not to be. Two women came in whom Kate and Genevieve had never seen before. Dr. Bold promptly left the girls in their care. It turned out they were Swedish masseuses. They proceeded to strip the girls of their nightgowns and massage every inch of their bodies, except of course between their legs. Each toe was lovingly tended, as was every other part of their bodies. Relaxed, fatigued, and massaged, they both soon fell into a deep sleep.

In the morning, they awoke refreshed.

"I had another strange dream," Genevieve told Kate.

"I was trying to get out those doors to walk in the garden in the moonlight, but they were locked and I could not get out. In the background, I only heard 'Not time, not ripe.' "

Curious, the girls went and checked the doors. They opened easily.

"It was just a dream," Kate affirmed.

As for Lord Fortinrod, he was not nearly as formal as they would have thought. He made very silly jokes during meals and thought nothing of pulling these young ladies onto his lap to tell them strange exotic stories of Africa and the Indies. Nor did he think anything amiss about chasing them down and then pouncing on them to tickle them until their bosoms were heaving from hysterical giggles and they thought they might faint. Sniffing salts would be summoned as if it was all the most usual thing in the world.

Kate and Genevieve got easily accustomed to their new routines. They had their lessons and meals by day and constitutional time by night. It seemed there was no escaping either the rectal thermometer or that odd potion, and so they soon got used to them both.

As for Genevieve, she felt she was becoming more sensitive. She could feel her whole body and see everything like she never had before. Her art was taking off in leaps and bounds and seemed to be gaining in depth and dimension. Similarly, gardening had come alive in a whole new way such that she was beginning to feel like the plants were talking back to her. They were starting to have their own distinct personalities and Genevieve could now sense in her own skin what it was they needed and how much moisture they preferred.

Kate was not sure if there was some spirit alive in the castle or whether it was just the culture and ways of the place, but she was gradually becoming more free and less inhibited. Her voice was becoming more free also. Now, when she sang, it just bubbled out of her. As for her relationship with the stallion, Longhorn; it was only becoming more intimate and passionate as time went on. She loathed leaving him at the end of the day.

It was for that reason, that she was late one evening for her constitutional. She had lingered in the barn with Longhorn, who seemed a bit restless and impatient, stamping his hoofs and switching his tail, even whinnying at times. Kate tried stroking him and feeding him an apple but it did not seem to help. Looking down, she saw that his large member had slipped out of its sheath and was like a very pink fleshy protrusion of startling size; standing out like a horizontal pole. Kate had never seen such a thing before and was fascinated. This was clearly part of his male apparatus and related to baby horse making, (from what she could glean from the very limited info she had ever been given or hinted to on the subject). Attuned to the magnificent beast, she realized that this was the likely source of his restlessness today. 'Dear Longhorn, if only I could make you more comfortable and contented.' Looking around, and noting she was alone, it occurred to Kate, that maybe she could. Mightn't he like it if she touched it? She could not be like a mare, but perhaps if she pet the inflamed implement like she pet the rest of him, it might give him some relief.

Kate got up very close and gently took the member in her hands. A bit tentatively at first, she started to explore what strokes seemed to good effect. Tuning in to Longhorn's particular snorts whether derision or pleasure, she was able to tease out when she had a good motion going. Kate gained confidence as she went along; instinctually, speeding up as the horse became more positively agitated. Suddenly, Longhorn reared up and Kate was left trying to hold on while simultaneously needing to keep herself well out of the way. Longhorn came up on his front legs, and then thrust some extra pointed thrusts in quick succession. Out came a splat and spatter of white fluid, after which his phallus shrunk and went limp in her hands. All this took Kate by surprise. But that surprise paled in comparison to her surprise when upon hearing a noise, she turned to find Sir Maxwell there avidly watching her. She looked down at her hands and realized she was still holding Longhorn's limp rod.

"You're a curious one, aren't you?" Sir Maxwell smiled. Kate blushed bright red and stammered in mortification,

"I ju-ju-just wanted to help Longhorn."

"And well you did, Kate, well you did." "I tell you what, Kate, I won't breath a word of this to anyone, but I hope you want to help me as much as you helped Longhorn…"

Kate gestured holding out her hand, questioningly.

"Actually, I had something else in mind." But seeing Kate's fright, Sir Maxwell added "Don't worry, I won't take your maidenhead." Then under his breath, he murmured, "That is already spoken for."

With that reassurance, Kate nodded her consent and proceeded to follow her instructor's instructions; laying herself down on her back on a pile of fresh hay. As Sir Maxwell's hands went to his trousers, Kate modestly closed her eyes.

"Don't you want to see mine, now that you have seen the horses, Kate? Open your eyes."

Kate did as she was told and saw Sir Maxwell's admirably shaped member. Although much shorter than the stallions it was still quite substantial and protruded itself up and out with a jaunty flare. Sir Maxwell knelt down and straddled Kate's face. To her great surprise, he then proceeded to part her lips and slide his ample cock right into her mouth, aiming up and toward the back so that she would not gag, he pressed into her soft palate and eased down her throat. He was a clean man, so his scent was very fresh and Kate was surrounded by it. How distinctive and sweet but also animal it was in some kind of way. The sensation was oddly compelling and between that and the unusual position she was in, of this rubbery hard but somehow still human fleshy rod sliding in and out of her mouth, Kate was fully absorbed in the moment. A natural suction occurred between her mouth and lips and Sir Maxwell began to pump harder and harder, until he came, ejaculating warm semen down her throat.

"That stretch to your soft palate should help your high notes, Kate." "Oh, and Kate? You had better get to your room for your constitutional. The doctor has been looking for you."

In a complete daze, Kate sat up and tried to get her head together to go face the thermometer.

While Kate had been away, Genevieve had had some adventures of her own. Dr. Bold, finding her alone, had decided to try his new Granville gadget on her, a common new treatment for hysteria.

"But I'm not hysterical, Dr. Bold." Dr. Bold did not seem to think that mattered at all.

"I'm sure it will heal anything that ails you, whatever it may be." He had her raise her legs. She tried to keep things covered, but Dr. Bold impatiently pushed the sheet aside to expose her rosy privates in their little nest of soft hair.

"You do not need to be shy with me, Genevieve. I am a physician."

With that, he turned the strange silver machine on. It made a frightful hammering noise as the black knob on the bottom bobbed in and out at rapid speed. Dr. Bold placed the bobbing metal knob gently on top of her naked privates, near the top where tender flesh met her mound. There was no escaping the pulsating impulses tapping their impression on her there. Genevieve was perplexed at the range of feeling stimulated in these normally all but ignored regions of her physique. The tapping clamored for her attention; evoking sensations that shifted and changed from moment to moment.

"What is this supposed to do, Dr. Bold?" gasped Genevieve. Dr. Bold barely noticed her question. "You'll see," he said absently. He was absorbed in concentrating on the little machine in motion and observing her responses. Genevieve began to feel the sensations become more wavy like electrical currents that seemed strangely pleasurable. Ripples of these currents were starting to pulse with the vibrations from her privates to her breasts and all the way down to her toes. She also felt like some extra sensitive part was raising itself up from the top of her privates, like a little knob raising its head. 'What in the world?' Genevieve thought. She shifted her hips so it would not be quite so sensitive. Then, all of a sudden, the waves of rolling intensity converged and she was involuntarily thrusting her hips and arching her back in an intense climax. It was shockingly good, and she emerged dazed and breathless. "Success!" exclaimed Dr. Bold.

At that moment, Kate came in the door, and Genevieve hastily pulled down her nightgown. Kate and Genevieve did not make eye contact. Neither was sure how to tell the other what had recently transpired in their newfound lives. They got their thermometers duly inserted and took their droughts of medicine. Kate told Genevieve that she had a lot on her mind and so would go sleep in her own bed tonight. Relieved, Genevieve said that was fine.

That night, Genevieve again had the dream about trying to get out and heard the words "Soon, not time, not ripe." This time she realized that perhaps it was not so much a dream as sleep walking, because she woke with a start to found herself pressed with her breasts tightly wedged against the glass doors. Genevieve went back to bed, only to find herself dreaming the other dream again. This was the one where someone comes in with a candle and pulls the covers down to look longingly at her. As it turned out; however, that was not a dream either. Waking just enough to know someone was there; she kept her eyes closed at first.

"What a pretty thing," murmured the voice of Lord Fortinrod. He bent down and caressed her face, hair and then down to her breasts, cradling them, lingering there, and then traced his hand down her tummy and to between her legs which made Genevieve do a little jolt.

"It's alright. I see you're awake, dear," He said conversationally. "Of course I won't take your maidenhead, (that is already spoken for), but I am allowed another pleasure." Then a little more sternly, "You would not want to keep me from such a pleasure, would you?"

By now, Genevieve had opened her eyes and was staring up at the commanding presence of Lord Fortinrod, who also seemed quite kindly at the same time. She nodded, "No." She would never want anything to do with keeping him from pleasure.

"Good, dear, then we have an agreement".

So saying, he gently rolled her over. He raised the soft muslin fabric of Genevieve's nightgown to expose her tender, shapely bottom. Opening his breaches, holding his substantial member in one hand, he parted her cheeks with the other, then started to rub the head of his pre-cum dripping rod on the little rosy furrowed opening. Then ever so slowly, he began to push in, exerting enough force to overcome any resistance but being fairly gentle at the same time. He knew he was large, and about halfway in, he paused and asked,

"Genevieve, are you alright?" Genevieve nodded that she was okay but asked a bit shocked,

"Does this really give you pleasure?"

"Oh yes," he answered with emphasis and then with one big push, he made his way the rest of the way in. Lying on her that way, lodged up to the hilt, firmly up her ass; he moved her hair aside and began to kiss her neck as he pumped languidly in and out of her backside. By this time, Genevieve was strangely aware how his action, in that formerly very private place, had begun to please and stir her in ways she had never known. She did not just feel it in her ass, but in her pussy and tummy as well. The sensations seemed to be spreading out in pleasure waves and adding to each other exponentially until she started unconsciously to moan. He gradually worked up his speed and intensity, such that he began thrusting hard into her tight buttocks and then all of a sudden, he gave way to a shuddering orgasm that made him jerk and thrust in little jolts and then squirt copious accumulated gooey seed, from all the time he had been visiting and waiting for her, straight into her. Turning her around, he kissed her sumptuously on the lips. Then holding her chin, and looking deep into her eyes, he said,

"Things are going to go quite well for you here, Genevieve. You will see what gifts will unfold for you."

The next morning, the girls were plum exhausted and both overslept. They ended up late to their lessons. Neither Sir Maxwell nor Lady Lucy was pleased. Genevieve and Kate were shocked to find themselves being told to line up and lift their dresses and bend over, wherein they were then soundly spanked like children. Sore aggrieved at this treatment, they later went and complained to Lord Fortinrod. He listened to them attentively and then suggested that perhaps, if it was so difficult to be on time, they need not worry about dressing properly. Next time, they could just go in their nightgowns and robe.

"Are you sure that would be appropriate, Lord Fortinrod?" "Certainly. I decide what is appropriate and clearly, according to your professors, it is more essential that you be on time."

The incident did end up helping to bring the two of them back together from their recent alienation. They hardly had to talk about it, it was more in the way they looked at each other over lunch. They remembered lovingly that they were sisters after all, and had always been so close. Kate and Genevieve realized that there was nothing that could come to pass, that the other too might not be subject to. At any rate, with all those instances of their bare bottoms being so exposed, really, how could they be embarrassed or ashamed in regard to each other? No, they were assuredly in this together, with both its wonders and strangeness.

They soon forgave Lady Lucy and Sir Maxwell as well. They knew what immensely good teachers they were, such that the good far outweighed the bad. Kate found out Sir Maxwell was right about her high notes and found her voice improved yet one more notch above the previous level just the day before, such that she could now sing with a fully free ecstatic soprano voice that knew no bounds. Kate could also ride with greater ease and speed than she had ever dreamed.

As for Genevieve, she felt fully able to recreate in art, whatever her eye could see or heart imagine and she had begun to make beautiful hidden forests with all manner of plants who had now become her friends. So magical did they look, that Lady Lucy said she could swear she had seen fairies and nymphs playing within them.

That evening, there was a flurry of attention over their thermometers. Dr. Bold seemed very excited as he read the reading and called in Lord Fortinrod who watched as the thermometers were reinserted a second time into the young women's bottoms, just to make sure. It was all taking even longer than usual. Kate was still dutifully staying on her tummy but her buttocks were getting little goose bumps from the chill.

"What is it?" Kate asked, but all that Dr. Bold would say was,

"Just progress. Your temperatures are a little elevated, but it is just as expected," he said mysteriously.

With that and a little more whispered consultation, the girls were then required to down 3 large tablespoons of the green odd tasting constitutional this time, instead of their usual one. Kate and Genevieve both felt a little dizzy and nauseous afterwards, and so lay down quickly, trying to still their heads and stomachs. The Swedish Masseuses came in soon after, and did a particularly thorough job massaging every inch of their bodies and may have gone on doing it for hours for all they knew, for they were soon fast asleep.

It was not a peaceful sleep; however, but a hot, flustered and fitful one. Back they were at those French doors trying to get out, but this time, they heard "ripe and ready enough to begin," and the doors opened easily. Eager and almost gleefully, they ran and ran barefoot through the gardens until they arrived at a little forest. There, there was a bunch of what appeared to be nymphs or fairy folk (Genevieve even wondered: had this dream been suggested by Lady Lucy's ideas about her art?)

They were very beautiful, graceful, and women-like creatures; all completely naked. They gathered around them, touching their hair and being very affectionate. The nymph creatures offered them beautiful fruits and goblets of wine, even lifting it to their lips. Such hospitality! The girls did not even consider declining. Instead they drank deep and delved into the juicy succulent fruits, which stained their lips with sweet colorful juices. Kate and Genevieve figured this was a dream and so surely no harm could come, whatever myths might say about imbibing fairy fare. The succulent fruit was almost startlingly delicious and the wine made them feel very relaxed. They began to feel warm and tingly all over. They began to notice beautiful music seemingly wafting in and out around them from the surrounding forest. Kate thought she could see some strange half animal, half man, hiding here and there behind trees, but could never see him clearly.

Kate lounged in the forest and gradually fell into a daze listening to the melodic peaks and valleys of the music and trying to discern that mysterious presence. Meanwhile, some of the nymphs gathered together and began laying hands on Genevieve. She thought they just wanted to touch and squeeze her but then all of a sudden they had lifter her. They carted her bodily off to the edge of a deep pond. They began pulling at her insistently to go into the water. She waded in a little but tried to hold her nightgown up to keep it from getting wet as they playfully began to bathe her. Genevieve could not help giggling in surprise at the lusciousness of this seeming dream as the nymphs cupped water and trickled it between her breasts and splashed the water up between her legs and then slid their hands as if to wash between her thighs while others cradled and caressed her, their wet hands lifting her hair and using flowers like sponges to rub the water on her neck and back.

As if a shadow of urgency passed over them, in a moment it was as if Genevieve and Kate could both sense that day might be breaking in the other world and that they needed to go back and wake up. Genevieve disentangled herself from the water nymphs and she climbed back out of the water. She found Kate and they both ran from the nymphs, who looked very sad indeed to see them go. They ran until the girls had stumbled back into their room and into bed.

Almost instantly, it seemed, the maids were there trying to wake them. Exhausted, and remembering their spanking and what Lord Fortinrod had said, they asked the maids to bring their breakfast to their classrooms, and decided to just go as they were. They arrived all disheveled and in their nightgowns, not even having remembered their bathrobes.

"Well," said Sir Maxwell "I wonder what you two have been doing all night?" They blushed. As if he knew! Lady Lucy smiled and drew Genevieve into the other classroom.

Feeling quite naked in the classroom in merely a light muslin nightgown and no stays or bloomers, Kate almost asked if she could go back and dress properly, but Sir Maxwell had already begun running her through her vocalizes. "Excellent, Kate. You sing very well. Really, you are almost at the end of what I can teach you." He came up behind her, as he had done before, and wrapped his arms around her front, and had her keep singing for a while as he did so. This time, though, he also began to gingerly fondle her breasts. Kate could feel Sir Maxwell's bulge, hard against her buttocks. She began to pant slightly, making it difficult to sing and as he ran a hand down to touch her between the legs, her singing cut off in a sharp intake of air.

"Oh, Kate, are you getting wet down there?" Kate nodded, 'yes' and asked, "But what does that mean?"

"Ah. That, Kate, means that you are excited and… ready for pleasure." So saying, he began to rub slow circles in the soft flesh over and around her clit. She might not know about that special spot, but *he* sure did. He continued that swirling touch with one hand as he stroked her breasts with the other. Kate sighed and relaxed into him.

Still working those artful circles, he gently led her to lean over a table.

"You know I cannot take you in your cunny, Kate." (Kate was not sure but she thought she knew what he meant and 'Why not?' was all she wanted to ask.)

"But there is another way." Kate was bemused to find that after a whole life of being sworn to protect her maidenhead, she was almost yelling inside, 'Take me, take me!' She wanted him to ravage and penetrate her in an animal sort of way.

Still with those circles, Sir Maxwell reached behind and under her. He stroked her pussy once luxuriously from front to back, gathering a scoop of her own cream, which he smoothed up her crack and also onto his, by now, extremely hard member. He was so erect, he needed no guide to stick his cock right to the spot of that tight little pink opening, and pulling her cheeks a bit apart with one hand, he slid force ably right into her ass with one strong glide. Kate gasped with a shudder, but then Sir Maxwell's hard cock was already all the way in and a fleeting ache rapidly changed to feeling a rare kind of good. The pointed imposing sensation seemed to be combining with the tender circle feeling such that Kate found herself moaning and moving without even meaning to as the pleasure took hold of her. Of their own volition, her hips began pumping and her buttocks squeezing. Kate little understood the contortions that took over her whole pelvic region, nor the sweet noises bursting from her lips, that she could not restrain. It sure felt good, though, as she gave way to her first ever orgasm. Sir Maxwell came also, causing him to thrust more heavily in, until he spurted his wad hard into her. Sir Maxwell kissed her cheek and said,

"I really enjoyed that, Kate. Thank you. And you, did you like what just happened?" Kate smiled and nodded still fresh with her own surprise,

"Oh, yes!"

Then on quite a different note, Sir Maxwell paused and said quietly,

"Well, Kate, I think this may be the end of our lessons"

"But why, Sir Maxwell. Don't you like teaching me?" Kate asked in distress.

"Very much so, Kate, and it is not I who would be the one to leave you…I just wanted a chance to say goodbye."

He hugged her close and kissed away her tears.

"Kate, there are other delightful things in store for you"

But he would not say what.

While all this was happening, in the other room, Genevieve was having some rather different adventures. Lady Lucy had slipped out of all her elaborate clothing, and laid down in front of Genevieve with her legs spread so that her pussy was fully exposed.

"Draw all that you see, Genevieve."

Genevieve had never seen a woman's privates like this in all her life. It looked like a large fleshy flower. It was quite mysterious and exotic. She recognized something important about it that reminded her of Dr. Bolt's gadget.

"What is the little ball at the top, and what is it for?"

"That is a clit and it is purely for a woman's pleasure." Genevieve was a bit touched and amazed. The idea that women had something like that, a little ball on their privates that was just for pleasure...Genevieve studied and drew and studied and drew. Then Lady Lucy got her a mirror and said,

"Alright now. Time for a self portrait."

Genevieve protested. She was not sure she wanted to see, no less draw, hers. What if it were ugly? But with much encouragement, she looked.

"Oh, Lady Lucy, it's beautiful!"

And so again, she studied and drew. At the end of that, Lady Lucy reviewed with Genevieve the key points of what she had learned about art and plants, and then in her own way, she also said goodbye. She hugged Genevieve tightly against her grand bosom, and told her what an excellent student she had been and what beauty is hers to create wherever she goes.

That evening, they were again given the three large tablespoons of green fluid. Once again, it made them feel quite dizzy and nauseous until the masseuses massaged them into dreamy oblivion. Again, also, they found themselves running gleefully through the French Doors, into the garden and deeper into the woods. The nymphs were there waiting for them, with even more delicious fruits and wine, which they imbibed unlike they ever would have in regular life. It was all so delicious and delectable. They drank and ate their fill until they felt a bit blissfully sluggish. Like before, they were also soon separated. Those nymphs really seemed to want Genevieve in the pond and so had soon carried her off. Kate was perfectly content to keep hearing the beautiful music and stay with the group of nymphs in the woods.

They tried to slide Kate's nightgown off, but for some reason she thought she should leave it on in case she ran out of time and had to rush back for class. The nymphs came up close to her, such that she was in the middle of a tight circle of them, feeling their luscious breasts against her own, their panting breath, their silky hair. They danced like this in this tight circle. It was some wild and wonderful dance in which they moved very quickly but were still so close together; almost like one body. All the time, there was that ecstatic music. Kate felt moved to begin singing with it, and the trills of her warbling operatic coloratura voice wafted up and intermingled with the transcendent sounds of the music, which at times seemed like an entire orchestra but at others, just a flute or a pipe.

Kate knew what it meant to be aroused now, and noted to her surprise, that she was actually aroused. Her nipples were erect and her pussy was wet, even as she sang and danced with the nymphs. There was somehow an additional source of excitement in the mix, almost a tantalizing scent. She kept catching glimpses of the half man, half goat. Was he the one making the music? As they grew tired, they all lay down together. They were like one body, rolling and rolling over and around each other. Suddenly, they unfolded their circle so that Kate was on her back in the middle of all of them. There was a peaceful moment now, as they cuddled and lounged beside her, giving her still more wine and feeding her more fruit. They giggled and whispered to each other while stringing flowers in her hair. There seemed to be a sense of anticipation in the air.

Then they leaned her all the way back and she realized that they were cuddling each arm but that meant that they were also holding her down. She wondered why they would hold her like this, as she looked at the sky, which was a beautiful pink color. She soon grew distracted by all the dazzling wonder around her and relaxed again. She was noticing all the fertility and abundance of the place. There were multitudes of butterflies and dragonflies mating. Some even began to land in her hair and on her body.

It was in the midst of all that beauty that she saw him; the half goat half man, towering above her, as if inspecting her. It was definitely *his* smell and *his* music. He looked powerful, with large muscles and horns, standing with a kind of weighty agility on strong animal legs with hoofs. Not only that, out of the animal furry half of him, sticking out with complete defiance of gravity, was a somehow more impressive cock than she had seen before (in all her limited experience). It was not so much long as the horse's but rather thick and almost like it could have had a real bone lodged inside. That is how solidly erect it was. As for him, he looked to Kate, like there was a singular wit and cleverness in his eyes that took in every aspect of her being. He nodded, and the Nymphs turned Kate onto her knees, so he could take her from behind. Kate was trembling a little with both fear and expectation. She could feel and hear him smelling her all over, feel his warm breath as he sniffed and licked her privates. He could taste the fertility of her juices. He could also taste that she was already ready for him. The nymphs hurriedly parted Kate's pussy lips as she felt the Satyr, put his formidable rod to the mark, and shoved into her a little part of the way and then with another push right through her virginal hymen. Kate cried out a little with that sudden stretch, as the nymphs stroked her, but soon Kate was just taken up with all the intensity of this huge rod up her cunny and how very good it felt.

All the other sexual experiences she had had lately, seemed suddenly trivial. If she had known more anatomy and terms, she would have known that what was rocking her body so powerfully, was that he was both doing deep tissue massage on her G-spot while also hitting her cervix hard. But, all she knew was that the penetration was so full and thorough, she could only uncontrollably shiver, pant, and moan with excitement. It was like he was sending ripples of powerful messages throughout every cell in her body, claiming her. He would have her completely now.

This only seemed to come home further as he rammed her harder and harder, faster and faster, and then howled, as he shot gushing spurts of potent, thick semen, into her cunny. It was then that he reached around and squeezed her nipples, and sniffing her hair, felt her lips. His weighty member slid out and the nymphs turned Kate around, smiling joyfully as if to congratulate her, and offered her more wine and fruit. The Satyr gave her a knowing smile which, like the rest of him, was quite booming. The satyr joined in as the nymphs pulled Kate down again to lie with them in a huddle and they all fell asleep together. Kate tried to stay awake so she would be ready to wake up from this goaty scented dream and go back, but she could not do it. She drifted dreamily off while she felt a tickle. From the copious supply of seed he had pumped inside her, a little bit had overflowed and dribbled down her thigh.

While all this was happening with Kate, Genevieve was off at the pond. The water nymphs had played with her in the water among the lilies and lily pads, with frogs croaking, birds singing, and a similar profusion of butterflies and mating dragonflies. She noticed also that there was an abundance of floating fish eggs just drifting in the water. Life had been very busy in these parts, with the business of Spring. Everything seemed to be about procreation, propagation and progeny. Life was calling life to life. Genevieve could sense the thrill of it, even if she did not understand what it all meant. She could feel every living thing telling its own version of this message to her, as surely as she had learned to listen to plants. She could taste the excitement in all these different languages, whether of frogs or butterflies.

At one point, the nymphs held Genevieve such that her head stayed above water. They gently spread her legs while a school of fish came and started nosing her all over, darting in and out and bestowing on her what felt like innumerable cool kisses, even in her nether regions. So absorbed in this novel experience, Genevieve did not notice for a moment, the rumbling and foaming of water from the mysterious depths below.

Then, He emerged. He was wild and a deep green color all over, with all matter of plant matter commingled in his long hair. He had bright, deep blue eyes like dark pools of water. The nymphs held Genevieve steady as he studied her. Then he came and touched her face and breasts. Genevieve felt strangely unafraid. She was taken with the beauty all around her and soothed by fairy food and drink. Also, though, she could feel him resonating with the same message all around her. He came a little closer and her body began to respond to this fascinating and clearly powerful creature. Genevieve could not see well in the water but she did see what seemed to be the shadow of a large green member. It looked very thick and the head curved in toward his belly. This wild man of the deep came up still closer to her; so close, she could smell the heavy organic plant matter smell of him. The look in his eyes was mesmerizing, such that she began to find it difficult to complete any trains of thought. The eyes told her to just give herself to this, give herself to him.

  The nymphs held her afloat in the water, positioned exactly as he would wish. He took hold of her hips, and situated the large fleshy green head of his member right at the opening of her vulva, and nestled just so between her sweet pussy lips, he lingered there without yet going in. He pulled her face to his and slid his long tongue into her mouth. Soon, it seemed he was inserting some kind of fluid down her throat that she could not help but swallow and swallow as he kissed her. The taste was a very green plant taste, but fresh and lightly sweet like blended greens and apples. It was oddly compelling.

  In fact, she was so absorbed in this new and unexpected pleasure, she almost forgot the presence of his member lodged between her legs. Then, with a seeming load of power behind him and holding her firmly, he thrust his member all the way into her, pushing his way right through the tightness of her cherry with just a little yelp from Genevieve. He held her tight as he thrust deeply into her. He was so large and it was so intense, that Genevieve realized she was biting her lip. He noticed also, and smiled at her, and then put his hand behind her head and pushed her lips to his again to kiss her some more, sliding more of his special syrup down her throat.

    Meanwhile, he was thrusting and pumping down below. He was so thick and hard and the angle was so amazing, he was ramming this point inside of her which seemed directly connected to all the pleasure centers Lady Lucy had taught her about. Not only that, but his extreme member seemed to be teaching her pussy how to have a whole new kind of pleasure, as if waking her cunny up from a long dormancy. With each thrust, he was flooding her with trills of sweet sensation. The whole thing seemed to be attracting a lot of blood, leading to a strangely happy swelling in her parts. This was actually now increasing the pressure and tightness as he pushed in and out. It felt like an eternity of bliss. Surely this was all she could have meaningfully done her whole life? The slow build and burn continued until, in an explosion of contractions and thrusts, he jolted a copious wad of thick, gooey, potent semen deep into her cunny. Then, he kissed her again luxuriously before he pulled out of both her mouth and pussy.

He looked deep into her eyes, and she returned the gaze, fully naked and open to him, as he plumbed her depths in still another way. Then he took her hand and began to pull her down into the water, but the nymphs seemed to be letting him know "Not yet," because they held onto Genevieve tight and pulled in the opposite direction to keep her head above water. He appeared to graciously acquiesce, kissing here again; then releasing her hand. He turned to go on his own; descending back down into the depths from whence he had come. The nymphs gave Genevieve more wine and fruit, then pulled her out of the pond onto the soft grass, and in a huddle they all went to sleep. Like Kate, Genevieve thought she should somehow stay awake in this dream, but sleep soon overtook her.

Eventually Kate and Genevieve awoke and ran back to Genevieve's room, through the French doors and into bed. When they awoke, what seemed only a moment later; however, Genevieve made a very telling discovery. Her nightgown was damp, but had it been just that, she might have thought she had just sweat in the night. Even stranger, there was a dried green spot on the bed and looking down, she noticed a trail of the same viscous emerald fluid, not yet dry, on her inner thigh. Kate made her own discovery as there were still exotic beautiful flowers woven into her hair. For both of them, their pussies felt somehow different and a little raw. They looked at each other with weighty glances. Last night was not a dream.

Kate and Genevieve went to see Lord Fortinrod. He was not at all surprised to see them. He took in their questioning faces, and said

"How do you think my grounds and castle have flourished so? I have a deal with the two Fairy Kings who rule this land, that I will supply them each with a beautiful virgin once every 20 years. With that, they allow me, and a few chosen associates to live forever and retain all this bounty. You two have been the perfect pair and will do quite well in your new lives. We will miss you, but you can still come visit. That is if, once you get settled, you yet have time and inclination."

They knew what he meant, because they were already quite anxious, yearning, really, to get back. But they still had more questions:

"And what of that awful constitutional?"

"Oh, that is a fairy brew the kings give me to help with the task. It aids the transition and conversion to fairy blood. The massages help the body better absorb it with more ease and comfort. We have been learning over time, how to make things as smooth and easy as possible. We know that once the rectal temperature begins to rise, the serum is taking its proper affect. We also know the limits of what we are allowed to take for ourselves and what we must save for the fairy kings."

"One last thing, Lord Fortinrod, what was that whole thing with the spanking, when you knew it would be impossible for us to be on time?"

"Ah, dears—-sorry about that. But, it is the only way we have found to make sure our very distracted visitors still find their way back for their last doses of medicine and last classes. You two did very well, really. Have a beautiful time in your new lives. I know you will make lovely nymphs, and the kings will be very happy with you."

Kate and Genevieve could not help but be delighted that they would get to stay in the nymph paradise forever, and so, they really could not fault Lord Fortinrod for any prior subterfuge. They both gave him a big hug goodbye.

Then, as fast as they could, they went; following the same path of their dreams, knowing now; they need not wait for nighttime.

The nymphs let up a cheer at their arrival and they all giggled joyfully together as they dined on more wine and fruit.

LOVE NOT WAR (3)****

(Or The Alien Elixir is Quite a Fixer)

Colette was once again on the verge of tears watching the news. Children were suffering in the latest conflict on another continent. It was as if they were right there in her living room, but she was helpless to save them. She turned off the TV to pray and breath. "Please, make me an instrument to help!" Colette was not politically active. She had found the processes involved too discouraging and disillusioning, but she cared tremendously. She just had not found her path to do anything about it yet.

She heard A key turn in the lock. Her live-in boyfriend, Mike walked in. She greeted him kindly with,

"Hello, honey. How was your day?"

"The usual, I guess." Mike replied, absent-mindedly.

Colette came up to him and coquettishly stroked his cheek and neck, trailing her fingers down past his navel to his zipper, toying there for a moment. Mike had paused a moment, but now resumed his landing at home activities. He put down his briefcase, took off the shoes. Colette unbuttoned her top, and unhooked her bra so that her rosy nippled breasts bounced out and presented them to him.

"You know that is so very nice, babe, but I am really tired." Mike cupped a little and squeezed, then picked up his laptop to check his email.

Colette was really horny today. Maybe it was where she was in her cycle. She always got really randy right in the middle, at peak fertility and also right before Aunt Flow came to visit. Or perhaps it was just because she was over-due for her weekly session. Colette ascribed to the belief that a bonk a week keeps horniness at bay. 'I think it has been over three weeks,' she sighed. Solo activity was nice for maintenance, but only if she had been thoroughly pumped on a weekly basis. Her whole body craved it. 'It must be all those pressure points a dick hits on the inside'. She knew she had read about that somewhere. Now those points were probably all clogged

---

* (Love not War) This Sci-Fi epic contains non-consensual sex due to viral compulsion as well as alien abduction and tentacle sex.

up. Anyway, it was no use bothering him. He would only do it when he was good and ready and she loathed a duty session anyway. She wanted him to want her. That was the biggest turn on ever.

Colette attempted to turn her mind to other things. She took a strange sparkly object out of her pocket. It was something she had found in the street earlier that day. The little token almost glowed when she picked it up. It turned different colors, mostly pink, blue, and green. Really, it was quite mesmerizing. She ended up putting it under her pillow for some reason, but throughout the evening, Colette kept going back to peek at it.

She decided to pamper herself and take a bath by candle light with lavender oil in the water. She shaved and trimmed her pubes, washed her hair. She used the detachable water spigot to relieve some tension, applying the massage spray function to send circular ripples all around her clit and lips. She was already so horny. What with the combination of the warm water, and thoughts of one of her favorite functional fantasies, like alien abduction, it did not take long for her to orgasm. She slid her fingers into her pussy afterwards, feeling her own warm creamy juices, and then gently sliding her fingers around her now sensitized clit. She felt her breasts also, just feeling how good she felt in that post-orgasmic way. Colette knew she was quite attractive 'and if I were a male, I would have me every night.' It seemed like such a waste…

Mike was oblivious to these activities and soon fell asleep on the couch with his laptop. Colette came over and covered him with a blanket and then took herself to bed, peeking at the little sparkly object one last time.

Later that night, after being sound asleep for some time, Colette found herself surrounded by those same colors, as if she were actually inside the sparkly object. She tried to move but it was like her arms and legs were all tied up. Her nightgown had disappeared and here she was, naked, and bound spread eagle in a kind of a bubble. Then this magnificent crystal sphere with her held fast inside began to levitate and rotate. As she rose to the ceiling, the roof of her house gently opened like a can being peeled by a can opener. 'That is awfully strange,' she thought as the ball with her so neatly captive inside, slipped easily out through the opening and then her house was carefully closed and sealed again. Surrounded by light and perfectly warm, her body was like a little star in the middle, gently spinning its way up and up toward the night sky and the moon. But wait, there was something else closer. She had never seen a spaceship but this looked the part; just like in all the books and movies she had ever seen on the subject. Despite being a bit dizzy from spinning round and round, she tried to see it more clearly. There was a mammoth sized metallic object shaped like a huge ball but with what looked like beaks protruding from on each side. The globe joined with a shuddering click of sorts to one of what seemed to be pointy space ship ports. Still held fast on a kind of transparent disc, she felt the sphere discharge her as she was shunted through a slot into a very quiet sterile compartment. A mask descended on her face and she felt a sting as a needle was inserted in her arm. She promptly lost consciousness.

***

Dustin, at 18 years of age, wanted sex all the time. At least it sure seemed like it. He would be walking down the street, and see a beautiful girl. Mind you, just about every girl looked beautiful to him. He really liked all kinds: plump, skinny, dark, light, short or tall. She just needed to be female. Anyway, so he would walk down the street and see a woman. He would already be fantasizing about bending her over the nearest car, whipping it out and plunging it into her right then and there. Of course, in the fantasy, she would go along with it willingly and then be glad she did. Any police around would just consider it community service.

Compared to women, men supposedly have an average of two times the size of that portion of the brain that seeks sex. John wondered if this made gay guys luckier. The ratio is different with rats, Dustin remembered. Rat males have five times the sex seeking brain apparatus as females. Dustin felt more like a rat in this respect; only much less successful. Perhaps it was his over-eagerness, but he had little luck getting women into bed. He wanted to be able to just strip away all the small talk and preliminaries and say: "Can I just put my dick in you now?" And have them graciously spread their legs. Handsome but socially unsavvy, he would find himself repeatedly pushed aside for more sophisticated and perhaps less rutty peers.

Sadly peering down at the umpteenth underutilized erection of the day, he looked past a little further and noticed a sparkly object on the ground. Picking it up, he felt a pleasant peaceful sensation as he looked at the play of colors. He slipped it into his pocket, feeling somehow better. He began to pep talk himself. He was young and inexperienced yet. He needed to give himself time to unravel the mysteries of the female sex and get more action. Watching the sashaying hips of another voluptuous female as she passed, he reassured himself: 'surely a fully sexually active future is in store for me; I just need to be patient.'

As luck would have it, Dustin would not have as long to wait as in that moment he might have thought. That night, something much stranger than his usual semen soaked wet dreams and much bolder than his raciest thoughts entered into his bedroom.

***

Colette and Dustin both came to in a very round and relatively small room, full of pink, blue, and green light with soft sides. There was some kind of membranous partition between them, so they could see each other but not directly make contact. Both were completely naked. Dustin, of course, really could not help staring at this unexpected gift that trumped any state of captivity. He was getting to look at a beautiful naked woman in the flesh up close for free. As for Colette, despite the strange surroundings, she could not help but enjoy Dustin's sexually charged stares. Her nipples became erect under that look and she flirted with him in the way she moved, giving him peek-a-boos of her pussy and languidly rolling around the soft floor. Colette was completely unconcerned with anything that should happen because she was completely convinced this was a dream. Dustin, on the other hand, did not think he had ever had a dream so truly remarkable. Seeing how she was enjoying his looks, he did not bother to even pretend to look away. Also, since there was no way to hide his substantial hard-on, he just let it stand audaciously out in the open.

Suddenly, a kind of round door appeared and a large octopus or squid-like creature entered one side, its many arms insinuating themselves all around the room, and largely filling up Colette's compartment. The arms were tentacled and seemed very agile and flexible, down to their small finger like wiggling points up to their more powerful larger width near where they joined this largely inscrutable creature with huge eyes but little else visible. There was a strong smell in the air also—-some kind of heady mixture of coconut, honey, and mint, with an undercurrent of something that reminded Colette of the smell of sex. It was like the post-orgasmic scent of combined juices. Colette thought she should be afraid. Instead, maybe because of that smell, she instead began to feel vaguely aroused and pliable, like whatever this creature wanted of her, she would try to do.

At the same time, Colette was no longer sure where to sit. It seemed that the creature had taken up most of the room and so she had naturally stood up to keep from being crowded. Slowly, two of the tentacled arms began to feel around her toes. Then, ever so slowly they began to wind their ways up her legs. The little suction cups gave purchase as they climbed and felt oddly pleasurable to Colette. She quickly learned, as they approached her soft nether regions, that when she tensed, the appendages became hard and almost prickly like steel, changing color to a dark red. But, when she relaxed again, they resumed their pink, blue, and green color scheme and became softly sensuous, moist warm and slightly sticky with those little suction cups. One of the arms slowly began to push aside her inner pussy lips, undulating as it went, inserting itself assertively. Having learned quickly the benefits of relaxing, Colette let it do whatever it was it intended to do.

Colette noticed that another arm was making its way up her back and it slid around her neck, and pressed past her closed lips into her mouth. It tasted much like the smell smelled and seemed to be secreting a lot of some substance. Whatever it was dripped down her throat, such that she found herself needing to swallow periodically. By this time, the one in her pussy had slid in deeper and seemed to be packing itself in, suction cups sucking, pulsating. Meanwhile, the other arm at first tickled at the tip but then earnestly began to work its way into her tight little butt hole. Colette gasped and started to tense but got the immediate feedback, and so relaxed. She let it enter her ass also, moistly pushing and sticking as it went. It seemed to go in very far and all three arms seemed to be pulsating and swelling to fill all available space as they went. As the one in her mouth started to ease itself down her throat, somehow bypassing her gag reflex,

Colette wondered if the arms would meet in the middle, completely going through her entirely, but not so. At some point they stopped and Colette got the impression that she was being held inside and out, and filled with some special fluid. She had gradually fallen and the arms had eased her down, were all around her now, touching and gently suctioning her all over. When one started to find its way to her clit, Colette moaned. It felt so good and so intense, she involuntarily started to move her hips a little. The arms seemed to notice and gave more focused attention to her clit. Colette was still swallowing in gulps that heady fragrant substance as the tentacled arms moved in and around her and rubbed her vulva and clit in the most sensitively sumptuous way she had ever experienced until she began to gulp and thrust in reverberations of pleasure waves throbbed and pulsated through her fully entered body. After she came, she felt a little woozy, perhaps from whatever it was on perpetual drip down her throat. At any rate, she dozed gently off.

    Meanwhile, Dustin had been watching absolutely fascinated, panting a little unconsciously as his hard-on strained off its base, balls hugged up tight. He had finally given way to touching himself. In no time at all, he popped like a cork. His cumming, seemed to signal another creature to enter. Either that, or it was just his turn, because there at the door of his compartment was another one.

    Dustin was afraid. It had been one thing to watch what happened to Colette but quite another, to think of what might happen to him. Similarly, he thought, the creature emitted its powerful scent and began its irresistible training of him. It turned the angry red at resistance, but softened to its most sensuous with cooperation. Dustin found himself yielding and lying down as the little tips of the arms found their ways into his mouth, winding up his legs and then creeping implacably up his butt. He was quite bemused to find himself hard again as he swallowed the juices flowing down his throat, and felt the tentacled arm stretching his ass hole as it entered more fully, pushing its way in. The arms crawled knowingly over his entire body, little suction cups on his nipples, cock, rubbing and squeezing around, undulating, and pulsing. Dustin's member began to feel much better than he was usually able to do on his own. The combination of suction and squeezing, the perfect balance of moisture and sticky friction, not to mention every inch of any other erogenous zone, including his balls being treated with just the perfect amount of pressure. It began to be too much and gulping and swallowing as he came, he thrust with waves of pleasure, riding them as they coursed through him; consuming him. Afterwards, he too was quite spent and drifted off almost immediately.

***

When Colette awoke, She felt good but like her skin was really sensitive. She also felt fully satisfied, like she had had some serious sex. Looking in the mirror at her own beautiful body, everything looked normal. She did not look like she had spent the night having sex with some octopus creature! She laughed to herself about having had such a wild dream. Then, with a start, she caught a glimpse of something. In the middle of her tummy, was a jewel, much like the one she had found on the street that day. Only, this one was embedded in her belly button.

"Wow, when'd you get that? I thought you weren't into piercings."

Mike had come up behind her, put his arms around her as she looked in the mirror. Ill prepared to share her growing suspicion that, wow, she really had been abducted by aliens, Colette brushed it off with,

"I'm so glad I can still surprise you."

His hand around her waist seemed to be triggering a chemical exchange because her mouth was watering and she tasted that taste from last night and also smelled that distinctive smell. Mike seemed to smell it also, as breathing in deeply, he made an "mmm" sound and she could feel him get instantly hard against her buttocks.

"Boy, you really are full of surprises, Colette. Is that some new perfume? It smells really good."

Smelling deeply into her neck and rubbing against her, Colette could feel her pussy cream and other tell tale signs of arousal trace themselves down her body from her nipples down to her womb, getting warm, tingly, and newly awake and sensitive. That heady scent seemed to be concentrating and expediting a process that normally would take some time and foreplay to kick in. Instead, Colette was already well primed, when with some urgency, Mike pushed her down so she bent over for him to take her from behind, and holding her hips with one hand and his very hard dick with the other, put the head of his dick at the opening of the warm, moist, little opening of her pussy, parting the soft lips with his member, and then, hardly containing himself, shoving it in for some serious insertion. Mike thrust the full way in and full way out, feeling the tight squeeze along the length, and not holding back, he went in each time with a decisive ram. Colette could feel it everywhere as he pumped her hard and thoroughly, holding her hips for leverage. Then, it seemed to Colette that her pussy was becoming tighter and more pleasure dense, like even her pussy was concentrating and intensifying. It was like a swelling inward so she could feel every inch of Mike's manhood sliding heavily in and out and her breath started to catch as the pleasure began to mount and she began to yell,

"AhAhAhnnAh"

with each thrust until suddenly, an orgasm just whipped through and took her breath away. Collette moaned uncontrollably as she happily convulsed with it. Mike soon followed, thrusting faster and faster until he,

"OoooooH!" and spurted into her.

He helped her stand up and reaching for her face, kissed her deep, with all that flavor of the scent still in her. He then looked a little confused and said,

"Oh my! I gotta get to work. I'm late" and pulling up his undies over his sticky parts, raced off to get ready.

Colette found herself an hour later after a shower, now at school. Before, the recent activities with Mike would have kept her nicely for a week. Instead, Colette found herself almost unbearably horny again, as if she had seen no action for months. Sitting in her Chemistry class, she found herself crossing and re-crossing her legs. She did kegels, wondering if she could make herself cum like that for some relief, merely by squeezing her pussy. Colette also could not help looking at everyone in the class. Strangely, everyone looked yummy to her. There were the guys. They were of all types and peeking at their crotches, she could imagine all different kinds of equipment. What would be the proportion of head to shaft? Was it going to go in like an arrow or stick in her like a mushroom plug? How would they lean? Up toward her g-spot or down toward her butt, or rub her more on one side. Which of those crotches contained the cockiest cock of them all?

Then there were the girls, who for the first time somehow inexplicably appealed to her also. 'But what would you do with one, if you had one, Colette?' she thought to herself 'You have never been bisexual before.' But they looked sumptuous, every last one of them.

Lastly, there was the professor. He sported plaid pants, a little bow tie and glasses. She was never interested in him before but now she was beginning to be convinced that he must have the biggest bulge of all. How had she never noticed?

What was more, her mouth was watering with that heady coconut, honey, mint, and sexy funk scent in her mouth and nose, and now she knew from Mike that others could smell it too. In fact, she could even tell it was starting to affect her fellow students. They were starting to stare at her and breath it in searchingly and some of the guys were starting to get hard-ons they were hard pressed to conceal. Luckily, at that moment, class ended and rather than incite some strange scene, Colette ran off to the Ladies room to gather her senses and perhaps wait for Professor Gladman's office hours. It smelled nicely clean and freshly mopped in the ladies room. She entered a stall and pulled down her panties for a quick pee, and was amazed that her clit was so strikingly erect, its pink perky little head standing out and fully sensitive.

Before she knew it, one of the girls from class had popped her door open, gleefully delighted to find her. She looked at Colette looking at her clit. The girl, Melissa, was very attractive and seemed to be just following her intuition and instincts. As if propelled by magnets, they came together easily in the little stall, Melissa hungrily finding Colette's lips, sliding in her tongue to catch that intriguing taste, with one hand feeling her pussy and the other, feeling her ass, then hugging her and rubbing her all over. Then, with a kind of impatient abandon, she knelt down and began to passionately lick Colette's clit and pussy. Colette came easily again, then knelt down a little awkwardly to return the favor. She had never done this before and it did occur to her to wonder, "what am I doing eating pussy?" But another part of her seemed to think this was the most natural thing in the world and the tangy taste of Melissa tasted good to her, as did the tender textures of her labia, like a little spongy flower or sea creature. Colette explored Melissa, teasing and pressing her clit and plunging her tongue into her opening, sucking on her pussy lips. Melissa came very sweetly with sighs and moans of pleasure.

They both came out of the bathroom stall a bit disheveled and smelling of sex. They tried to freshen up, amid some giggles. Colette had not really had time to look at the jewel in her belly button and so she stole some moments now, lifting her dress and studying it in the mirror by tilting her tummy and looking down. It was really beautiful and shown those same sparkling colors of pink, green, and blue. It somehow seemed very deep as if it had no back. Colette wondered what it meant, as she contemplated this undeniable sign of change in her life.

When Colette showed up at professor Gladman's office, he seemed glued to a textbook and did not even notice her come in. Already horny again, she was not able to retain her former sense of fidelity to Mike. In fact, monogamy now seemed alien as if it had been another person who had once lived that way. Instead, life now seemed about spreading oneself around, pleasuring and being pleasured. When Colette noted again her interest in this man, that was when the mouth watering and scent began. 'Oh, is that what kicks it off?' thought Colette. She watched it have its affect on him, even as he kept trying to read his book. Yet unaware of her, the professor was starting to squirm. She watched as a growing hard-on began straining against his pants. He seemed to be getting a little sweaty and be biting his lower lip. Colette waited for her new scent power to more fully claim him, before she came up to him to help him out of his perplexity.

"Hello, Professor Gladman."

"Oh, Hi Colette. I know this is supposed to be my office hours but I am afraid I am going to have to close early. So sorry."

The Professor hastily grabbed some belongings and made as if to leave, but Colette caught him and deftly undid his pants, releasing his fully erect member, while simultaneously pressing her breasts against him.

"But we're just getting started, professor."

Holding him by the dick, she led the professor over to his couch and gently pushed him to lie down.

"Don't you want inside, Professor?"

"I'm really not supposed to be doing this."

"But, do you *want* it?" Colette saw an encouraging answer in his eyes and promptly leaned down and popped his dick into her mouth. After a teasing little suck, she straddled him and began to rub her soft moist pussy along his rod while beginning to kiss him, immersing him further in that heady smell. Quite overtaken, the Professor started to moan into her kissing lips.

"Yes, yes, please".

Colette let him wait a moment more and then tilted her pelvis to hit the right angle to slide him up and in.

At that moment, a fellow student came in the door seeking the Professor and his office hours but beholding the scene, stood stock still in surprise. The sights and smell had an instant hardening effect on him but he seemed stuck in place. He was having difficulty remembering his academic question.

"It's okay" Colette said reassuringly.

She had never had two entries at once, (unless one could count the alien), and so surprised herself by spontaneously saying:

"There's room for one more."

Uncertain, he stood a moment more but then as if taking a dive, rushed forward, and unzipping his pants and taking out his cock, he came up behind her, smelling her, kissing her back and butt. He was a handsome young thing and Colette could almost feel in her own body the heat of flaming desire igniting in this new visitor and it heightened her own already sparked excitement. Colette reached behind and daringly pulled her cheeks apart for him. He was like 'Wow, really?' But took the cue. Putting the head of his member there, he rubbed it a little at the opening, pre-cum moistening the way, and then beginning to slowly push it in, squeezing himself in by inches at a time. Not only did this intensify things for Colette, but the Professor could feel the increase in pressure also. The men thrust in and out of Colette, which felt absorbingly wonderful to Colette— certainly one of the most thorough fucks she had ever experienced, every erogenous zone all at top tingle. They came in quick succession like a cascade of catapulting orgasms, each feeding off and contributing to the others and all bundled intently in the tight space of Colette. The men slipped out of her, satisfied and a little exhausted. Colette stood up and adjusted her clothing. She gathered her things, and smiling, kissed their bemused faces each goodbye and headed out the door.

As she was rounding the corner of school, Colette was shocked to find herself face to face with a gun.
"Give me your laptop and your money, or I'll shoot".
Colette could not believe she was being mugged and hurried to comply with his demands. Despite the fright, she still had the presence of mind to access just a little thought about her recent activities. With that, Colette was able to start her newfound watering mouth/smell production thing going. She knew it was having the desired affect when her would be mugger, dropped the (thankfully) unloaded gun. It landed with a loud "plop," startling them both. He came confusedly up to her, and pulling up his mask, sought her lips to kiss her, surprisingly tenderly given his recent approach. He touched and fondled her breasts, in very nice fashion and now the watering and smell was coming of its own. Lying her gently down, parting her legs, and sliding her panties aside, the man, still kissing her and drinking in her strange juices, began to enter her. Colette was amazingly already ready for more and so the mans nice member was very welcome up her pussy. She also somehow felt and knew things about him as he pumped in and out of her. It came to her that his name was Max, and that he was actually deathly afraid due to owing money to some kingpin he had previously worked for; selling drugs. He had never abused substances himself but had borrowed some of the funds to help his Mom keep her home. Now he was trying to get back the short fall the only way he knew how before they came to kill him. Colette seemed to be receiving these messages like little clouds drifting into her mind as his dick went silkily in and out. Seeing his goodness and how he was trying in life, despite outward appearances, Colette began to stroke his hair, neck, and back with all the compassion she was feeling for him. She kissed him fully back. They came together very luxuriously in waves of strong and long pleasure. When the last contraction had spent, Colette leaned up on her elbows and said,

"I'll help you, Max."

"What?" Max was taken aback.

"I will come with you to face them."

Max was not at all sure how she knew what she was talking about or if that was a good idea but then he realized that nothing today had made sense and it had still kind of worked and even felt really good…so maybe nothing was as it seemed anyway.

"Can I at least know your name?"

"Colette," she said with a smile.

Max could not believe it but he allowed Colette to push his gun into a gutter drain with her foot.

"So, Max, when do you want to go?"

Max decided he would rather go tomorrow. That would give him time to tie up loose ends and say goodbyes in case things did not work out.

"These are dangerous people, Colette."

"I believe you. But what I got is, well, out of this world!" With that burst of cheerful confidence, Colette kissed her new friend on the cheek, told him where to find her, and headed home.

Colette was surprised to find her home empty and instead, find that special smell all about the place but especially in the bedroom. 'But I thought that was *my* scent' Thought Colette. She followed the trail of it out the backdoor and into the yard, where she was surprised to find Mike deeply involved in coitus with the singularly attractive neighbor girl, Julia. She was flat on her back, with her breasts sloping to the sides, and jiggling with each thrust. Colette could see her pussy spread wide around Mike's impressive member. He was holding her hands above her head with one hand and supporting himself with the other, staring intently into her eyes while he shoved purposefully in and out of her. Fascinated and strangely without a shred of jealously, Colette sat down to watch. 'Oh, this is going to be fun' she thought. 'I want to see him gush into this girl.'

She noticed the smell was really strong and it had started her own going so she was swallowing it down the back of her throat. Who knows how far it was traveling, this scent elixir, wafting around the neighborhood, stirring folks up to sexual propensities beyond their prior dreams or imagined potential. It occurred to Colette, that if Mike could now produce it, it must be contagious. She thought of all her encounters of the day and all those newly sexualized people, wandering around town. Mike was somehow beginning to get into this intercourse even deeper and Julia was starting to make "uh" sounds at each thrust. She looked flushed and fully aroused now, her nipples erect and she had her mouth on his arm, like she needed something to suck on. The watering in her mouth, made Colette really hungry for contact and so she went up to the mating pair. Julia looked up with a creased brow of worry at seeing Mike's girlfriend appear, and struggled to juggle this new anxiety with all her built up pleasure and excitement. She could not have easily gotten away; though, being thoroughly pinned down by Mike's dick. Colette said kindly,

"Don't worry. You're exactly where you should be, Julia, and really doing a beautiful job."

Colette then leaned in and put her hands on either side of Julia's face, and pulling it gently towards hers, she started French kissing her deeply all the while Julia was being thrust and pounded by Mike. Colette could feel Julia gasping, and swallowing the heady mixture she was sending into her, and the quivers of pleasure running through her body as they kissed. For his part, Mike did not seem at all surprised to find his wife suddenly in the mix; he just smiled at the new addition. Building up faster and faster, Mike suddenly came in forceful jolts, spewing spurts of his juices up inside Julia as she took the full brunt of his last plunges.

Mike looked at the two women as if arising from a juicy dream, only to find it still true. Julia, freshly ravaged and still a bit flushed, was lying completely naked with Mike's semen dribbling from her sweet pussy while Colette was lounging in the only kind of clothing that seemed to make sense now: a mini dress with front hooking push up bra showing lots of soft cleavage and no panties to speak of. Mike gave them a broad lazy smile, and lay back on the grass, one arm behind his head.

"Nice to see you again, Colette. I don't know what you did to me, but I really like it."

Julia of a sudden emerged from her daze and exclaimed,

"Oh no, what in the world and what time is it? I'm supposed to be a bridesmaid at my friend's wedding."

She hopped up and began running around a bit frantically, trying to find her clothing, which was spread in bits from the house to the garden. Colette laughed as she tried to assist her but in her mind she was wondering how soon Julia's own elixir would start. Depending on the timing, she mused, she might just turn that whole wedding into an orgy…

Colette was enjoying this new state of affairs also. She did not at all mind knowing that special powers were bolstering her sex appeal. There was something quite delicious about knowing she could have anyone she liked without risk of rejection, that her desire would mean their certain desire in response. It *was* a little distracting, though, and so she had decided to drop her classes and take a leave of absence from College. She kissed Mike on the lips and dick and then went off to school to go fill out the required paperwork. She also planned, just for a lark, to seek out Professor Gladman again.

Professor Gladman, it turned out, was working on taking his own sabbatical. His classes had become absolutely impossible to conduct because they were always on the verge of orgy, which threatened the ethics of his position and made for frequent compelling interruptions in any lecture, no matter how weighty the content. He had decided that instead of continuing to try to teach, he would take time off to study the strange smell and taste that seemed at the genesis of this remarkable change. He had enlisted his friend and fellow scientist, a biology professor by the name of Mrs. Honey. Together, they were trying to get work done to determine the chemical components and impact of this new substance. Of course, every time some substance would get generated between them, they would need to take a break to resolve the tension and clear their heads enough to be able to proceed. They were on just such a break when Colette came in. Professor Honey was leaning over the lab table, with her lab coat and skirts hiked up and her panties pulled down while Professor Gladman, bow tie and all, was ramming her good from behind. Colette waited, again enjoying watching such activities. She noticed that such pleasures for her had become greatly increased and enhanced. This was an additional apparent benefit.

When Professor Gladman came inside Professor Honey, with a feeling moan and some hefty spurts, Colette politely cleared her throat. Professor Gladman looked around, surprised.

"Oh, Colette. Goodness, pardon me. But wait——-you were around when all this started……Let me introduce you to Professor Honey."

Said person hastily adjusted her clothing, and shook hands.

"You can call me Violet." Abashed, Professor Gladman said,

"Of course, Colette, you may call me Arthur, or Art for short."

"Well, what have you figured out?" Colette wanted to know, once she had learned of their research.

"Not much, Colette. It's unlike anything we have ever seen. the chemical elements are distinct from any we have in the periodic table and yet somehow they are able to trigger the production of various human hormones through some mechanism of mimicry."

"But even more bizarre," Chimed in Violet, "Is that then a virus like organism appears to rapidly invade the blood stream and alter the DNA of every cell it touches. Since all cells need blood for food, it gets to all of them sooner or later and converts them in ways that ultimately result in the infected person no longer resembling any untouched member of his species. We took samples of cells from Art's cheek and found that he is no longer genetically a member of 'Homo Sapiens.' I mean, one of the nice things is that it seems our cells will actually be so altered as to no longer be susceptible to our usual human selection of sexually transmitted diseases. That is quite a relief given how difficult it is to take precautions under current consuming and absorbing circumstances."

Violet tried to nip that thought, (about how consuming and absorbing it all was), in the bud quick lest she get herself going again. With the weight of this newfound knowledge spoken aloud, they all sat down for a moment to ponder.

"What about you, Colette, I hear that you were the one that introduced this phenomena to the campus. Can you tell us anything about how it came about?"

"I could, but I don't know if you would believe me."

And with that, Colette described to them her strange nocturnal encounter and showed them the jewel embedded in her belly button. The jewel seemed to be special. No one else had gotten one so that was not something that came from the virus. It had to have been implanted in her during her abduction. What did it all mean? In a way, they were all more perplexed than they had been before they talked. They all agreed, though, that whatever the implications, they were enjoying this new way of living.

"You know, Colette, when Art and I get back to work after our 'breaks,' we actually get more accomplished, are more attuned with each other, and have greater insights than we ever did before."

After the little interval passed, they all predictably got intensely horny again. The heady scent wafted all around them like a cloud, pulling them together as if sucking them into a whirlpool. In no time, Colette lay full length on the table and Art frantically slid the bottom of her dress up, feeling her pussy with knowing sensitivity, while Violet pulled the top of Colette's dress down, and began to squeeze her breasts and suck her nipples. Violet climbed up on the table to join Colette, and began kissing her until Art turned Colette over onto her knees, holding her hips. Violet pulled Colette's face down to her own pussy, already back out of panties. 'My goodness, why not just leave them off, like Colette does?' She thought. Colette graciously took the hint, and began to work her tongue around Violet's creamy caramel folds, sucking gently on her clit, tasting her thoroughly. To her surprise, she had really gotten a taste for pussy. Violet squirmed with delight

"Ooh, oooo,"

Meanwhile, Art slid his hand around her front and was artfully stroking Colette's clit, just as he force ably slid his ample member into her tight juicy cunny with one push. Colette's face still buried in Violet's pussy, she let out an,

"Uum,"

as she felt him slide it all the way in. They were already all so cumulatively aroused and ready to go, it did not take long for them to all cum in what turned into an amazing group orgasm. At the end, staring around at all the petri dishes and other trappings of the lab, they began to giggle at the silliness of it all. Violet looked at Art,

"We have become the most exciting experiment of our careers!"

After exchanges of contact info and reassurances that they would keep each other updated, Colette took leave of her new friends. Heading home, she decided to take the subway to save time. She was eager to get home to freshen up and also search for any clues that the aliens might have left. Taking the subway turned out to be an interesting endeavor. It took so little to turn her on and as soon as she got turned on, everyone else did as well. Colette avoided any new entanglements for a while by switching cars every time things started to evolve. This meant she left in her wake one car after another full of confused and heavily aroused folk.

When she got to the last car, she noticed someone sitting on the side, looking very nervous and clasping a large army colored bag. He was furtively looking around, peeking periodically at his watch. She even noticed beads of sweat on his temple. In an urban environment, it took little to suspect that this chap could well be up to something unfortunate, and others on the train looked worried like they were thinking the same thing. Colette had the additional benefit; however, of having this newfound intuition that had come with the change in her chemistry and which she had been learning to trust. In this way, she knew without a doubt that this young man had access to a bomb and intended to use it. Colette looked around and discreetly found the Subway alert phone, let the authorities know there was a "situation of concern" in her train car. Then she set about trying to help in her own way with her newfound powers.

Colette began by turning her mind to sex. This was just so easy to do these days. All she had to do was review the highlights of her recent activities in order to spark the spin into action. Her pussy became instantly wet as her mouth became flooded and she started to taste and smell that distinctive scent which had become her new friend and companion. Once it was all in full motion, Colette went and sat near the man. She was not yet close enough to alarm him, but close enough to give him a larger dose. She watched his confusion as, in the midst of his anxiety and efforts to be very cerebral and coolly execute his plan, he was instead faced with fact that a hefty portion of blood had just begun to descend en mass into his lower regions, making him feel a bit dizzy while his pants had gotten very tight. To help things along further, Colette turned towards him and began unbuttoning the top of her dress, unhooked her bra in front so her tits came tumbling out. Bag man was not the only one who gasped. He had to put the bag down as he tried to cover his face and avert his eyes, but then he kept peeking; no longer at his watch, but only at Colette. She came up and sat closer to him. Putting her hand on his bulge, she began to caress him there as she sought his lips and began to kiss him, infusing him with still more of the otherworldly substance and heightening his desire.

    The man was too distracted to notice as some on-the-ball fellow rider, snuck in and took the bag in order to give it to the subway police as they entered. It was so convenient for them to be able to go do a check on the bag without any hassle from the owner. They only caught a passing whiff of the elixir during their moment in the car. It was just enough to be pleasantly pleased at Colette's state of undress, rather than think there was some need to cite her. When the officers had left, Colette continued her activities, more from pleasure now and a preference for completing what she had started. His very hard erection and the intense desire in his eyes was working its wonders on her. Now she seriously wanted him inside her. He had stopped fighting it and was giving himself over to this new experience. His name and something of his substance came to her. It was "Duma" and he had really been trying to sacrifice himself for what he thought to be the most righteous and worthy cause. He was also a virgin.

    "Let me give you some Heaven on earth right now, Duma," Colette said to his widening eyes as she unbuttoned and unzipped his pants. She freed his dick, such that it popped out and stood majestically upright. The riders watched entranced by the scene and all were so involved in the lusciousness of the moment, that no one had a thought to be self-conscious or question anything about such blatant intercourse on the train. In fact, they really wanted to see Duma's member enter Colette and were waiting breathless for her to be penetrated. Colette held up her little dress as she straddled Duma, feeling for him, she lifted herself up to place her pussy opening on point, right on the head of his substantial member and then pushed and eased herself down the length until she hit bottom. Her tits bounced sweetly as she began to pump up and down, her hands on his shoulders, as she still tried to catch his lips for kisses as she went. All the recent sexual activity was like pussy calisthenics so hers was all tight, as it squeezed him nicely. His cock was so at home in all that moisture, warmth, and pressure. The more she pumped, the more Duma's eyes bulged, and he began to breath in excited pants until all of a sudden, the pleasure took total hold of him and he began to thrust and moan uncontrollably, shooting his wad into Colette in pulses of gooey pent up seed. A very disciplined young man, the only other time Duma had ever had an orgasm, he had been asleep in the midst of a wet dream. Duma was stunned at how good it was. 'How could this be? Had she indeed been sent from heaven?' All he could do was sit open mouthed and ponder for a while over what had just inexplicably happened. 'But it had to be a sign…' With this conclusion, he was not dismayed or surprised to discover his bag gone. He already knew his world had changed.

Colette looked around and noted some members of the train were now flirting very heavily with each other. 'Was it transmitted via the air, or only through the exchange of bodily fluids?' wondered Colette, as she kissed Duma on the cheek and snuck out of the train, which had just arrived at the station. Checking in with the subway office, just for curiosity, she was able to confirm that yes, it had been a bomb and they were headed in now to arrest the would be terrorist. Colette wished she could save him from such a fate but then realized that even that outcome would soon be transformed, because he had the elixir. Nothing could be expected to go along typical lines. She decided to let it be and continued on her way home.

When Colette finally arrived, Mike was out and she had the house to herself. This was great because she was a bit tuckered from all the recent action. She took a quick shower, grabbed a bite to eat, and without even bothering to get dressed, laid down on the bed and took a power nap. When she awoke, she noticed that there was a green, pink, and blue glow of light and at first was like 'Oh no, have they come back for me?' But then she realized it was coming from under the bed and so hopping down and getting low down on the floor, she looked under the bed. It was a brilliant green object that looked much a like a huge head of curly cabbage but as she pulled it out, she saw that it had a larger version of her belly button jewel, in its center. It also had a little card attached with a picture on it showing where to place her fingers around her belly jewel while she looked at the larger cabbage patch one. Colette's curiosity would never have let her resist and so she took the position, each hand with fingers on either side of her belly jewel and looked at the larger jewel.

    Colette began to see images floating across the face of the large jewel, amid its interplay of light. First they started simply by telling her things she knew and that had already happened, so that it was clear she was able to read and understand the images. Then they progressed to greater complexity. Colette saw how this alien species had been observing her planet for generations. They desperately needed the very chemicals that for humans were waste products, in order to restore the eco-balance of their own planet and grow their food. At first it had seemed so logical to them that since these were things that humans wanted to get rid of and that their people needed, they would be able to just come and pick it all up.

    With further study; however, they had realized a number of complex issues that would threaten such a plan. There was the fact of rampant greed and the drive to make profit across various circumstances contrary to the interests of even our own species. Then there were the different factions of humanity such that if one group was won over, there was no guarantee of another. Most importantly, there was the tendency toward violence as a key problem solving method. Looking at these elements among our species society, they saw that sadly, there could be no easy exchange at our present level of development.

    They were forced to study humans more thoroughly and reevaluate their methods. Gradually, they had looked into the human genome and managed to successfully engineer an effective way to impact human behavior. They would make alterations in our DNA to emphasize sexuality over aggression. They successfully designed a carrier virus that would both trigger immediate hormonal changes to expedite spread as well as actually transmit the genetic changes into human cells until all human DNA would be altered. The aim was that humans would be much more pleasant to do business with and the Tulliotipoptizumi would then be able to come and easily cart our waste products away. It would be a great service to both peoples.

Furthermore, she was informed that the jewel in her belly was for communication and consultation as they conducted this process. She was shown in images how she could request contact or other aides. Colette immediately tried out making a request, which involved tapping the face of the larger jewel and then focusing her thoughts carefully as she held her hands in the proper position on her belly. She wanted to find her fellow abductee, so they could chat and support each other in this awesome new role. They would be Earth's spokes people during the course of Humanity's vast sexualization and pacification. It was such a lot to digest...

No sooner had she made her request, then she heard a knock on the door. Running to the door to answer it, she only remembered she was naked, when she was standing in the doorway and saw Dustin, her former co-abductee there. Vapors of the scent smoked between them as he looked her up and down with immediate need. "Hi, Colette. Wow. It's really nice to see you again." The scent grew even more dense between them. Dustin came in and summarily picked Colette up, placing her on a nearby fake fur rug. Eagerly, opening his pants with one hand, while he pushed her legs apart with the other, with no preamble, he began to jam his cock into her pussy, kissing her hungrily. He rammed into her hard for a while. Then he slowed down so that she could feel every inch as he slid meaningfully in and out until he gradually worked up his speed again. Somehow, he was managing to hit both her G-spot and clit in a wonderful concert of friction that was quite perfect. Colette started to get transported by the swelling and mounting of pleasure and

"Uh, Uh, UUUMMMmmm!"

She cried out as she came and Dustin was in full orgasm soon behind her, squirting loads of jism into her pussy.

Afterwards, they chatted. Dustin had a jewel in his belly button and had received a similar piece of equipment glowing under his bed also but had put off looking at it. Dustin was a little more hesitant about new things and all this was so new. But, he was interested in what Colette had learned, so she filled him in.

"Oh" said Dustin, "They're turning us into Bonobos!"

"What?"

"I saw a documentary about it. Bonobos are the only other primate species besides Chimpanzees that are like 99.6% related to us but they are really different from the more war-like and aggressive Chimps. Bonobos use sex to greet, connect, resolve disputes, and release tension. These aliens must have found a way to shift our genetic material in a similar direction." Then he added: "What are you going to do about it, Colette?"

"Well, I'm going to cooperate in full, Dustin. I like this idea of peace on earth through sex. And then, getting rid of toxic waste is really an awesome additional benefit."

"Yah," said Dustin, "It does seem pretty win-win and all but it just also seems kind of weird."

Dustin had mixed feelings about having lost considerable control over his life and urges. On the other hand, his wishes had come true. That old adage about being careful what you wish for, was not lost on him. Now he really could approach any female he might like and bend her over a parked car and take her from behind and have her like it. The world of juicy females was open wide for him. Even while he needed a little time to mentally adjust, ultimately he knew it was really worth it...

Soon after Dustin left, Mike came home. He could smell another man's semen on her and was mildly annoyed someone had gotten to her first, but also instantly intrigued, and titillated.

"What did he do to you, Colette? Did he fuck you hard?" Colette nodded slowly. The coconut honey mint vapors were misting around them, mouths watering.

"I want your ass, Colette" Colette submissively lay on the bed on her tummy. Mike raised her dress, exposing her soft butt cheeks. Colette let out a surprised "Oh!" as he slapped them once, for no reason, just to see them jiggle and get a little pink. He massaged her butt, squeezing the cheeks and pulled them apart to peek at the little pink puckered spot in the middle, making it open slightly.

"Looks good, Colette. We've never done this before, have we? But I think you're up to it."

His dick was already dripping little drips of pre-cum and he rubbed it around the head to moisten it. He put the head right at the opening of her ass, just leaving it there for a moment, letting her feel its size, and then he ever so slowly started to push the large head in. Colette quivered a little as a chill went up her spine as he began to push it in more firmly and relentlessly until his ample meat was all the way in. Then he began thrusting into her in earnest, building up steam until jolts of pleasure cascaded as he spurted cum up her butt. He lay on her a moment, still inside her, kissed and nuzzled her ear and neck. He slipped out and hopped up to go take a shower. Colette joined him in there briefly, just long enough for both of them to get all sudsed up and then wash each other off. Colette got out while Mike went on to shave and wash his hair.

As she dried off, Colette realized from her well-penetrated and highly sexed state, that she still needed to somehow prepare for assisting Max with his kingpin issue tomorrow. She had the inspiration to invite Julia. She said goodbye to Mike and went next door to visit. Opening the door, Julia smiled to see Colette. Julia had already nested in for the night and was in a rose pink negligee that showed the color of her areolas through the lace. They hugged in greeting and Colette could feel her breasts and nipples so softly pressed against her.

"So how have you been, Julia?" Colette asked as Julia hospitably made tea.

"You can probably guess, Colette, because somehow, I think you are in on it. Wow—-what is going on? I literally cannot leave the house without having sex; I mean really good sex."

She went on to tell tales of the wedding. Just as Colette had guessed, it had turned into an amazing orgy and Julia had had sex with various men and women in the course of frolicking in her satin full skirted bridesmaid dress. She had even ended up giving the groom a blowjob but her best friend did not even mind, being similarly quite occupied with his best friend.

"I don't know what happened there but I have never seen anything like it."

Just thinking about it, made Julia a little flushed. Colette observed that Julia's nipples were now erect. She could imagine what was happening down below also and the thought reminded her of the sight of Julia's pussy. The familiar honeyed scent crept up on them densely as they drank their tea. Still, they took their time, looking each other over slowly as they chatted. Colette drank in every detail, and could tell that Julia was doing the same with her.

Colette made the first move, getting up and coming up behind Julia, gliding her hands over the negligee, touching Julia's breasts luxuriously through the silky material, sliding her fingers underneath to better feel her nipples. Julia was in a lounge chair, and so Colette pushed and made it recline, laying out Julia in front of her. She grabbed some rose massage oil she saw on a bureau and began to massage Julia's painted toes and dainty feet, massaging her legs, doing large sweeping rubs in circles up her legs, and gently parted them, pushing aside her lacy underwear to see the sweet little lips surrounded by soft pubes. Colette began to kiss and smell and nuzzle Julia's pussy, to Julia's delight.

Colette climbed on top of Julia and laying against her lovely body, while she stroked her pussy, talked to her about joining in on the Max appointment the next day. Colette frigged Julia into ecstasy, doing it expertly just as she herself liked it done, using fingers inside and her thumb working circles. She felt the contractions and squeeze as well as the tremors beneath her as Julia came, and to Colette's surprise, squirted.

"You squirt?" Julia looked a little shy about it.

Colette reassured her it was actually quite novel and endearing.

"I'll come with you, Colette. Just come and get me. I will stay inside and save myself for it."

Colette gave her a long, deep kiss good by in thanks, and then headed back home.

Mike was in bed asleep when she got home and she quickly followed suit. She woke in the middle of the night to find him spooning her and slipping his dick up her pussy from behind. She arched her back a little to make it easier, and he held her tight around her tummy, came quickly and fell again fast asleep.

The next morning, Colette went to fetch Julia and off they went to join Max. Max had already experienced the bloom of his own unfolding chemistry and had been very busy with all the wonderful sex that seemed to come to him everywhere. As such, he had had little time to be afraid and had had no inclination to attempt any old style solutions to his problem. He was delighted that Colette had brought such a beautiful friend with her. He said her name slowly savoring it, "Ju-li-a." Off they went to meet the scary head honchos.

They came into a dark, dank building that seemed to signal enemy territory. Catching her first glimpse of the men in question, Colette thought their reputation had hardly done them justice. They were larger than life, so imposing, and ripped. They looked like their whole existence had been about being the biggest fishes in the pond of life. Here this little trio was, coming to disturb the waters. She looked with a little awe at these big men with burley muscles adorned with elaborate tattoos. Abruptly, the largest of the three men said,

"Ah, Max. What brings you here?"

His voice did not go up at the end of the question so the words just streamed out in a straight line. Then, with a little rumble in his low voice:

"You have the money you owe?"

It was very quiet for a moment. The trio knew that time was their friend, time for the elixir to kick in and work its wonders. It was easy for Colette to get her interest going. These men were so well built and with such physical presence. She could not help but think about their hidden parts and what it would be like to be held by them; what it would be like to be entered by them. The elixir production was so contagious that with Colette starting to spin out the magic, Max and Julia soon followed suit. Since they knew what it was, they could already sense the release into the air of the smell as it began to generate; the watering in their mouths.

"Well?" The leader barked impatiently but already his voice was less weighty as the blood was dropping down elsewhere, easily observed with the stirrings in his pants. The fragrance was building and thickening in the room and the visitors watched as the three toughs began to succumb, their bodies visibly softening as sensitivity and arousal claimed them.

Colette decided to help things along,

"We brought something better," she said sweetly and picking the biggest, toughest one, went over and climbed onto his lap, felt him harden even harder beneath her as she sat. She kissed him, flooding his mouth with the elixir. Julia then took her pick and followed suit. She picked the one with the goatee.

Max was not sure what to do, but saw the last tough looking at him very intensely, almost passionately. Max had never been looked at by a man like that and was not sure he was ready for what might happen. Still, he found himself to also be very drawn to this man. He was fully erect now himself and felt naked before him. He had never been interested in men but now things were so different or maybe this man was different. The man came to Max, and gently but firmly hugged him. With all his muscles, it was a powerful hug. He stroked Max's back and his hair. Then he began to kiss him slowly, sliding his tongue into Max's mouth. Max could feel acutely, little charges of electricity as his body responded. Max looked down hesitantly as the man gingerly undid Max's pants, slipped his hand in and began feeling his privates, then stroking up the trail of his hair, up his tummy and chest and then pulled him firmly in close to kiss again. Awash in the elixir and barely able to think himself with arousal, Max allowed the man to turn him around, pull his pants below his buttocks, and start to kiss his butt. There was a foam futon on the floor and The burley man pushed Max gently down onto it, and lay on top of him, his erect dick hard against Max's ass.

"Let me in, Max, and all debts forgiven. I want it bad"

Max caught his breath but then said,

"Okay, but gentle. I've never done this before."

The man said,

"Don't worry, I will."

Pulling out some lip balm from his pocket, he smoothed some around the head of his dick. He parted Max's butt cheeks and Max felt the slithery feeling as he slid a finger of the balm right up Max's ass. He followed up with something a bit larger, starting to press his very erect dick slowly through the little furrowed virgin opening, widening it as he went, easing his way slowly in that tight, private spot. He worked his cock in just a little and then paused, giving Max's insides time to adjust, then pushed in a bit further. After he was all the way in, he reached a hand around and under to hold and rub Max's dick as he pumped languidly in and out of his butt. Max was pleasantly surprised and a bit bemused at how good all this felt. Something he had, like so many men, regarded as a thing to be avoided at all costs, now in actual experience felt so good. He began to moan as pleasure intensified in places he had never experienced it before. Max began to cum in waves around the same time as the man did and they thrust together as the joint orgasm took them, Max milking the man as he came, and the man shooting his wad into Max's butt.

Colette little noticed anything outside her own pleasurable tryst. They had taken their time, kissing and as the kiss went on, Colette received the man's name: Theo. She received the message about his leadership skills, how he tried to be fair and good at what he did. Violence had been such a big part of how things worked in his world, that he had gotten progressively trapped by it. Theo began to run his hands around Colette's body, feeling her beautiful breasts and tummy. He smelled her hair. Undoing his pants, he freed his formidable equipment. Easily lifting Colette up by holding her under her arms, so she could spread her legs, Theo then put her down right on top of his cock, penetrating her as he brought her gently down. He filled Colette up thoroughly, in fact it was almost too intense for her when he was all the way in, but then he would lift her again, Lifting her by the hips and pulling her back down. Theo took in her tits and face with wide eyes as he felt the squeeze of her tight pussy on his member. He felt like his entire body was being squeezed by her pussy—-so well did the pleasure touch every part of him. Colette found Theo extremely attractive and enjoyed being pliant in his arms, for him to do his will with her. Eventually, Theo was able to recline in the chair he was in, and Colette came forward, bringing her legs together and closing her thighs with him still inside her, making his large size penetration a bit more manageable but keeping him tightly nestled all the same. They kissed and made love in this way for what seemed a very long while, with Colette undulating her body, sending ripples of pleasure through them both. Eventually, Theo began to have an intensely pleasurable orgasm, and he held her hips as he thrust into her.

Julia was having a great time also. The man she was with had told her his name, Ryan, and he had been very tender with Julia. They had kissed a great deal also and so had been immersed in the elixir. Ryan had undone Julia's clothing to see her better.

"You are so beautiful, Julia."

Cradling her on his lap, he slid his finger up her and felt her creamy pussy from below, then smelling her scent on his finger. He tossed his coat on the floor and had her lie on it, her legs spread. He felt and suckled her breasts, then made his way, jokingly nipping her inner thigh, he kissed his way in and started to go down on her, licking her clit out of hiding, thrilling her pussy lips and making her tremble on the verge of orgasm. At that moment, he whipped out his sizable dick, and forced entry in one large thrust that made Julia cry out. So aroused from his oral attentions, the feel of his large dick lodged inside her of a sudden sent a shock of pleasure through her whole system. Ryan was full of vigor as he slammed her hard and the floor held her fast with no give so that she received the full brunt of his administrations. Julia could not hold back the orgasm when it came like a tidal wave as he kept plowing into her at full speed, sound ripped out of her with a

"Uh,uh, oh my oh uh,UUUUUHHHHHHHH!"

Ryan held her hips fast as he finished himself, pumping faster and faster until with a few spurts and a whoosh, he had gushed a bunch of creamy cum into her pussy.

In the afterglow of sex, no one was in a hurry to leave and so they ordered pizza and lounged decadently half clothed. The toughs no longer seemed quite so tough. Theo, Ryan, and the third man named Reese were flirting and laughing as they all got to know each other a little more.

"So what is this really all about?" Theo wanted to know. Colette said,

"It's just a virus from outer space to make us have sex a lot." Assuming she was kidding, of course, Ryan piped up,

"But who needs a virus?"

After a bit more mingling and a few more rounds, Colette, Julia, and Max said their "Until next times" and all headed home. Max was very appreciative.

"Thank you so much for saving and infecting me, Colette. I will never be the same but I am so much happier!"

Colette contacted Violet and Art to swap updates. They had the idea that it would be helpful to keep a register of infected folks for future notice and so Colette tried to give them an account of the recent newly infected, from the growing list of those she knew about. Violet reported that they had learned through some little experiments they conducted, that although the olfactory particles of the virus were enough to trigger profound arousal, actual fluid exchange was necessary for a full on infection, but it could be just saliva via a kiss.

Violet and Art were fascinated to hear from Colette news of the communicated aims of this operation, and like Colette, were all on board. It was a relief to know this was a means to achieve something yet larger that they fully agreed with.

"This relationship with the aliens in which they want our waste, reminds me of aphids and ants," said Violet enthusiastically.

"What do you mean?" asked Colette.

"Well," said Violet, authoritatively,

"Ants and aphids have a symbiotic relationship in which ants provide services and support to aphids, including for example, giving the aphids a lift up the stems of roses. In recompense, the ants are then able to harvest from the aphids the sweet honey dew they excrete after gorging themselves on plant juice."

Colette was not quite sure she liked the image of being an alien's "aphid," harvested for honeydew in the form of toxic waste. So, she just gave her new scientist friend a polite nod.

Colette preferred to focus on other aspects of this marvelous development. She could now see a bright future as a kind of ambassador. She would travel; first to Israel-Palestine, parts of Africa, and any war torn or violence ridden location. She had the power to stop the poaching of elephants, the trafficking of humans, the suffering of untold children——all through the power of an alien elixir combined with her native sexual attributes. She would go on to accomplish great things; easily entering the quarters of heads of state, via her celebrity status, and leaving world leaders blissed out and invariably altered by the encounter. But all this would be with the happy knowledge that she would not be alone. A veritable army of a highly sexed new species, fully committed to conquering through pleasure instead of pain, would soon be taking over the world.

*****

As for the aliens, they did prove good to their word. With breathtaking ease, they hauled away epic quantities of toxic waste humans had been inadequately harboring for generations. They took it far out to outer space to their own distinct eco system where it provided vital support to all manner of exotic alien agriculture. Relations between the peoples flourished such that illuminating scientific discoveries were shared and an arrangement was made to enable future periodic exchanges. The aliens never had cause to tamper with the human genome again, since humans had become much more evolved citizens of the galaxy and so much easier to work with.

Colette, Julia, and Violet, like many others, would go on to birth the first generation of babies that were genetically a brand new species. They would raise them in supportive groups and find them remarkably easier to parent. These babies would turn out to be less fitful and aggressive than homo sapiens, and instinctually more affectionate and generous. These generation "O" children would blossom across their lifespan into profoundly effective communicators; loving and powerfully independent, yet simultaneously unified and deeply connected adults. They would fulfill the mission embedded deep within their DNA:

Love not War.

BONUS TALES

Including More Rousing Romps to Titillate and Tickle Pink Any Excitable Parts......

SISSY IN SEXXTASY (1)*

PART ONE: Sissy and Johnson

"Unh, unh, unh" Sissy was moaning
"Quiet, or you'll wake your parents,"
Johnson tried to remind her as he plowed into her from behind. She turned her head to try to muffle her sounds with a pillow. She couldn't help sounding. It felt too good. He had his big beautiful cock in her deep, pushing her hard into the bed, and she could feel what he was doing to her pussy from her head down to her toes.

"Unh, uunh, unh"
He had his hands on her hips and because she was a petite person, his dick looked even larger proportionally, he thought, enjoying how the length of it would disappear between her legs; as if it were penetrating straight through her. It felt so tight. Damn Sissy was good. Her pussy was like gold and he liked to tap it every chance he could get.

He had had to climb up her wall after a whispered conversation in the night like Romeo and Juliet. He was pretty buff so it wasn't too rough a climb, although he had almost bit it when his jacket snagged on the window frame. Sissy had hurriedly gotten him into the room, and kissed him gleefully. Her sweet tits were showing through a little pink camisole and her cute butt with the little dimples at the top, sporting only a G-string.

"Oh, Sissy,"
Was all he really could say, sweeping her up, feeling her up, kissing her all over and then throwing her onto the bed. He had pushed her onto her tummy, struggling to get his jeans unzipped as his hard cock was just bulging to be where it belonged. Sissy was lying on her stomach now and she put her hands behind her thighs and pulled herself apart so he could easy make the mark, and he lunged his dick straight in.

---

* (Sissy) Although all characters are 18 or over, key characters start out still in high school and living at home, making them just barely legal.

Now he wanted to savor it, wanted it to last, wanted to feel every inch going into that delectable tight juicy pussy. He leaned down to lay on top of her, feeling her boobs with his hands from the side. "Oh, Johnson, it feels so good..." Sissy was almost purring.

Johnson started to ram her harder and harder and for some reason it actually felt tighter and tighter--perhaps that yummy engorgement thing that can kick in and suddenly you get a juicier squeeze, even more friction, like sexual stars have come together and wow--

"Damn you feel good!"

Johnson started to moan, himself, even while he was trying to check it. What if her parents found out?

"Oooo, unh, unh"

They were only a couple rooms away in a small house...Johnson felt like he was going to explode, the pleasure was so intense and it was coming in waves, he was riding them and then...

"Whooeee"

Johnson chugged loads of cum into her cunt, while she enjoyed those last thrusts.

They heard footsteps in the hall, and in a flash, Sissy rolled under the covers and Johnson rolled under the bed. The door opened.

"Sissy? Are you all right? I thought I heard noises."

"No, Mom, I'm fine---I was just yelling back at the TV but I turned it off and am going to bed now."

Sissy did not like to lie, least of all to her parents but, Sissy loved sex. She just loved everything about it. She loved the attention, the sensations, the pleasuring and being pleasured. She had been fascinated with the subject from a very tender age and her interest showed no signs of abating now that she had turned 18. In fact, for her it seemed to only be intensifying. She still needed to live at home awhile more and her parents were not quite on the same page, so she regrettably saw little choice in the matter. If she were to have sex, she would end up having to lie. She had made a pact with herself, in fact, that she would only lie if it had something to do with enabling her to have sex. That way, she hoped it would not become a habit.

"Okay, honey. Well you sleep well," Her mother said as she left the room.

"Shit, that was a close call," whispered Johnson.

"Oh it's alright," Sissy said. "It was bound to happen sooner or later"

"Well I better head out in case everyone is on high alert now."

"Yah, that's probably best. At least we got to do it again."

"Yah, thank you, Sissy. That was awesome."

Johnson put one hand on her cheek and holding her close, gave Sissy a parting kiss, sumptuous and lingering, before heading out the window for his descent. Sissy watched him go, one hand absently on her pussy. She could still feel the luscious residual feel of Johnson's cock all the way from her nether region on up to her tummy. He had really fucked her good, she thought.

It was difficult to wait for the next opportunity but there was no sense in risking her house again too soon. They were both seniors in high school and so the next chance they had was between classes. They snuck up to the roof for a quickie. This was tricky in other ways, being that they were not the only ones to consider such a plan. Then there were those who preferred to try and catch other folks doing it and snap a picture, and the school staff who might sneak up there for yet other purposes, perhaps to catch a moment of solitude. Timing was everything. Sissy and Johnson were willing to risk it. They were really close to graduation and could not imagine getting into enough trouble to botch it. They felt like adults now. It was not their fault they had no decent place to fuck.

Meeting at the appointed time, sissy ran over to Johnson. She was so excited. She knew this would, like, make her day and make physics class seem much more interesting.

"How should we do it?" asked Johnson.

"How about like this?" Sissy undid his fly "Can you pick me up so we can do it standing? I have a skirt so worst case scenario, we can say you were just carrying me around."

He picked her up straddling him, and with a finger she pulled her G-string aside, and located his nice hard rod and lifted her hips up to line up her pussy slit with the head of his dick, and then eased herself down. "Ohh," they both moaned. She had her arms around his neck, and could use her legs to help pump. Johnson braced himself against the wall. He was in deep. He kept hitting the top of her pussy with a thump and they were in that high friction tight squeeze mode again. They fit together so well. Sissy's nipples were erect and she had goose bumps, even chills as he sent thrills up her spine stimulating her deepest nerve endings. 'Everything must be connected to my pussy,' she thought. 'Otherwise, why would sex make everything feel so good?' Johnson was experiencing his own brand of ecstasy via the amazing vehicle of his dick, which seemed to concentrate every pleasure sensor possible. He came inside her in no time this time in a quake of thrusts and jolts, spurting cream up her pussy.

They both quickly adjusted their clothing and shimmied down the stairs just as a professor was heading up. He looked at them a little suspiciously, but they just smiled.

Next they tried Johnson's place during the day on a Saturday when his folks were off shopping in the city. They went into the one lockable room in the house. It was a den with bay windows streaming in sunshine. Johnson had thought this through and put a towel down on the sheepskin rug just in case. As much as Johnson loved Sissy's pussy, he was in an adventurous mood today.

"Sissy, I've been wanting to try something."

"What is it, Johnson?"

"Well, could we try it in your butt?"

Sissy had read about that and had been a bit curious...of course she had read about a lot of things. Time would only tell if she would try all of them.

"Will it hurt? I mean, don't you need lube or something?"

Johnson had thought of that too.

"It's okay, Sissy, I snagged some butter like they used in that movie 'Last Tango in Paris' I think we just gotta start it real slow, like ease it in. I read about it in a book. How about you curl up on your side."

Sissy was pleasantly surprised that Johnson had been doing his homework.

Johnson gently helped Sissy turn on her left side and dipped his fingers into a pat of butter and eased it into her ass hole. 'It feels kind of novel already,' Sissy thought. Then Johnson lay beside her spooning her, but this time he knew he was aiming differently than usual. He used his thumb to part her butt cheek, and began to rub the head of his dick on the tight little closed and puckered little hole, making it open a little. He wanted this to feel good to her. He wanted to be very careful not to hurt her, even though his big hard dick was starting to urge him on. "In, in, in," his dick was telling him. But he held back and ever so slowly and ever so gently, he began to push in.

Sissy was amazed how sensitive this spot was. At moments it seemed like it might start to hurt but Johnson was doing such a good job of going slow that it was like her butt had a chance to relax and realize this reverse motion could be okay after all. The more he got in, the easier it was to get in farther. Even though it was feeling really good already and the urge to thrust becoming quite intense, Jonson managed to still restrain himself and kept pushing in only as he found ease in, then when it would get too tight again, he would ease up pressure. Her virgin ass hole was so tight that it took some time and patience.

By the time he was in all the way, it felt so good to Johnson, he knew it was well worth the trip. Now that he was in her deep, he used his hips to he roll Sissy onto her tummy so he could have better leverage to pound her. The new position with him on top pumping, felt even better. Being up her ass was even more tight and had a different feel than her pussy, with something like spirals of friction. It felt really good.

As for Sissy, once he was all the way in, she began to really like how it felt also. It was like a thick hot block of pleasure crammed up a very personal place. It was surprisingly sensitive. She could feel how this unexpected spot was definitely connected to other erogenous zones, like what he was doing with her butt could be felt in her tits and pussy also. Since she loved being penetrated, it was neat to be entered in yet another way, taken in the ass. It made her feel that much more desirable also, somehow, that he even wanted her ass like that. Sissy reached one hand around the front so she could play with her clit while this was going on and oooh, it felt really good to be getting it in the ass while she worked circles on her clit. Sissy, who rarely came unless she was doing her own thing with a vibrator, actually came first this time. It snuck up on her like a tidal wave electrically ricocheting pleasure catapults from her butt to her clit, "ummm" Sissy uncontrollably squeezed and thrust, her pelvis having a will of its own, her buttocks clenching, and inadvertently milking Johnson's dick in the process; propelling him into his own oblivion. Johnson shot his wad up her ass, just as Sissy was spent and in a very relaxed blissful state.

Sissy and Johnson continued to expand their repertoire. Johnson had the delightful quality of being able to revel in and enjoy how easy and sex-loving Sissy was, without looking down on her for it or talking about her behind her back. The only exception was his best friend, Jim, who was a virgin. He loved sharing with poor deprived Jim, how awesome sex was. So it was that Johnson had another burning question for her, the next time they got together. This time they had met at a rarely utilized picnic area of the local regional park.

"Sissy, would you take pity on my friend Jim and give him his first time?"

"Are you sure you wouldn't be jealous?"

"I don't know, I don't think I would be jealous if I could be a part of the whole thing. Can I watch?"

Sissy rather liked the idea of deflowering a fresh virgin boy. How cute! She had met Jim, and he was a really sweet guy and quite handsome.

"Okay, but we need a good place. I mean like super comfy and private with no chance of walk ins."

"Absolutely, Sissy. I will work on that and keep you posted."

Meanwhile, on their menu selection for the park, they had in mind trying 69. Johnson was new to pussy licking but had really been starting to get a taste for it and Sissy loved a nice cock in her mouth although she hated having to choose one thing or another and she liked having everything all at once. So, this seemed like it could be a good solution neither had tried before. The library was so helpful!

Johnson put his nice thick jacket down on the picnic table and picked Sissy up and put her down on her back. He unzipped his pants and took out his dick and then straddled her face upside down, easing his member into her soft lips where she began to hold it with her tongue and suck on it. Meanwhile, he pulled aside one of those dinky little G-strings she wore under her skirts and Johnson slid his face into position for nuzzling her pussy. He began to lick on her clit and pussy lips in nice circle motion, the way he knew she liked; taking cues from the motions of her body for what felt most especially awesome to her. He knew she could not say a word with a fat cock in her mouth.

Sissy sucked in earnest, feeling her face just filled up by Johnson's impressive manhood, and surrounded by all the smells and textures of that region of his body. While she was sucking, the feeling of what he was doing as he slid around in her cream on her clit and lips was quite thrilling, and once again in seemingly no time at all, as the thrills pulsed through her body, she began to have an orgasm. While she came, she sucked harder and harder. He plunged in and out of her mouth and throat as she sucked trembling and rode waves of pleasure shaking and convulsing her body. Johnson was tipped over his own edge like a domino and ejaculated loads of cum into her mouth while she was in the final throes of orgasm. She sucked it all in and swallowed it, gasping.

"Wow, that was good," Sissy said, a bit breathless.

"Sure was, Sissy. It really was."

Johnson flipped around and lay beside her. He drew the coat around her shoulders and they cuddled on the picnic table for a time.

It took a little while to get together the preparations for Jim. They were all so busy. Soon; however, they had a time and place arranged. Jim's parents were away on a little romantic getaway of their own and were unlikely to show for a full twenty four hours. Johnson had confided to her that Jim had considered jacking off prior to their session; for fear of being over excited. "Absolutely not!" Sissy had exclaimed. "Tell him not to be a bore like that. I want him as excited as possible."

Sure enough, when they arrived Jim appeared acutely excited, like he was going to blow at any moment. Just thinking about this special appointment all day, had put him in a prolonged pending orgasmic state. "Hello, Jim." Sissy Gave Jim a hug, and he could not help but hold her close all body for it, and she could feel his boner against her tummy.

"My goodness, Jim, you are well hung!" Jim blushed.

Sissy did not worry about Johnson's feelings because they both knew he lacked no confidence when it came to his equipment. Squeezing Jim through all his baggy clothing, she was pleasantly surprised that this seemingly nerdy guy was actually well toned.

"Jim, do you work out?" The blush deepened as Jim said "Well, I like to swim...."

"Very good. I want you to concentrate on all of this like you concentrate on swimming."

Jim was trembling a bit, and maybe some instruction would help him focus. Sissy caught the whiff of his excitement and it made her catch her breath also. Really, desire was the ultimate aphrodisiac. His mixture of both fear and longing for her was so palpable. Sissy was not about to rush things.

"Let's go really slow, Jim. I personally think a mild game of footsie is a nice way to start."

Johnson had meanwhile made himself comfortable in the background, already quite intrigued and erect himself. He had long known how much he liked to watch. He was a very visual guy and he and Sissy were so close in so many ways, he did not feel at all insecure. This meant he was fully free to just lay back and enjoy the show.

As for Jim, he had no extra neurons to even remember Johnson was still there. He was completely consumed by the visual high of Sissy's female flesh and sparkle. She was wearing only a soft fuzzy bathrobe and the view kept changing as the garment fell one way or another and her tits shifted in and sometimes a little out of it.

Jim submitted himself to a game of footsie. Lying next to Sissy, she guided him through gentle touching that required him to come out of his head and actually inhabit his body. How else could one transform size twelve usually ignored clodhoppers into sensual implements? But he got into the flow of tickling and soothing with his toes, and communicating through his body, attuning to the subtle rhythm of lovers and unspoken language of bodies and pleasure. When he had that mostly down, Sissy added fingers and after a sweet time of that, put his hands on her breasts inside her robe, showing him with her hands the nicest ways to squeeze and feel those delectable endowments. He reveled in the weighty soft fullness of her tits as he cradled and caressed under her nonverbal instruction.

Then, with a gesture from Sissy, he undid his pants and took them off. Sissy smiled at his choo-choo train boxers. She rolled on top of him, straddling and dry humping him through the soft fabric. Sliding the robe down her shoulders, she let him see the swell of her boobs from below. Jim's eyes were bugging out. Life had never been this good. Then, she lifted the bottom of her robe so he could see her pussy lips pressed against his boxer shorts and the little spot of cream she had already printed on his shorts. The visual combined with the sensation of that soft pudgy pussy flesh pressing and rubbing on his dick intensified his desire. He was practically buzzing when reaching her fingers through the slit in his boxers, she felt around the fuzz on his balls, his inner thigh, caressed his pubes and then pulled his dick neatly through.

Sissy brushed the head on her pussy lips and clit, and then began to rub her creamy pussy up and down the length of it, leaning forward so her tits were hanging over Jim. Sometimes she would dip a nipple in his mouth for him to catch a suck. She gave such good cues; it was easy for him to follow her lead. Then at one point, when she had rubbed forward, she tipped her hips to catch the head of his cock nicely in her tight juicy opening, and scooting back, pushed herself fully onto his swollen hard member. Jim could feel every inch of slide down that moisture rich passage and gasped, instinctually grabbing her hips, starting to thrust his own hips into hers. Sissy sat up so he was penetrating as deeply as possible, ramming right up her middle, making her tits bounce with each thump.

Johnson was so excited now, it had become difficult to just watch. He came up behind Sissy, nuzzling in her neck, whispering,

"Sissy, can I please enter your ass?"

Sissy had never tried that before, two dicks at once, but she was willing to try.

"Jim, you okay with it?"

"Anything you want, Sissy, Anything you want...."

Johnson knelt down, and pushing her gently forward with one hand, reached under her with his fingers took some of the cream from her pussy. As plugged as it was with Jim's large member, there was still pussy juice seeping a little out the sides. Johnson stroked her little butt hole with her pussy juice, and then pulling her ass cheeks apart, he began to press his dick slowly up her butt, even while Jim was still thrusting in and out. Sissy used her hips to slow him down for a minute, to ease this other entry which was one tight squeeze. Soon; however, the guys were thrusting in and out in tandem. Sissy had never been penetrated this fully before. She could really feel it everywhere, and so could the guys. They slowed way down to delve fully into all that friction and pressure. Sissy had shivers of pleasure go up and down her spine and she kept having these kinds of pleasure shudders, that would momentarily take her breath away. Then the guys began to speed up again and Jim could hold out no longer, he felt like his dick was going to shoot off like a rocket. In a way it did, starry meteors in his head as he had the most powerful orgasm he had ever experienced, convulsively squirting loads of cum into Sissy's pussy. Johnson came next. He lay forward on Sissy, holding her hips for maximum leverage, shooting his wad in sticky streams up her butt. Sissy felt like she was in the middle of some sexy love sandwich, with them less erect now but rather soft and warm and gooey still all up her parts and with her hugged so tightly between them.

    Johnson reported to Sissy later that week that Jim felt enormously more confident about sex and dealing with females now and that he had successfully made the move on a sweet girl by the name of Ophelia. He had shown her the footsy game too...

    As for Johnson and Sissy, they thought the whole endeavor had been such a success and so much fun, they decided to extend the offer to other 18 year old virgin males in their school. Johnson was in charge of initially vetting prospective applicants. They had to be virgins, accept Johnson's involvement, understand it was a one-time deal, and well, "Not be jerks!" Sissy had exclaimed. That last criteria meant even more specifically, that they were kind and respectful and were capable of some modicum of discretion. Quite strategically, as their own underground service project, they began interviewing candidates, setting up dates, and deflowering the nicest 18 year old virgin males in the school.

    This kept them quite busy for the remainder of their senior year but then summer was suddenly upon them and the sad prospect of a long distance relationship loomed in their minds. Sissy had not applied to college. Application time had been before she met

Johnson and she had planned to take a year off. Johnson, on the other hand, had a summer job at Yosemite to earn money for college, and then he would be headed out of state to attend college in Vermont. As attached as they were, they were not yet prepared to make the major decision of matching paths. Nor were they thinking that Sissy should somehow follow Johnson around, although at times she sure was tempted. She had no funds to speak of; however, and there were no more summer job openings at Yosemite, (she had checked). So, it really looked like they would not be together like they had been, at least for a good long while.

Their last night before Johnson left, was the most poignant, intimate, and intense ever.... Johnson was in tears as he ate Sissy's luscious pussy. She clung to him and let him do whatever he wanted with her (she kind of did any way, but that night, even more so). They served themselves up on golden platters to each other and gave full play to their tender love-struck emotions. It was prolonged, heightened, sweet, and kind of agonizing at the same time.

After he left, Sissy did not have sex for two weeks. It is not like she lost her drive. She was extremely horny and in abject withdrawal also. She knew she could have called on any one of those former virgins. They would have counted themselves unbelievably lucky. But no, for those two weeks, she was trying to hold out and really just wanted Johnson. Her whole body and being was in shock from not having his cock in her mouth, not having his smell surrounding her dreams and imbedded in scent filled spots in her bed, not having him claiming every inch of her every chance he got, not having their various activities, adventures, and common mission of sexing it up at every opportunity. She felt quite lost and bereft. The rare times she could reach him in Yosemite; however, she could tell he was already getting laid via someone else. She knew him so well, that, well.... She just knew.

PART TWO: SXXI Corporation

One day, in the dark depths of this crisis, her mother came running to her with a first class priority letter embossed in gold, that she had had to sign for.

"Honey! You got into college after all," her mother said with a touch of eager hysteria.

"Mom," Sissy sighed, "I didn't apply."

"Then maybe you got a job offer, dear. It looks special, whatever it is."

Sissy was really too gloomy to imagine that it could be anything worthwhile, but when she slid open the envelope; she was intrigued by what turned out to be a very mysterious invitation.

Dear Mrs. Sissy Samantha Stardust,
You are one of the elite few selected for a prestigious honor. You are cordially invited to a special event. Do come alone. All details will be revealed. A limousine will be at your house at 9:00AM tomorrow morning to pick you up for the informational and orientation. Plan to spend the day and evening. Meals and evening attire will be provided. This is regarding an employment opportunity.
Regards,
Philip Randolph Lexington
Chief recruiter for SXXI Corporation.

"Well, which is it? Is it an honor, event, employment opportunity, or orientation?"

"I think dear, it is all of it and you should go see."

"But what if it is a hoax? Or some kidnapping scheme?" Sissy's mom was far more afraid of her daughter sinking into a depression and ending up lying in bed all summer than of her getting picked up in a limousine. It was hard for her to imagine that could spell trouble. "If it is, they have so much money to burn, they would probably find another way to get you anyway," her mother teased.

"Aren't you curious? You know, I think the worst it could be is if it turns out someone thinks you actually have money and ends up trying to sell you a vacation or a time-share all day. But really, Sissy, it will still get you out of the house!"

In the end, it was decided Sissy should go. If for no other reason, than that they would both be too curious forever if she did not.

It took a lot for Sissy to wake up on time the next morning and she tried with minimal enthusiasm to dress up. All she could think was 'Johnson' and spasmodically sigh at intervals. The limousine showed up right on time, just like the letter said. There were no men in masks inside so she got in. Actually the only other person in the limo was the driver. "Where are we going?" Sissy asked casually. She was just testing if she might get some additional info. "To SXXI Corporation headquarters." Yah, Sissy, thought--that was helpful. Why bother to ask more. Surely she would find out soon enough.

Indeed she did. SXXI Corporation Headquarters was housed in an impressive 20-story skyscraper in the heart of the city and equipped for holding extravagant events. Coming into the elegantly decorated entryway, and standing on very cushy plush carpet, Sissy was struck by the grandeur that made it seem so large and imposing. Yet the immensity of it all was juxtaposed with an attention to detail via artistic décor, including statues and beautiful paintings that made it somehow cozy and inviting at the same time. Much was in a crimson red and royal purple but with such variety of shade, and texture, nothing was too much and all was a delight to the eye.

"Sissy Stardust, how nice to meet you."

An attractive woman, likely in her fifties, but wearing a beautiful gown with plunging neckline and all the poise to carry it off, extended a warm hand and greeting to Sissy.

"My name is Kendra Davenport."

She in turn introduced Sissy to a gentleman, who happened to be Phillip Lexington himself. He was dressed in a very refined suit except on closer perusal; Sissy could see that his tie had naked pinup girls all over it.

"Nice to meet you," Sissy said politely, "But I'm really not sure why I'm here..."

"Sissy, we promise to explain absolutely everything to you very soon. But, so that we do not have to do it a million times, we have an orientation just for that purpose. After the orientation, we will have a private meeting in which you will have the opportunity to ask any remaining questions you may have. For now, we would like to take you to the lounge where you can meet the other girls and get some refreshment. Is that alright with you?"

Sissy agreed, and so off they went.

In the lounge, Sissy got to meet up with a bunch of other women. They were all around her age, with a range of body types and styles but somehow seemed to her like kindred spirits. What was it about them? Well, they seemed very open and warm and friendly…but there was something else. 'I know what it is,' Sissy realized. 'They are sexy. I mean, they are really sexy and they know it.' Sissy had actually never been with a girl before but 'Man, I would be with any of these girls in a heartbeat.' They were all so attractive. It was the way in which they were embodied, like they knew every inch of their flesh and liked it and they knew what felt good. Then there was their charisma. It was the kind that comes from loving yourself and loving others, and not being afraid to show it. They seemed to feel the same about her, and invited her easily into the fold. In no time, they were all cuddling, chatting, and fixing each other's hair.

"Yah, we have no idea why we're here either," A more gothic styled chic named Fanny, with tattoos, piercings, and jet black hair said. "But once we saw the place and the company, we figured it must be something good." Another girl, Tiffany, in a fitted suit dress, seconded that sentiment "I don't know what it is, but I just feel like I belong here." Maria, from Brazil, and many others nodded their heads.

Their hosts soon arrived equipped with a projector. A little throat clearing and Phillip began the orientation portion of the day. "You are all here today because we have reason to believe you love sex. Not only that, but you love people and delight in the pleasures of the flesh in a way that is generous, sincere, and shameless."

('This was starting off real interesting,' Sissy thought.)

"We operate a revolutionary escort operation in which those qualities are fundamental, cultivated, and encouraged. As you know, prostitution is now legal, but that has not ended the traditional trappings and pitfalls of many an entry-level profession. Too many lackluster employees who hate their jobs and only do it for the money, too much suspicion of exploitation, a general lack of support or retention of the classiest personnel, erratic quality of service and an unfortunate reinforcement of guilt and shame for all involved. Well, that is not how we do things at Sexxtasy International. First, we are highly selective and secondly, we provide a level of support and expect a degree of quality unparalleled in the history of human kind. There is so much to share with you and much will have to wait for the tour, but there are certain things we like to disclose right up front."

"First of all, we require all our escorts to have surgical implants." An uneasy hush fell over the room.

"These are purely for your benefit; however. Think of it as having a remote control under your skin. There are four different microchips that you can turn on with a sequence of 3 rapid nerve signals in their direction. They are imbedded in your digits but will function even if your toe is sprained or otherwise unable to move-- you need only intend it to move to activate the signal. One is a GPS to signal your location. Mind you, we only need to know where you are when you are on the clock or you want us to know for safety. You are the one who can turn it off or on at will. We do make it our business to be able to get to you fast if you need us and so this is critical. Call that button "G".

Then there is "M" for Microbe clear. When activated, this button purges all new bacteria/viruses/fungi on your person. Note: it only rids you of recent arrivals, so it leaves your resident flora and fauna untouched. We expect you to activate this after your session with each client.

The third button is "R" for Repair and Heal. This button triggers an expedited healing process in your body. For example, if you have been at it rough and you are starting to get a little raw, you can activate that button and it will greatly speed up your recovery."

One of the girls yelled "You mean we can do it all night if we want to?" Phillip did not miss a beat. "That is exactly what I mean, girls. You are in charge and you get to work that pussy as much and hard as you like.

The last and definitely not least button, we call "P" for Pause. Picture a perimeter six feet around you. You press this button and anything within that circle, except you, receives an energetic pulse which causes a painless very mild seizure."

Someone raised their hand: "Oh my gosh. Do the clients know that can happen?"

"In answer to your question, yes. That is, if they read their user agreements before clicking accept. Of course, we assume you would only use the pause button if something really unfortunate were happening that could not be better resolved another way...."

"These implants are done surgically and then escorts must train in their usage so that it is second nature. Part of that training is thinking through and applying problem-solving to different scenarios."

Some of the young women who had considered walking out at the mention of implants, were now fairly glued to their seats.

"So let's see. What else do we require? Yes, we require that you continue to love sex. If you find you are no longer into your work with clients for whatever reason, we ask that you come to us and let us know, and we will put you to work in a non-direct service department of our agency. If on the other hand, we hear about it via the customers and it is corroborated over time, in that case we would have to let an employee go. We do not tolerate complacency with mediocrity in our agency. If something is wrong, you should let us know so we can help remedy it. Okay. Any more questions at this stage?" There was total silence. Sissy thought folks were just kind of stunned. This was all so different.

"Kendra, I think they're ready for a tour" Kendra responded by beckoning the girls with an air of expectant excitement, "Well, let's go then." Soon they were padding down the plush carpet and looking into myriad rooms. Sissy felt a little like she was in the middle of Willy Wonka's Chocolate factory except that it was all about sex.

First stop was a cozy little room with naked women lounging on big velvety comfy chairs around the perimeter. A large bouncy thick mat was in the middle. Sissy wondered what this class was. The women were holding mirrors up exploring their pussies while A woman, presumably the teacher, was standing in the center with her legs spread and a stainless steel mini barbell of sorts hanging suspended from between her pussy lips. "Wow," Sissy thought.

"That is just not possible..." Looking around, Sissy was amazed at all the variety of vulvas, like fleshy flowers, they were as shamelessly beautiful as orchids on display and just as open and varied. There were the ones with dark inner lips, protruding out like plush rippled petals, with deep pink on the inside, the lighter toned varieties like caramel beige with creamy insides, and an almost mauvish lavender one tinged with brown, and then one pussy that was all pink pudgy outer lips like pillows and just a cute slit in between. There were big clits peeking out of their hoods and tiny clits well hidden.

Sissy felt a bit dazed, a bit in wonder that women everywhere were hiding these secret wonders between their legs. What must that be like for men, to know that women everywhere were walking around with these completely decadent and untamed carnal pleasure blooms just neatly hidden away in their panties but primed for the slightest touch and waiting for a tumescent member to enter and sample their delights? The woman might not even think she is waiting, but then she has this amazing equipment evolved over centuries for that purpose and so there it is. It is inherently waiting...Surely pussies are not meant to be wasted! 'Well no risk of that here,' Sissy thought. She wanted to ask some questions, but realized that in her musings, she had already fallen far behind her tour and so no one from her party was anywhere around to ask.

Rushing to catch up, she was newly touched at the care and luxury of this operation as Kendra showed them a twenty-four hour beauty complex which included a full service salon with every possible head to toe offering, including waxing, nails, and massage. There was also a lingerie room, brimming with beautiful skimpy garments in all possible styles "Escorts may claim one new outfit per work day. We want you to feel and look your best."

Next, on the 19th floor with a stunning view, she showed them a gym that was clothing optional and which was stocked with every kind of exercise equipment, a small pool, sauna, and Jacuzzi. This was also one of the few locales on the tour that was open to VIP clientele. These were club members who paid extra for the privilege of being able to come watch the girls work out or work out themselves alongside them. Other things could happen there also, but there were certain rules of etiquette that VIPs must follow to maintain their gym membership. Sissy noticed that over in a corner, a very well muscled man was pumping more than iron. Rather, he had his rod well into a girl lying on a bench press, and you could tell it felt really good to them both. They were super sweaty, like they had just stopped mid workout. She was clasping him with her legs, and he seemed to be working it in deep. They were so absorbed; they did not seem to notice the tour at all. Pleasure was written all over their faces. Her lips were parted, his eyes glazed with sex. What was more, Sissy thought she could actually smell their sex. Sissy let the tour go on ahead for a moment.

"What is wrong with me? Have I just turned into the ultimate voyeur?" Then she realized 'Oh, yah, it's been over two weeks since I got laid.' In the wake of this revelation and just as she was trying to pull herself away from those tantalizing sights and go jog to catch up with the group, Phillip Lexington appeared right next to her. Apparently he had been watching them also. Or, had he been watching her? The older man smiled with a kind of charismatic charm,

"Looks good, doesn't it?"

"Yes, it does," Sissy admitted with a sigh.

Sissy sensed that Phillip had not missed anything. 'I think he knows how much I am craving sex,' she thought with chagrin. He looked at her in a way she had never been looked at before. There was an audacious fiery passion to it with an undercurrent of both reserve and tenderness. Because of the latter two, she could not be indignant at the first. Regardless, however, it effectively gave her both goose bumps and a pleasurable twinge and tingle in her lower belly culminating in an even wetter pussy than she had had before. Somehow Sissy could tell he knew about that also...

"I am so glad you could come join us today, Sissy."

"Oh, yes, me also," murmured Sissy.

"Do you think you will stay? I personally think you would be very well suited to Sexxtasy."

His voice lingered over that last word. Sissy cleared her throat.

"Thank you, Mr. Lexington. I am still learning about employment here, but it does seem very nice."

He nodded and smiled and then promptly disappeared off into a side room; leaving Sissy to rejoin the tour.

"Up here is the health section of the tour, with a complete health and dental clinic." Kendra was saying, "All new employees pay a visit there for a check up and to review their birth control options." Then she showed them another large section with beautiful windows taking in the view, and where there was a library full of every sexy book and video available the world over. 'I am going to have to get back here and check this out when I have more time.' thought Sissy eagerly.

Next, there was a travel resource office. Apparently escorts could decide 'I would like to go work in Greece' or any other country in which Sexxtasy does business, and sign up on the list and then the first job for that destination would be theirs. Then, they would go to the travel office where all arrangements could be made.

More interestingly, right next to a comprehensive sexy toy resource center, there turned out to be a "Try it out" room.

"This room is in case there is something you would like to try in a low pressure exploratory manner outside the context of customer relations, you can do it here. We have staff at your disposal to help you work out the kinks, so to speak."

Kendra smiled very proudly at the pun. Sissy peeked in the room and sure enough, a girl was on her stomach with another woman stroking her hair while a guy was talking to her soothingly as he engaged in the process of slowly entering her ass with his dick.

Then on the other side of the room, partitioned from the other group but easily viewable from the hall window, a woman was all bound up and somehow suspended by sashes around her thighs in a kind of swing with her legs apart, while another woman licked her pussy.

In yet another section, similarly veiled from the others but easily viewable from the hall, through a system of mirrors, was a woman on her hands and knees, who looked almost strung between two dicks because one was full length in and completely filling up her mouth, and the other was lodged deep in her pussy. The man in the front was up on his knees, and supporting her head with his hands. The man in the back had his hands on her hips and was pulling her back and forth.

Between these three scenes, Sissy could have stayed watching for a long time. She realized that actually, she had been busy having a lot of sex in her life, but had never had the pleasure of watching in vivo action and she admitted to herself that it was really fun. She felt her own body empathetically respond as she saw the hard members penetrating, the lips quivering, and heard the sighs and moans. She was not the only one to linger behind, but she was the one who stayed the longest.

Right when she thought her horniness was actually getting a bit unbearable and she felt she might start rubbing on furniture soon if she did not get relief, she felt a breath on her neck and some warm, large presence and turned to see Phillip Lexington had reappeared. He asked, "Are you enjoying the show, Sissy?" She really did not have to answer. His eyes swept over her slowly, lingering on her erect nipples and the way she was breathing, helplessly panting a little with excitement.

His own voice a little husky, he asked, "do you mind if I touch you a little?" Sissy did not want to appear too eager but part of her wanted to beg him to do it, to say, 'no, no, I really don't mind. Please, touch me all over, touch me a lot, just do it now.' Instead, she just nodded demurely, and he brushed her cheek with his finger tips, tracing them luxuriously down her neck, and into her cleavage, then, as Sissy caught her breath with pleasure, softly cradling and squeezing her breasts only to continue his tracing down her tummy, finding her belly button, like he was finding the center of her being. In his touch, she already knew his mastery, his experience. To be so gentle and so firm all at once. It was like his senses were heightened to every subtle contour of her body and they could proceed with perfect confidence to chart the secrets of her flesh. He hugged her from behind, so she could feel his well-hung erection against her buttocks, seeming to strain against the confines of his slacks. Then, with a final caress, he smiled and walked smoothly away again.

Was he toying with her, using restraint, or simply called away on business? 'Well,' Sissy thought, 'At least he seems interested. Or, does he do that to all the girls, kind of sample the merchandise?' Meanwhile; however, Sissy was left hot and bothered. All she could think was 'Two weeks is too long. I need dick or I'll die!' and then she chuckled to herself at all the drama. But really... Sissy wanted sex.

Kendra showed the girls briefly down a hall where there were many hotel-like rooms for use for in-house client calls. There was also a gourmet cafeteria open all hours with all manner of yummy food. "This is where we will be stopping for lunch. Make yourselves at home"

Sissy picked a tray full of first class sushi rolls and went and sat down next to Maria, the Brazilian.

"So what do you think?" Sissy asked.

Maria thought for a second and then said, "I think it looks really nice. I'm just not sure it's for me. I think even though I love sex, I still want to know what they pay and more about what they expect. I want to make sure it's not golden handcuffs..."

"That makes a lot of sense," said Sissy, as she chowed down the truly scrumptious sushi. But actually, she was thinking, 'Golden handcuffs in this job? Bring them on!'

After lunch, they went to the business office, where they got to see the computer software and how billing works. "We only work with the most wealthy clientele. Of course, we provide a distinct service. Clients know our escorts love their work and truly want to be doing what they are doing. This makes the experience the next closest thing to a guilt-free actual love affair but with none of the strings and complications.

Additionally, prospective clients must go through an extensive vetting process themselves to become members of our elite club. They put down a weighty deposit and money is withdrawn commensurate with services received. Escorts do not have to deal with or talk about money at all. The way it works is like this. If you have just completed a job as an escort, you call the office after the session. You get on the phone with one of our operators, (Kendra gestured to a row of women in headsets), and chats with them like you would to a girlfriend about how it went. We try to be fair and consistent with everyone but basically customers are billed according to three criteria: amount of time, amount of labor involved (if; for example, he just wanted you to lounge around and read in the nude in his hotel room, that would be less money than if he wanted 5 blow jobs during that same amount of time), and how pleasant it was. For sure, easy gracious customers pay less, as they should. Escorts keep all tips and get one third of what comes in. One third is reinvested into the girls and pays for all the amenities and services you see before you. The other third goes to the agency."

Kendra began handing out papers. "This is a questionnaire about your sexual tastes. We give a different one to prospective customers. You can see the questions detail the most commonly requested sexual acts and inquire if you have done it and if so, do you dislike it, tolerate it, like it, or love it and in case you have not tried it, if you are open to it. For readily understandable reasons, we prefer girls with a broad repertoire of sexual tastes. There are pages at the back that you can consider 'bonus questions.' They are in no way required, but can help us meet demand for more specialized tastes."

The group quietly worked on the forms. It was a self-score kind of quiz, which stated clearly the ballpark score that was a good fit for Sexxtasy International. Sissy had a shining score.

Kendra asked if anyone had any questions. Sissy raised her hand.

"Can we still have sex with whoever we want on our off time?"

"That is an excellent question and the answer is absolutely. We want you to stay fired up and inspired about sex, and what better way than to get to have it your way on your time however and with whomever you like. Additionally, you are entitled to use your implants even on your off time if you like and in fact, we request that if you are going into a situation that could in any way be risky, like a night club in a foreign country, for example, that you turn on your GPS button and that after any sexual encounter, you get in the habit of turning on your Microbe clear."

Maria then asked,

"How many hours do we work, and do we get vacation?"

"This is approximately a 40 hour per week job but we do not care when and how you put in your hours. For example, it is not uncommon to spend a weekend with a client and then have the rest of the week off. You can also stockpile time, in that, if you work extra, you get extra time off. Work time is any time you spend with a client. So, if you spend a week with a client in Hawaii, you have worked way more than 40 hours and so can take the next week off; perhaps have your own vacation."

Sissy was sold on Sexxtasy, so when Kendra came around offering contracts for review to those who were interested, Sissy quickly took one and read briskly through it. It was just a more detailed rendition of all she had already heard plus additional awesome stuff like benefits and even a pension if you stayed with the agency for 30 years. 'What a great job!' she thought.

When it was time for her private job consultation session, she really had only one question left. She asked,

"How did they find out about me?"

Kendra brought up Sissy's new profile on the computer and said apparently a Johnson Mathews had heard about their organization via one of their sex magazine ads, and he had called in her name on their special nomination hotline. Sissy was touched that he had been looking out for her, even while he was away.

Kendra looked into Sissy's eyes, gauging her sincerity as she reviewed key features and requirements of the job. Once she ascertained that Sissy was absolutely clear on the particulars, and was unreservedly prepared to say "yes," she invited Sissy to take the Sexxtasy vows.

Sissy repeated the words clearly "I vow to continue to love sex (or notify SXXI), treat clients and coworkers with kindness, exercise absolute discretion at all times in relation to clients and coworkers, adhere to all safety and hygiene protocols as specified in the manual, and otherwise obey the rules of SXXI."

Once Sissy had signed all the paperwork for new hires, she was taken to the special clothes closet where she got to select a stunning evening gown. Sissy went and called her Mom right away and told her she had scored an excellent position in an entertainment, event-hosting agency. It *was* kind of true. She also let her know she would now be living in a company apartment. Her mother was very happy for her. "Save some money for college, dear."

Sissy was then given a key to her special micro apartment on the tenth floor. She was welcome to live there but it would also serve as her dressing room and locker for her belongings and anything she needed for her work. As soon as she opened the door to her brand new little home, Sissy was surprised to find a large bouquet of beautiful different colored roses in a vase. It was so large, in fact, that it took up almost all the available floor space in the little room and filled her quarters with the gorgeous fragrance of roses. Walking gingerly around the flowers, she found a gold embossed card. It said only, "Welcome Home, Sissy---regards, from P.L."

Sissy went into the hallway, and knocked on her neighbor's door. This was Tiffany's apartment. She had decided to take the job also. "Oh, Hello, Sissy. You getting settled in alright?" Sissy nodded in the affirmative with a smile that brightened still more to note that there were no roses in Tiffany's room. Sissy and Tiffany traded a few more niceties welcoming themselves to their new lives and then Sissy waltzed back to her own pad. "It is personal," she thought happily. "I think Phillip really likes me." With an ear to ear smile on her face amid the wafting aroma of five dozen roses, Sissy set about arranging her things.

That evening was the welcome dinner party social. She arrived sheathed in her new evening gown; a flattering combination of lace and satin. It was the perfect color to offset her features. The music was engaging; nice syncopated dance rhythms with soothing vocals. Sissy began to move her hips to the music. The lighting, too, was sensuously tasteful. Soon, she had sampled a fine glass of pink champagne punch with cherries floating in it and a bubble had gone up her nose, which made her burst into helpless giggles. Sissy found her little cluster of more familiar girls. She was so pleased to know that Tiffany, Maria, and Fanny had all decided to join SXXI. They compared notes and chatted excitedly about their new lives. When the food arrived, it was a marvelous banquet of the most succulent and well seasoned faire Sissy had ever tasted. They just did not do pleasure part way in these parts! It arrived just in time, too, because Sissy was getting a little tipsy, unaccustomed as she was to alcohol and having imbibed the punch on an empty stomach.

After dinner, the girls headed back to their apartments together. Fanny, the cute gothic kind of girl, wanted to stop in and hang out with Sissy for a few minutes before going back to her pad. "Those are such beautiful roses!" she said as she came in the door and Sissy was relieved she did not ask where they had come from. Sitting next to her on the bed, the only place to sit, Fanny said,

"Sissy, are you, like, as horny as I am after a whole day of this?" Sissy nodded "Oh yah. Big time."

Fanny had skipped the evening gown and was wearing a short plaid skirt with a little tank top that had lace on top. Sissy noticed her bra straps were showing and they were purple. There was a little tendril of a tattoo peeking out above her bra. What could it be? Sissy wondered. Fanny noticed Sissy's eyes glued to her bosom. A little tipsy herself, Fanny graciously aided her view by pulling the lacy straps of her tank and bra straps down in turn, the soft flesh of her breasts ending up bulging over the top; her nipples sticking out. The tattoo was an art nouveau kind of ornate octopus twirling its tentacles around her breast as other tentacles were finding their way down her midriff to her belly button and around her side. Sissy felt an unspoken invitation and began to trace it with her fingers. She had never felt another woman's breast before and was surprised at how very soft it felt. The softness was somehow more consciously so, being another person's skin. Getting into this, she began to squeeze and fondle Fanny's tits. Fanny sighed and relaxed.

"I really needed this."

Looking at Sissy's evening gown, Fanny asked,

"Isn't that a bit tight?"

"Yes, it kind of is. Can you help me get it undone?"

Fanny nodded, "Of course" and so Sissy turned around on her knees, while Fanny moved her hair around to one side and slowly undid the long zipper of her dress. Easing the dress down her shoulders, Fanny surprised Sissy by suddenly unhooking her bra. She slid her hands around the front, under the bra and began to caress and squeeze Sissy. Sissy was so horny and it felt so good. Fanny knew just how to do it, too. 'Is that because she has tits of her own?' She wondered. Fanny let her fingers slide down further, rubbing Sissy's clit gently through the silky fabric of her panties. "Hmmm" Sissy moaned. Encouraged, Fanny slid fingers from her other hand up Sissy's pussy from below, while still diddling her above. Fanny pushed Sissy forward onto her tummy, and with one hand on her ass, began to finger fuck her from behind, while Sissy took over rubbing her own clit. After awhile, Sissy rolled over and began trying to pull down Fanny's panties but Fanny had a garter belt with thigh high stockings on, so the garters had to be unfastened first. Sissy looked very industrious getting them undone so she could finally pull those lacy undies off and toss them in a corner.

Seeing all those pussies earlier had made Sissy curious to explore. She saw that Fanny's pussy looked a lot like the rest of the young woman herself---very pretty and a bit exotic, with a little delicate golden ring on one of her soft pussy lips, and an audaciously perky clit sticking out of a swirl of rose pink. Sissy knelt down and began to lick Fanny's clit, and the surrounding super soft flesh, making little circles, while she stuck her thumbs inside Fanny's cunt. She tasted the tangy truly female taste of her and sucked gently on her clit; making her own swirls and paying attention to what seemed to give the most pleasure. Fanny was very responsive and so gave many clues.

They played like this until they happily managed to get each other off, and then snuggled sleepily together. Sissy had really enjoyed herself, but could not help it. She still craved cock. Cocks were just so perfect for penetration with their width, texture, and length. The ingenious creations were just hard enough and just softly fleshy enough. You would think they were just made for pussies. Maybe, because they were! They really are quite wonderful things, Sissy thought as she dozed off into some rather cocky dreams.

Fanny got up to go and Sissy gave her a sleepy hug as she extricated herself from their cozy cuddle to go brush her teeth and go to bed in her own pad.

"That was fun. Thanks, Sissy. See you around."

Sissy fell back into a deep sleep.

The next day was going to be big day. First there were various classes she was to attend. It was going to basically be like the orientation but much more in depth. Then in the evening, she would undergo minor surgery to put in the implants after which everyone would go to bed. The next morning, they would begin training in how to use the implants.

****

Sissy had been awake for a little while and was getting ready, when there was a knock at the door. It was Phillip.

"Mr. Lexington, hello." Sissy said. She was so happy to see him. "Thank you for the beautiful roses."

"Oh, your welcome, Sissy. It was a pleasure. You may call me Phillip."

"Please come in, Phillip."

There was little room to be had in the tiny apartment with the flower vase taking up all the floor space. The only spot to be was on the bed. Phillip knowingly pulled down a panel that turned into a shelf and put the roses up there.

"Do you want me here and in your bed, Sissy? I have been meaning to tell you that you should feel no pressure. I am your superior in your job but this has nothing to do with your position and you should feel completely free to decline my attentions. I only want you to accept them if you want them."

Sissy did not know what to say.....she wanted him so badly, she was afraid she would collapse into begging.

She gave up.

"Yes," she said.

He took her chin in his hand and tilted her face so he was looking deep in her eyes.

"Yes what, Sissy?"

"I want you, Phillip. Please take me."

He wasted no time and promptly picked her up in his arms and put her on the bed. He began to strip off her clothes, kissing her at intervals, then stripping her some more. Sissy, delighted, and already creamy for him, just gave herself over to whatever he might do. He stood up and took handfuls of the heads of the roses and crumpled them free of their stocks, dropping little loads of rose petals on her breasts and tummy. He rubbed them luxuriously into her skin as he nipped at her nipples and kissed a voracious trail down to her pussy. Sissy cried out when he landed his hungry lips on her clit and pussy lips, stimulating knowing circles into her yet sex-starved tissues, setting them aflame with desire. Whipping out his large cock, so hard, he stroked the head against her moist pussy, coating it with cream, then he plunged it mightily in, the heavy hard weight of it pounding solidly into her. They could feel the nice tight friction, greater because of his larger size and because in her arousal, she was squeezing him so tight. It was automatic because her whole body wanted him. As he went back to kissing her, he started out real easy so they could both feel every point of blessed contact between then as he entered her. Then, gradually, he built up speed. He was soon ramming her from below as he held her succulent lips in his own lips, tasting the sweetness and thrusting his tongue in her mouth. He could feel his other thrusts all the way up her body, and in her gasps and moans muffled by his mouth.

Phillip worked up to a frenzy. He held her arms cradled above her head with his arms around them, propped up on his elbows as his strong pelvis drove his cock into her in faster and faster strokes. Sissy could feel him hitting every point, unplugging every untapped center; surely he would fuck her into oblivion. She had not realized she was making so much noise until her breath caught and she felt a sudden intensification of pleasure that transmitted itself both inwardly and outwardly at once like an electric wonderful surge and she was thrusting her hips and rolling and wriggling in delicious orgasmic climax, right as Phillip hit his. He shuddered, gushing a fountain of steamy cum deep into her pussy, which just kind of lapped it up in its own happy contractions. Phillip kissed her sumptuously some more as the last little after shocks of pleasure rippled through their bodies.

It turned out that Phillip was actually fairly insatiable and he would let himself into her micro apartment at all hours. Sometimes he would make slow love to her and other times he would just come in and pound her pussy in an ecstatic quickie, taking her from behind while she was sleeping, so she would awake to find him already driving his member home.

Sissy was in a blissed out state of perpetual satisfaction now. She got through implant implantation and training like a breeze. Soon, sex was not only her favorite hobby, but also her profession, one in which she took great pride and pleasure. Her clientele were some of the happiest at SXXI and she became legendary for exemplifying the company values and highest aspirations.

THE TAMING & TRAINING Of JULIA (3)****

Xanadu, as he had been fondly nicknamed by a previous newbie, was looking over the latest arrival. Like all starters, she was suspended lengthwise in a water-filled tank with a tube in her mouth bringing in both oxygen and nutrition, and a tube up her rear end to remove waste. She was sedated and would remember nothing of this stage.

She was quite beautiful, Xanadu thought, even for a human. He really liked everything about humans. They were such succulent delights. That was exactly why his species had come to prefer them for their sexual playthings. Xanadu considered humans and sex similar to the way humans viewed chocolate and food. Fellow Xazaxz were of course necessary for reproduction, but he knew not a single one who would not actually prefer sexual activity with a human instead; if it were purely a matter of pleasure.

Xanadu looked at the girl's hair all spread out in tendrils floating in the water. He used the controls to rotate her slowly, staring at the contours of her butt cheeks where the tube entered and disappeared, the rounded hills of her breasts peaking with protruding nipples, how her lips were spread around the mouth tube. Her eyelids fluttered a little in sedated sleep and he wondered at the delicate eyelashes. The lighting of the tank made her skin glow in a kind of goldish blue. Xanadu just could not wait to break this one in.

First, she would have to undergo some special procedures. The Xazaxz liked things to be as easy and painless as possible, but also to get their way in every respect. They had studied humans extensively and knew all about every neurotransmitter and pleasure sensor that affected their behavior. As such, they were able to outfit their captives with special additional dosing mechanisms that were implanted in key parts of their anatomy that would then be under Xazaxz control. Xanadu knew the details really well as one of the key trainers, but skilled Xazaxz equivalents of surgeons would actually insert them. One went in the base of the human skull and cancelled out fight or flight instincts, leaving only freezing as an option in case of fear. Two more would go into the g-spot and

---

* (T&T of Julia) This unique sci-fi tale includes alien abduction, brain washing, physical alterations to effect response, dubious consent

clitoris, to increase pleasure sensation on Xazaxz command. Then another would go a little deeper in the brain to increase dopamine, to promote lust, risk seeking, and general gusto for life. Lastly, they inserted two triggers to increase oxytocin, which would enhance a human sense of comfort and safety. That was the same neurotransmitter released for both parties when a human pets a furry animal or breastfeeds a baby. These triggers were normally placed in the nipples. Xazaxz were an extremely advanced and ancient species, which had had a lot of time to explore and experiment. They were at their peak when it came to being experienced with humans. So, there were no side affects to these alterations; only the intentional result in which the human was rendered utterly submissive to the Xazaxz every desire.

Xanadu imagined this sweet girl all altered and under his command, and he started to get very aroused. This meant the hard prickly casing retracted and his large slimy reddish member slid out of its inner sheath. Leaning back on his large beetle like outer wings as they helped to prop him up, he used his feelers to stroke the meaty exposed member. His extremely long tongue unfurled also to help out, its stickiness adding sensation to his feelers and soon, with the help of the elegant visual still suspended in front of him, he was at last able to climax, jetting streams of gooey Xazaxz seed on the side of the tank. Bemused, he hurriedly wiped it off with his feelers and left the room.

"You really like that new one, don't you?" Pax wing-nudged Xanadu in the space ship's dining area.

"What do you mean?"

"Oh, I saw you on the camera. Yah, you really like her, alright."

"I guess I do." Xanadu admitted balefully.

"Well, aren't you eligible now with seniority and everything to get one of your own? You should just put in a request. I think we have plenty in our stores at present and so she might be kind of an extra."

"Thank you, Pax. I think I will."

Xanadu submitted his request through the ship computer and received an instant response. "Thank you for faithful service- tenure granted-request honored-you may claim number 345239123- feel free to transfer to your compartment when item is post alteration."

'Oh, wow,' Xanadu thought. He would have one of his very own...He knew he could not help but do the best job ever on her, since he would get to enjoy all the results for her lifetime. That night, Xanadu was so excited that it was hard to sleep. He knew she would be getting altered tonight and be ready for training in the morning, albeit a little sore. Every time he thought of that tender human flesh, his casing would pop open and his member would be sliding out again. It made it difficult to get comfortable with the heavy weight of it all engorged and it's yearning. Hot and tumescent, it spent the whole night flopping around seeking a proper nest, but instead being lodged on his uncomfortably hard abdomen. His member so wanted a warm, juicy, and fleshy spot to go into. It wanted that girl...

****

Julia woke up feeling achy all over, but especially her head, her pussy, and her nipples. She was in a small warm room softly lit in lavender light and she was completely naked with her arms bound behind her back. Julia tried to figure this out; like when you lose something and have to retrace your steps. 'Let's see,' she thought, 'where was I last?'

Ah.... She had been traveling. She remembered with pain why she had been traveling. With only a month's notice, her mother had died of cancer. Julia had been raised solely by her Mom. They had been very close. After her passing, Julia found herself feeling quite shattered. Suddenly, she was the caretaker of the family home and affairs as well as heir to a modest inheritance.

It was just the summer after high school graduation. All her former plans; plans she had labored for to an extreme, appeared to be completely meaningless and futile. Ill prepared to attend Stanford, she requested a deferment and elected to go travel for a gap year. Turning over the care of the home and other business to her few remaining relatives and with a combination of determination and desperation, she had thrown herself into planning a very cost effective trip. She had taken off at the earliest opportunity to travel all over South and Central America.

After amazing adventures in Costa Rica and then in the Amazon, she had entered Brazil and made it to the Northeast, where the pristine beaches called to her with their epic dunes and deep blue waters. Then there was the music---all that wonderful music day and night! She had danced at nightclubs, the wonderful dances in which legs are between legs and no space between bodies. Young handsome men, suavely moving their hips, would sometimes dance "armado" or "armed" meaning erect, so dancing became like having spirited dry hump sex in public, which made for a deliciously giddy and titillating experience, even without benefit of sugar cane whiskey.

As people were so hospitable to this winsome gringa wherever she went, a warm and enthusiastic family scooped her up and took her in. They constantly tried to feed her and fussed over her in every way to make her feel at home. They even got her to shave enough to fit into a tiny bikini, the "fio dental" or dental floss g-string variety. There she was, piled into a crowded car in her bikini and off to the beach to sunbathe, climb sand dunes, and eat popsicles while wading in the ocean.

The handsome, robust son of the family, Rorjario, took a liking to Julia and wanted to "namorar" with her, or date. To him this meant taking her on his motorcycle to the beach at night. The moon was full, the air warm with the sweet smell of the sea surrounding them. They spread a blanket on the soft sand, and he began to kiss her, telling her how "linda" she was, so beautiful! She had had minimal sexual experience back in high school. She had been one of those busy super structured types. She certainly had never had so much affirmation of her attractiveness and male attention in general as she had received since setting foot in Latin America. But, Rorjario took it well over a notch with his crooning endearments and caresses. Between that and the beauty all around her, she was well prepared to let everything go. Really, what did she have to lose?

Of course, she had condoms with her just in case. Like all good girls from the San Francisco Bay Area in the era of safe sex, she never left home without them. Rorjario had never seen one before and was mildly horrified at the idea of putting such a thing on his cock. "Camisinha? Eu não!" (a little shirt? not me!) But as she had practiced with her best friend after sex-ed class on a banana, she took the rubber in her teeth and set about putting it on his dick with her mouth, which made him feel all together better about the idea; at least enough to keep his sizable erection. He assumed she must be very experienced, indeed, given this show of knowledge. She did not mention that actually, it was her first time. As he entered her, she felt a little bit of a pull and a slight burn, but then he was all the way in, and the novelty and intimacy of the experience swept her up along with the sound of the crashing surf and the beautiful stars in the warm night. They were alone on this exquisite beach and a man was inside her. A man had really taken possession of her most intimate parts and was excited, thrusting into her. Wow. There he was. What a marvel that after years of reading about it, this intercourse thing really worked!

Julia was pretty blissed out and just going with the flow, by the time Rorjario lifted her legs up above his shoulders to penetrate her more thoroughly. She thought nothing of it at first. It was almost too intense, though. He was ramming into her cervix really deeply. He was getting more and more rambunctious about it also, and coming out fairly fully before going back in. Suddenly, he came out all the way, and instead of going back into her pussy, he plowed his well lubricated cock right up her ass. Julia gasped and tried to speak but could not call to mind much in her limited Portuguese to apply to the situation. His gusto only intensified amid the tightness of that spherical squeeze, and her shocked facial expression was hidden in shadow. Julia was still speechless and so little was effectively communicated except his own pleasure as he continued to thrust into her, in and out of her butt. All of a sudden, in a series of jolts and convulsive shudders, he came, loading gobs of jism into what would be a very soggy and well worn condom, deep in her ass.

Rorjario slowly pulled out and rolled over onto his back to look at the stars. He smiled at Julia. Julia felt a little full with undigested experience, but nonetheless played it off by smiling back. He asked if she wanted to go return to the house now? She nodded.

Back at his home, sleeping in a different room in a hammock, (as if she were the chaste girl that young unmarried Brazilian women were expected to be), she suddenly felt a little awkward staying with his family. The next morning, she said her very gracious goodbyes and left some American dollars in appreciation of their great hospitality; which they tried not to accept, but since she was traveling light and had little to give them as presents, she insisted. Rorjario was sad to see her go, and why so soon? She just smiled and kissed him on both cheeks.

She ended up staying in a youth hostel the next night and decided to take a walk on a stretch of beach a little ways from where Rorjario had greatly expanded her sexual experience. Sitting on the beach, her pussy and butt still a little sore from all that expansion; she had watched the waves, thinking about her travels. Where was she going? Would she ever want to return to her former life or go to college as expected?

Then, seemingly out of the blue and ostentatiously right above the horizon, a powerful beacon of light appeared and began pouring radiance down the ocean in front of her. It was mesmerizing. Rainbows like fireworks dazzled through the streaming light. What in the world could it be? Leaving her belongings on the beach, she walked down to the edge of the water to get a better look. The water was warm and felt wonderful. She waded in a little further until she was in up to her waist and all of a sudden, Julia felt a sting in her left buttock and found herself unable to move. She fell backwards into the water and felt something coil itself around her chest and then pull her gently toward the light. At some point she passed out and that was the last thing she remembered before she woke up in this captive state.

Having thought it all through, she felt she knew little more than before. Now fully awake to her situation, she began to get increasingly anxious and actually feel a bit panicky. Where was she, who was keeping her here, and what would they do to her? Julia started to whimper and cry to herself but then something came in the room that made her scream. It looked like a huge insect with waxy thick wings, large shiny bulbous eyes and a pink spiral curled up inside what might be some sort of a beak in the middle of its face. It seemed to be waiting patiently for her to stop screaming. As soon as she stopped, she felt an immediate bizarre soothing and pervasive relaxation feeling take over her, it was even pleasurable. Still the insect thing did not move.

Julia really needed to pee. She began to wonder if she should ask it somehow how to go about it; but how? She did not want to just go on the floor. What if she had to live in this tiny room with that? She began to cross her legs. The strange creature pulled out from under its wings a large pink container and put it down near her feet. Julia hoped she had this right and would not elicit wrath from this scary beast. She daintily squatted over the container and peed, to her immense relief. The creature removed the container.

Now her stomach began to growl. She was so hungry. When had she last eaten? As if reading her mind, the creature presented to her three round jars of a creamed substance and holding it with these crazy long black feelers, put them under her nose in turn to smell. One was reddish and smelled surprisingly like pizza, the other was green and smelled like creamed broccoli, and the third smelled sweetly like ice cream. It dawned on Julia that these creatures must know an awful lot about humans. She really knew this to be true when she noticed the creature was saving the ice cream for dessert.

He, as she had come to think of him, took the red and green jars in one set of feelers, and unfurling his long curly tongue from his beak, he dipped the end in and then curled it back up a little so the paste was wrapped in a tube of tongue, and then he slowly headed it towards Julia's mouth. She thought she should be trying to get away or flail at it or something and yet, it was as if her reflexes would not kick in, and despite a bit of dread, she could not really move. Additionally, as he used a second set of feelers to part her lips, which initially triggered a wave of revulsion, she was surprised to find those icky feelings somehow transforming into the same soothing melting kind of comfort that she had felt earlier when the creature had come in. The creature moved the food only very, very slowly towards her and she was so hungry, she could not help that her mouth started to water, as the aroma filled her nostrils and it smelled great. If she could have closed her eyes, she would have sworn she was in some New York pizza parlor. She could not bear to close her eyes; however, as if she were under some compulsion to actually witness this food transport via massive insect tongue headed towards her lips.

To add to the complex mix of feelings, Julia started to feel the absurdity of the scene a bit acutely, and started to giggle a little, which for some reason made her mouth water even more. 'Julia,' she thought to herself, 'you are really going to eat that food off that thing's tongue. I really think you are going to do it.' and sure enough, by the time the tip of the tongue curled around the creamy food, began to press between her lips, she knew she would submit. The whole little package stuffed inside her mouth, Julia realized that there was no way for her to get the food out unless she sucked on the tongue. It filled up her whole mouth and felt a little sticky and meaty textured, but not unpleasant. She tried not to think about it too much. 'Only think about the food,' she exhorted herself. And so she began to suck, like a baby, on the tube made of curled up tongue until through pressure and suction, she was able to extract all the contents. It tasted so good, even better than it smelled. She really needed so much more. The creature dipped the tongue into the green jar, and this time inserted itself into her mouth much more quickly. She was voracious, and the faster she sucked and emptied the food, the more quickly he dipped and reinserted his tongue into her mouth. Soon, it was the most normal thing in the world, and she had finished all the pizza and broccoli---if that were what they really were. Now, it was on to the ice cream. Julia had been so hungry; she still had plenty of room and was really looking forward to that ice cream.

  The creature paused for a moment. Julia heard a twitching, flicking noise and suddenly a shell like pod snapped open at the base of the creature's abdomen. A slinky sleeve like sheath seemed to be pulsating to life. Growing turgid and starting to bulge out of it, emerged a reddish beefy member, looking very moist and kind of raw. The head was like the size of a small fist, and it stood imposing. Fascinated and a little horrified, all Julia could do was stare. Then she felt something kick in that frightened her a bit more. She was feeling a delicious feeling in her clit, and pressure in her womb, like she wanted to have sex more than she had ever consciously been aware of feeling before. Those connections had not been previously activated for her yet. How could this make her feel that?

  Before she could try more to figure this out; however, the creature had dipped the head of his formidable rod into the ice cream and taken out a swirl. Pulling her gently down to her knees, he then slowly headed his other head toward her parted lips, where her jaw was unconsciously hanging open, and she was again quite frozen. He went very slowly so she could see for herself that she was not resisting, and again, that her mouth was watering for the ice cream. Sure enough, when he put the head of his alien dick between her lips, she naturally started to suck the ice cream off. He fed her all the ice cream in that way.

He left her for around half an hour, but for her it seemed like eternity. She was learning that she felt better when that insectoid alien thing was there. The whole time he was gone, she fretted and waited for him to return. Add to that, she was starting to really need to go the bathroom. He came back just in time, and as soon as he entered the room through the sliding door slot, she immediately felt a bit better emotionally.

He had a strange contraption in his feelers this time. It looked like a vacuum cleaner with a long hose. He came up behind her. She was again anxious what he would do. She noted wryly; however, that being anxious these days seemed to just mean she would be even more still for whatever he had planned. She was incapable of mustering the slightest resistance.

He pushed her bound hands up a little, and then she felt the feelers pulling apart her buttocks and sliding the nozzle of the machine easily up her butt. All of a sudden she was being suctioned. It was surprisingly quick and efficient and a total relief. She began feeling waves of gratitude toward this being. All the while, she argued with herself,

'But he is your enemy! You should not be thankful he is taking care of you. You should be angry at him for keeping you captive.'

But somehow, she could not feel the appropriate feelings to go along with those thoughts and so they were like empty meaningless words. Or perhaps they were just about a distant former life.

*****

Xanadu was very pleased with the results of his efforts. The majority of the work was already done. She must first realize that she was dependent for every comfort on him and that his very presence gave her pleasure. Then, as a result, she would begin to feel that his form could not be nearly as repugnant or strange as it initially appeared. Lastly, she must learn that she belonged to him completely and utterly. Once all these lessons were strategically in place, everything else would be easy. He could already tell also, that her body was starting to take over the extra hormonal boosting triggers. Initially, he had to intentionally activate the extra oxytocin and dopamine, but now her body had come to associate those things with his presence. That meant that now, whenever he was with her, her body would automatically produce more of the hormones, using the implanted additional sources and receptors for production and exchange.

Soon, she would not want to live without him and he would be able to do whatever he liked with her in every way. Xanadu was deeply looking forward to that final possession of her. It was very important to take everything slow so her whole being had a chance to catch up to current realities. For that reason, he would not be rushing it. But still, he felt profoundly pent up and unrequited as he made it through the steps of the taming and training process.

Giving her a little time alone, gave her a chance to feel bereft without him so she would be all the more motivated to please him and do his will when he was present. It was difficult for him to stay away also; however, and he returned to her with relish. Today they would share names. Xanadu pointed all his feelers towards his upper abdomen and buzzed out "Xanadu" which was a much easier name for humans to say than his real name in his language. Then he pointed towards her and she took the cue "I am Julia." "Juuleeyaa," Xanadu buzzed out in a creaky voice. Xanadu came up very close to Julia, and began to feel her gently and again slowly, all over with his feelers and tongue.

"Juuleeyaa," he crooned as his feelers touched her hair, face, lips, traveling over her breasts, toying with her nipples, entering her mouth. The sticky tongue touched her a little between her legs and immediately, her pussy responded more intensely pleasurably than ever before. One feeler even went a little up her nose, and she sneezed. "Xanadu!" Xanadu, seeing her responses so favorable and her submission quite full in effect, then set about undoing the binding on her hands. Julia felt more waves of gratitude to find her hands free. "Thank you, Xanadu." Xanadu then guided her hands to explore his body, inviting her hands to feel every inch. He helped her explore the glossy hard parts, as well as the softer parts. His wings twitched in pleasure when she hit a good spot.

He knew now that the time had come. He used his feelers and bulk to maneuver her down to the ground. His long tongue unfurled and went its sticky way down to her pussy. Julia cried out in pleasure as that very capable tongue began rubbing her pleasure button, sliding stickily around her pussy lips, and even inserting itself into the juicy depths of her opening, exerting pressure on her g-spot. The sensations felt so good but they seemed like they were building and needed an outlet beyond this yummy foreplay alone. Xanadu knew he was large for her and she needed to be so mad with desire that the discomfort of the stretch would be as nothing for her. Meanwhile, his feelers were squeezing her tits even as his tongue did more and more concerted swirling circles on her pussy and clit. Soon, Julia was writhing, her pelvis grinding with yearning. She knew she needed it and only he could give it to her. "Xanadu, please," she began to beg. Some deliciousness was being wound up tight and there had to be a plug to set it loose.

At last, Xanadu, who had long ago popped open his case, stuck the mammoth head of his member between the inner lips of her creamy pussy. Wings twitching, he began to push it ever so gradually in. He was so large, Julia necessarily needed to relax entirely to make room; as her body quivered in a heady combination of anticipation, a little fear, and acute arousal. With just the head in, he was already hitting her newly sensitized g-spot, and she felt almost delirious with desire, and actually started to orgasm but tried to stop because contracting at this stage with him being so large, was a little painful. He slid out a little to catch more cream, and then she felt the luscious friction as he headed back in, so solid and full. He pushed and crammed this time until he was all the way in and the penetrating erogenous rubbing again propelled Julia inexorably toward orgasm, she started to thrust herself and rode a ripple of contortions and contractions which only intensified things for Xanadu also.

Fully inspired, and holding her tightly while deeply entered into her human flesh, Julia was surprised to see his magnificent wings spread to full breadth and then feel them lift a little and then actually leave the ground as he began to take passionate flight around the room, still thoroughly engaged in thrusting his huge rod pointedly up her innards. Julia had never been airborne like this—and to be doing so in the throes of acutely pleasurable penetration. It was deliriously intoxicating. Xanadu seemed spurred on in his flight, darting here and there in the room, and in a fit of buzzing, he pounded harder and faster, until XZZXZZ! he shot his large load of alien cum into her pussy. A little dizzy with bliss, he then brought them fluttering slowly down to the ground again.

Now that Julia had passed her training with flying colors, she was awarded greater freedom. Xanadu took her on a tour of the spaceship and for the first time she got to see the countless stars of the galaxy through crystal portal windows. She also got to meet fellow humans with their masters. They looked so sweet, like they were in love. Was that how she looked? She wondered. Although Julia found it satisfying to meet and see others like herself in her same situation, she had no desire to visit with them alone. In fact, Julia only liked to do anything with Xanadu nearby. This thankfully worked out, because he liked to have her with him at all times anyway and her whole function and job in life now was to please him.

Xanadu was himself acutely attached to Julia. She had fulfilled his highest hopes; given herself entirely to serving him and was his optimal and ultimate companion. At some point, he had realized he really could not imagine having intimate relations with his own kind again, but he did need to reproduce. He went and discussed implantation with the ship surgeon. It was decided that Julia would be prepared for hosting and birthing his fertilized eggs. He had explained what would happen to Julia as best he could with antics and the little bit of Xazaxz she was starting to understand.

"It would be an honor, Xanadu."

Xanadu watched as they put her under anesthesia and then surgically put Xazaxz eggs into her womb through the opening in her cervix. They also put in Xazaxz chemical dispensers to promote the appropriate hormones and uterine environment. Xanadu was then free to ejaculate his seed into her, knowing his babies would sprout in her womb. His case could barely stay shut, it kept popping open all the time just thinking about it. His erection was almost feverish. She had been stretched enough to accommodate him now, although it was still always tight. She craved him as much as he craved her, and so it was always extremely good, but this time, there was another level of rapture for him, knowing he was pumping his seed into her in a way that would give fruit, make her heavy laden with it, and that she would be bearing his babies.

Julia had a powerful orgasm as she always did, but this time was a bit different for her also. Immediately afterward, there was this warm tender feeling in her womb, probably the hormones getting primed. Julia felt a bit nauseous and dizzy, even as she still felt tingly with post-orgasmic bliss. Xanadu had made a special comfy compartment for her with all kinds of super comfortable furniture. He really did not want her to be uncomfortable and had his own plans to put her under if it got too be too much. She could go through the rest of the pregnancy in suspended animation if necessary. It turned out to be okay; however, and when she felt too pregnant to withstand the brunt of his rod; she eagerly and dutifully sucked him to completion whenever he wished. Her body responded much as it would have with a human pregnancy, and soon her belly was round and her breasts were swollen with their own plans for future milk.

One day, a gentle labor started and through a series of contractions, Julia secreted nine, slimy pods, which Xanadu asked that she keep warm near her belly and breasts for a time. Soon enough they had cracked open and the new babies were starting to flutter around. Xanadu said it was not their normal food but they would probably enjoy it and benefit from it, so Julia expressed milk from her engorged breasts and as it let down and dripped, the fluttering baby Xazaxzs unfurled and dipped their tongues in it to taste it and then curled their tongues around her nipples to steal sucks.

It was hardly the life she had planned, but through all this adaptation and submission, Julia had ended up feeling connected, well utilized, and fulfilled. As the babies buzzed and fluttered around her and Xanadu echoed his own buzzes in pleasure, Julia felt waves of satisfaction, and even, not a little joy.

SEXING IT UP ABOARD THE AQUADELIGHT (2)**[*]

(Or Love and Lust in a Submarine)

June felt the young man's strong arms around her middle, just under her breasts, tugging her to safety through the ocean water. After all the fear and excitement, she felt a wave of relief. She also began to experience other sensations; however. June had seen so few young men and certainly none so vital in their physicality. When this man had gotten her through the water to the submarine, the next step was to help her get on board. This of course involved more of his touching her. In the course of saving her, he was grabbing, holding, supporting, and feeling her. Her clothes provided little buffer from such inevitable contact. They were already soaked through. She noticed with some embarrassment that the water was making her lightly colored blouse see-through. Where she came from, they did not wear bras. He could probably see the shape of her breasts very intimately and even a little bit of the color of her nipples.

The discovery submarine, "The Aquadelight" was a new generation of deep sea diving self-propelled vehicle operational by a smaller crew. It was significantly lower maintenance than its predecessors. Billionaire sponsors had taken a liking to the idea of financing an exploratory voyage after an epic sized octopus was sighted surprisingly close to a Caribbean tourist destination. Now the all male crew had been mostly undersea for months with only passing glimpses of the gigantic cephalopod. In between sightings, they took samples and studied various other flora and fauna for smaller scientific projects. The fact was, though, that there was hardly enough important work to go around and the men did get a wee bit cranky at times. Being subject to close quarters, boredom, little privacy, and a lack of the female sex took a toll on even the most devout lover of science.

---

[*] (Aquadelight) Mostly conventional love boat situation but includes following elements: voyeurism, boss/employee power differential, medical advantage taking

First among the crew was Todd Brighten, one of the best and brightest marine biologists of contemporary time. Being a man of two professions, he also wore another hat as the ship medic. Then there was Brent Strong, a maintenance man; and Ralph Heimlich, the cook. The head of the ship was a certain Captain Dick Smart. He was supposed to keep the small crew in line and see to general logistics. At the head of scientific research, was the esteemed Professor Liam Deeply. The men had a convivial relationship, which made management of the ship relatively smooth. That was at least until the wee hours of the morning on April 1st. At that time something happened that would cause the crew's interpersonal dynamics to become a bit topsy-turvy.

The men were rousted from sleep by dramatic turbulence as the little submarine was buffeted about. Jostling to their posts and straining to see, they were able to determine that "Harry," as they called the octopus, was clearly the cause of the tumult. His immense muscled arms loaded with tentacles were flailing and whirling in the water. The men backed their sea craft up as far as they could from the chaos while still keeping view of their study subject. It was difficult with all the churning water, but as the beast retreated back to lower depths, they saw to their dismay that a boat had capsized near the water's surface and a number of people were trying rather unsuccessfully to swim.

Submarine to the rescue! The crew jumped into gear. They got their craft as fast as they could to the surface and site of the shipwreck. They were all good swimmers and this was the most exciting and meaningful thing they had done in months. Todd, Brent, and Ralph jumped into the water and threw themselves whole heartedly into rescuing the stranded people. The victims turned out to be three young women who looked to be barely into their 20s. They were trying with difficulty to swim. Their clothing looked like a throwback to pilgrim's times. When they spoke, you could hear their rare lilt of an accent.

Captain Smart directed the whole operation and had the women brought into the submarine as efficiently as possible. The men, all fired up with adrenaline, could not help but enjoy the feel of the women's bodies as they held them, swimming valiantly to get them to safety. What man would not enjoy rescuing a woman like that, her nipples erect from the chill and poking through the wet clothing, the wet clothing a bit translucent and clinging to her body, her obvious helplessness and need? Once in the submarine, the women were loaned the men's dry shirts and trousers, given blankets, hot tea, and food. At first no one was sure where to house them in such close quarters. There was really no way to keep them separate. They would have to rely on the men's honor and discretion. A set of berths was cleared close together on one end of the tiny sleeping quarters.

June, greatly relieved after the rescue and all comfy now in dry clothing, blankets and a cup of tea, whispered avidly to her friends,

"I can't believe we made it out of there. Now we get to begin our new lives. No worries now. The colony will never find us underwater."

Prudence nodded,

"We did, we made it and did you see how we're surrounded by cute young men?"

"Do you think they will make us their wives?" Asked Grace, shyly.

"I don't know what men out here do, Grace," replied June. "Although, I would like to find out...."

The women had fled from a cultish colony which had become increasingly oppressive, kicking out all the young men as boys, and requiring all the fertile women to marry only the eldest and most prestigious men in the clan, who of course already had loads of wives. June, Grace, and Prudence had gotten ahold of a book and learned a little of the life outside. They became less willing to go with the program. The book stimulated their imaginations such that they ultimately made the momentous decision to plot their escape. After extensive strategizing, they secured a boat and made a run for it. In all their planning, however, they had just never reckoned on an epic octopus.

As for the men, they were on fire. After months away from any sign of a female, now a bundle of young and beautiful ones, seemingly completely unfettered, inexperienced and curious, had just landed in their laps. How to make optimal use of this bounty?

The men were watching and awake to any possible flirting opportunity.

The cook, Ralph, was a little more mischievous than most, and had soon rigged cameras up to the women's private dressing areas as well as the shower. In the digital age, the cameras could take photos silently via remote, and soon there were many such photos being taken of the beautiful women's lithe bodies---their bosoms, buttocks, hips, thighs, all in various states of undress, and all while completely unself-conscious, not knowing that their images were later being consumed by the ravenous crew like first foods for starving men. Ralph only showed the images to Brent and Todd who swore they would not tell. Really, who in their right mind would tell? Who wanted to be a tattletale and then have to be cooped up on a submarine with an angry cook? If the photos were going to be taken and seen by men regardless, what was the harm of one more set of eyes seeing them? In short, there were plenty of rationalizations to support the viewing of these beautiful girls. Of course, the more the men saw and knew of every lovely angle, freckle, beauty mark, and curve, the less they felt satisfied with pictures alone.

Captain Dick Smart and Professor Liam Deeply, being in positions of authority, were oblivious to the whole photo operation. They were aware; however, that the crew did not seem to be focused on the expressed ship mission of studying the octopus anymore. Everyone was distracted, restless. Of course, that included Smart and Deeply. They wasted no time in inviting the girls to the officer's quarters for a special meal.

After introductions, while food was being served and even a little wine, Dick and Liam vied with each other to be warm, inviting, and witty. Dick asked,

"So, where is it you said you came from?"

June seemed the most at ease to speak,

"We come from Tolloweg and our people are the Tollowights."

"And why did you come?"

There was silence this time and Liam aimed to eliminate any awkwardness.

"Well, don't worry about it. You can stay here."

"What?" asked Dick, but then he quickly got the point.

"Goodness, it is isn't the military. If we wish to hire more help for the mission, I'm sure we could justify a few more positions. I tell you what: if you girls would like to stay aboard, one of you can assist Ralph the cook, another can report to our maintenance man, Brent, and the third can help clean and tidy the ship. What do you think, Liam, does that work?"

The professor nodded and gave the captain a look of enthusiastic approval. Grace, or Gracie as the other girls called her piped up,

"I want to cook".

"We knew you would." Prudence smiled. Gracie was a wonderful cook.

Prudence, said,

"I'll do maintenance."

For her part, she thrilled at the idea of being involved with the inner workings of the ship and getting to be close to a hot engine. That was just the kind of thing girls back home would never have been allowed to do. Additionally, she suspected that it was Brent who had rescued her. She could still remember the feel of his hands on her body. Prudence blushed just thinking about it.

That left June to clean and tidy about the ship. That suited her fine. She would like being more self-directed and having the freedom to get to know everyone and everything.

"Who will I report to?" She asked.

"June, why don't you report to me." The captain replied.

That made a lot of sense, but still the professor wished he had thought of a way to make her report to him.

Business tended, the two men stopped asking questions for awhile and instead told stories about how they had gotten the expedition started; strange and wonderful things they had seen. The girls were soon at their ease, laughing at the men's foibles and wondering at their gumption and audacity. Full of good food and mildly intoxicated with wine, of which this was their first taste, they became less inhibited and words flowed more freely. Liam, feeling the shift, broached again

"So why were you running away on that boat?"

Prudence replied,

"We wanted to have young men!"

Hearing how that sounded, the girls all burst into a fit of giggles but then June explained,

"Well, we wanted the freedom to marry who we chose, not just do as we were told our whole lives."

Gracie, who was looking less shy by the minute spouted out "And we wanted adventure!"

"Well girls," the captain said with a wink, "I think you will have it all."

They headed back to their quarters and since their own clothing was all dry, they decided to change into their underthings for nightwear. Gracie tried to cover herself as she changed, like overly modest women will. She attempted to hold a dress around her waist while she pulled down the men's trousers.

"Goodness, Gracie, it's just us!" Prudence exclaimed.

"I don't know, Prudence, I feel like I am being watched all the time---like the men can see me."

She did feel a bit silly, after saying it and so decided to let it go with an "Ah, heck" and just pulled the men's shirt off over her head, her breasts tumbling out in the open, nipples instantly erect in the night air. She turned and reached for her thin cotton camisole, but could not find it. Seeing the smirk on Prudence's face, she immediately knew she had it. Gracie lunged for Prudence, but Prudence was too fast and moving quickly about the small space, the little camisole all wadded up in her hands. Gracie was barely thinking anymore about exposure, just that she needed to get that under-thing from Prudence. She hopped and climbed over berths and furniture, her breasts bouncing as she went, until she finally pounced on Prudence, bowling her over onto the ground, and resting the top from her hands. The whole thing ended with Gracie straddling Prudence in victory, the article aloft in her hands and June clapping with appreciation.

"Gracie, I do believe you are coming out of your shell."

Later, when Ralph saw the photos of Gracie running after Prudence topless, it was almost too much. He was instantly so hard and aroused, he could have just bumped into a piece of furniture and he would have cum. His rod was loaded and ready to go off. Soon after that, the captain let him know that Gracie would be under his direction to help him in the kitchen.

Brent likewise heard that Prudence would be joining him in maintenance. It would be very close quarters but he could not remember a time he did not like an attractive female with him in close quarters. According to the Captain, she was also really interested in learning about maintenance. Really…wow. He also could not remember the last time anyone had been remotely interested in what he did. Brent himself had also had the pleasure of seeing the recent images of play between Prudence and Gracie. "That Prudence is a feisty one, isn't she?" He had remarked admiringly.

With key crew members getting new employees to manage, the ship doctor and marine biologist Todd Brighten, felt a little left out. "I think they should all have full physicals like all new employees do." He informed the captain. These were arranged and the girls were given appointments.

June came to hers first. She was quite curious. In the colony, no one saw a doctor unless they were ill beyond cure by home remedy. She really did not know what to expect. The exam room, like everything on the submarine, was very tiny. Todd had to practically climb over June to get to the blood pressure cuff. He was looking very official, having donned his doctor's robe. After taking her blood pressure and temperature, he said, "I'll step out, while you get into this exam gown." Then, he waited for a moment in the hall. June looked skeptically at the typically small patient garb but nodded. Still, she was prepared to go with the program. It was all so interesting. When he returned, he was happy to slip his stethoscope down the front of the gown to listen to her heart. "Oh, that's cold!" June said, as he placed it right where her bosom began, having her take deep breaths.

"Have you had a pap smear?"

"What is that?" June wondered.

"All women of childbearing age should have them. Have you ever had intimate relations?" June blushed,

"You mean, down there, like married people do?"

"I will take that as a no. Don't worry. That just helps determine what size speculum it is best to use".

Todd selected the smallest one. Thankfully he had brought that size. Really, it was unlikely he would ever need such things in the course of his work on the sub, but he was a man who liked to be prepared for everything. Here he was being rewarded.

"Here, just lie back"

Todd helped her lie back and put the pillow under her head.

"Then raise your legs, like so."

He pulled out the stirrups at the bottom of the exam bench, and helped slip her feet in. Putting a little lube on the speculum, he slowly eased it into her narrow virginal opening, all the while taking in all the beauty of her privates. My goodness. She had such soft, tender, and fresh female flesh, sweetly clinging to itself and nestled into little curly tufts of hair. It was all so rosy, and for a moment, Todd was a little dazed. He just want to dive right in, and immerse himself in June from bottom to top.

"Is everything alright?" June asked anxiously.

"Oh, yes, it's fine. I mean more than fine. Everything looks great." He said earnestly. 'This was a view the other guys don't get to see', Todd thought with no small satisfaction. Todd felt mildly guilty knowing June did not really need an exam, as a virgin and all. He was rather aware that he had really done the exam purely for his own pleasure. He argued back in his head, 'It is perfectly fine to enjoy the perks of your work, isn't it? and what harm did it do?' Todd slowly slid the speculum back out.

"Have you had your yearly breast exam?"

June nodded 'no.' Goodness, was this what they did outside every time they went to see the doctor? June was feeling all flushed and vaguely excited like she did during the rescue. She was used to doing what men directed when they seemed to know what they were doing. That was how things were run back home. Thus, it was natural for June to be yielding and allow Todd, in his medic role, to slide his fingers gently pressing over every inch of her breasts. This "palpitating" of her flesh seemed to make her heart palpitate strangely in response.

"Are you alright?" Todd asked earnestly in concern, as he noted her quickening breath.

"Oh yes, I'm fine," June said, and blushed again.

Todd was very thorough with examining her breasts and really took his time.

"Okay, you are all set. Please let me know if you have any problems or concerns I can help you with. I want you to be comfortable, healthy, and happy on the ship"

June thanked him and after he stepped back out, slowly put on her things. She had never been seen or touched by a man like that before and she thought it had just not really felt like the routine medical procedure it was apparently supposed to be. June wondered what Todd might like to do if he was not trying to have it be all official and appropriate. June felt so intrigued, she thought she might come up with some excuse to visit Todd again and see if she could figure it out.

Meanwhile, Gracie had already reported for duty with Ralph. "I have an extra apron, let me help you tie it on." 'Goodness, Ralph looks handsome' Gracie thought. He was kind of a rugged man with a dimple in his chin and a twinkle in his eye and she was already quite taken with him. They set about doing some cook prep in the confines of the miniature kitchen. Ralph was immediately impressed. He could tell she knew her way around an onion. She cut with speed and efficiency, and demonstrated an evident gusto for the culinary arts. He was not used to having company in the kitchen, but found comfort and enjoyment in hers. That was even beyond the undercurrent of playful titillation he was getting at every turn as they squeezed past each other. The arousal factor was had been primed and enhanced by his having previously viewed pictures of her naked body. Particular images would reinsert themselves in his mind's eye at will.

"How did you get this good, Gracie?"

Gracie smiled at Ralph.

"I always adored being in the kitchen. They could not keep me out. I've been cooking since I was a little girl."

She was a hard worker, too. Ralph could not help but admire her industry and the economy in how she moved. One moment, Gracie caught Ralph just standing stalk still, watching her. Confused, she asked

"Did I do something wrong?"

"Oh no, Gracie. I'm beginning to think you could do no wrong.....but let's move on to making the hot fudge."

They dumped loads of chocolate into a huge pot on low heat and added cubes of butter. Once it was all melted, they stirred in cans of sweetened condensed milk.

"You probably have not dealt with such large quantities before, so let me show you how to stir."

Ralph came up behind Gracie, and put his hand on her arm, showing her the motion. The space being so tight, he had every excuse to be up very close to her, almost snuggled close, his breath on her cheek, his loins pressed against her buttocks. Gracie blushed and a chill went up her back. This was something she had never experienced before. It felt good. She let his arm guide her stirring the hot fudge as the delicious aroma began to permeate the small room.

Ralph took a spoon and scooped up a sample, surprising Gracie by dipping his finger in and putting the fudge coated digit to her lips. She slowly sucked the fudge off his finger, just as he had hoped she would. Then, he did it again. Looking in her eyes, Ralph saw that Gracie was very receptive to him. There was no resistance. Still, he did not want to mess that up. So, he planned to take his time and do things right. He smiled, as Gracie returned the favor and began to feed him hot fudge as he sucked it off her fingers. 'I think this is going to be an awfully nice partnership,' he thought.

Prudence had a similarly auspicious start to her maintenance job with Brent, if perhaps a little less eventful. He seemed absolutely interested in teaching her anything and everything she wanted to know about the workings of the submarine. He found her a quick study. She realized that this would be a nice skill to have in the outside world, where it seemed girls could indeed do stuff like this. There was all the hands on stuff that involved cleaning and oiling but then there was also a bunch of techy stuff. Since Prudence had never even seen a computer, there was a lot of catching up to do. Brent was extremely patient with her, putting his hand over hers to show her how to use the mouse for the computer.

He too, could not help but think of what Prudence looked like under her clothes as he worked with her, and at times he had to try to hide an erection but for Prudence's part, since she had never seen one before, she would not have thought to look for it. She did feel a certain intensity in Brent's quality of attention to her, which at times was almost unnerving. Generally; however, he turned out to be a nice companion and an excellent teacher. He demonstrated such patience and genuine interest in her learning, which greatly aided all ease. They were soon having a great time together doing all the various tasks as well as troubleshooting issues and problem solving.

Liam was not to be outdone in having a chance at the girls. He decided to beat Dick to the punch, by inviting June to come and do some early morning cleaning in his room. She had not even had a chance to report for duty to Dick, but had her first assignment by an important member of the crew. It seemed best to just say yes. June arrived as expected while Liam was still in bed. He pretended to be asleep, while she set about doing the list of things he had assigned. He watched through slitted eyes with relish as she got on her hands and knees and scrubbed the floors, her bottom up in the air and moving in rhythm. She was facing the opposite way so she could not see how he had by now popped a tent. When she stood up, he quickly rolled over onto his stomach, thereby pressing his hard-on into the bed.

"Ohhh," he inadvertently moaned.

"Oh, Professor, are you awake?"

"Yes. Thank you, my dear. I was just waking up. I see you are doing a fine job."

"Thank you, Professor. I was just finishing up. I'll be on my way so you can get ready." With that, she briskly left the room; leaving Liam to renew his schemes.

June had warned Prudence and Gracie about the nature of the medical exam they were to receive and so Prudence was fully prepared with some healthy anticipation when she went in to see Todd the medic. He was similarly excited to see her. Prudence came equipped with some genuine questions. If he was a medic, he must know everything about those parts, she thought. She might as well ask him anything. He was a professional after all. A ways into the exam, Todd had just put lube on his fingers and the speculum, when Prudence came out with,

"Excuse me, doctor, but what are the different parts down there and what are they for? I mean what is the little nub at the top about?"

Todd was glad she was lying down, and that he had a doctor's robe on so she could not see the mammoth erection that was already straining against his pants.

"You mean this little nub up here?" Todd ever so gently touched her clit and rubbed it just a little with lube

"Ooooo--that's the one." Prudence said.

"What is it, Prudence, did that hurt?"

"Oh no, doctor, just the opposite."

"Well that is good, because that is just what it's for. It is a clitoris and it is purely for feeling good."

"Are you serious?"

"Absolutely! So, it is in good healthy shape and doing its job well."

He then kindly pointed out the basics of her anatomy, similarly feeling her inner pussy lips.

"Would you like to see it all in a mirror?"

"We can really do that?"

By way of answer, he whipped out a nice size mirror and showed her, her pussy in detail and even with magnification. She was understandably fascinated.

"Prudence, you seem like a very straightforward girl, and what if I told you I would like to give you a pleasurable experience with your privates, that is not part of your exam?" Prudence knew what this might mean and she was immediately on her guard.

"Will it lose me my virginity?"

"Not at all, Prudence, not at all. It is just something to enjoy. Here, let's wipe some of this lube off."

He used water and a rag to gently clean her off and then patted her dry. Todd made sure the door was well locked.

"Lie back down and relax, Prudence, and feel free to let me know if you do or do not like something. The whole point of this is for it to feel good."

Prudence could not believe that her most private parts were so exposed as they had been today. She was amazed that she was now crossing the boundaries of an exam into the unknown. Todd was putting his face down there so she could feel his breath on her inner thighs. What in the world was he going to do? This was all so novel. She reassured herself that it had been quite nice so far, so it would hopefully continue that way. Prudence could not have stopped the proceedings. She would have died of curiosity if she had.

Todd began to kiss her pussy lips and clit, pressing his lips to the soft, succulent parts, and then slowly working up to begin licking and taking them into his lips and sliding around, over, under, and around some more with his lips and tongue. Prudence had never felt anything like it before and was surprised to find his activities taking her breath away and affecting her whole body. She found herself arching her back and moving into it. There was some kind of delicious hum deep in her belly and little tendrils of pleasure even reaching her nipples.

At times, it was so good, it was difficult to bear and she thought of saying something, and then it would move into some other realm of good that was more tolerable, and then another kind of pleasure would hit, like layers of an orchestral production; there were so many different flavors of beauty to be produced and heard in the symphony being played upon her inexperienced body. Then Todd got into a more steady rhythm, that circled and circled in more intensive succession and suddenly something was building. "What could it be?" Prudence haplessly thought as she felt herself losing control. Her toes were jutting, her pelvis thrusting, and then a cascade and swoosh of ecstasy spilled over in her from head to toe, with her first orgasm. Todd rose and looked at her sweetly, the taste of her tangy pussy cream still in his mouth.

"Did you like it?"

Prudence nodded

"Oh yes." She was awash in stunned gratitude. "Can I come back for more another time?"

"Certainly, Prudence, we can make appointments for this as if you are getting some special treatment; which I suppose you are."

Prudence did not tell the other girls about the special bonus features of her visit to the medic. She was honestly just not sure what they would think. Surely she had gone beyond some expectable boundary, even for them in their new life. There really was no one she felt comfortable consulting on the matter. She was left perplexed about it all and yet completely attached to this fun and thrilling new activity.

June had finally gone and reported to the captain for her duties.

"June, so nice to see you again. Here is a list of the tasks that we could use your assistance with. Please review it, and see if you have any questions."

June looked it over, and noticed that per her wish, she would basically have the run of the place and everything was readily doable to her. She would have optimal autonomy.

"Allow me to give you a more thorough tour of the ship so that you can find everything on the list and also where the cleaning supplies are."

He was very supportive and encouraging, June thought, as he took some real time to show her everything.

"Are you interested in learning about navigation, June?"

"Oh, Captain, that would be wonderful."

"Then come to my study tonight after dinner and all your duties are done."

Work kept her extremely busy. The time had arrived before she knew it. After cleaning up a bit, she went to the Captain's small office, which contained a tiny circle table and two chairs. There was one of the few porthole windows, so she could see the black water of night through it. He had a charming little lamp whose light reflected off the glass of the window. His quarters were tastefully decorated in modest blues and browns, with mostly things of a practical nature. There was already an array of books lying about; which he had evidently been pouring over.

"Welcome, June," he said as he ushered her in and onto a chair next to him.

"It has been so nice to have you sweet girls aboard our ship. I hope you have fully recovered from your ordeal."

He very naturally put his hand on her knee, in sympathy.

"Yes, Captain, thank you."

"And the work is not too hard, I hope?"

"Not at all, Captain, not at all."

"And no one has been bothering you. You know that men can get a little rowdy when they've been months without any female contact. I would not want you pressured into anything that you did not want."

As he spoke, Captain Dick seemed to be looking closely at her lips which were a deep pink and parted. June licked them. She reassured him,

"No, they have all been perfect gentlemen."

His eyes had dropped to her bosom, which had begun to heave slightly.

"Well, that's a relief. You please let me know if you have any problems, so I can fix them. That is generally my job around here."

Dick stood up and grabbed a book, came around behind her and bent down and put it on her lap, so they could look at it together.

"See, we are here...and this is how we begin to figure out how to get to there..."

She could feel the whisper of his stubble against her cheek as he talked, and smell the wood scent of tasteful cologne, combined with mint and wine on his breath. That feeling now becoming quite familiar, of a bodily excitement, began to flush through her again. The captain offered her a little wine, and she accepted. As she sipped from the glass, she felt the heat of that touch of alcohol combine with her preexisting flush. Perhaps that was why it seemed so natural and easy to let the Captain slip the clip out of her hair so it tumbled loose and then let him play with her soft curls, like at some point he did, and then rub her back.

"You must be sore from all that cleaning you've been doing." Captain Dick said, as he rubbed a bit lower. He had a nice touch and it felt really good. June relaxed into it. He knew better than to push his luck. Better to leave her wanting more than to have her experience herself having to set a limit, so he went no further than this. He let his sensual sensibilities and desire communicate itself through her flesh alone, without words or consummation. He stayed purposefully away from those specifically erogenous zones he longed to touch and ravish. June naturally leaned in to him, in a trusting cuddle, and seemed as if she were about to fall asleep. Being quite strong, he neatly picked her up, and maneuvered the short distance through the tight passages to her berth, and put her gently to bed. Looking sleepily up into his eyes, she smiled and said "Thank you, captain."

Gracie's exam with Todd was more brief and routine as she was eager to get back to the kitchen with Ralph. The two had grown quite close, and were flirting as fast and hot as they were cooking these days. They had become an amazing team and everyone on board said that the food had improved since they had begun working together. Ralph was beginning to sense that the way was open for him to take special liberties. Gracie seemed to genuinely enjoy him, want to please him, and be willing to try new things. That was a very nice combination of ingredients which he kept well in mind the next time they made fudge together. It was now their secret joke and tradition to feed each other fudge with their fingers by way of sampling.

"I just love fudge!" Gracie exclaimed happily. "I would love to just have it everywhere and be filled with it"

"Would you really?" Ralph replied with a smile. "I think that can be arranged. Let's get naked"

Gracie laughed, and said, "you first."

It seemed like a crazy good idea and best to go for it while the moment was hot. Looking into Gracie's eyes as he did it, he unbuttoned his shirt and slipped it off. Gracie saw his chest and the distinctly male hair pattern on it, his peck muscles sticking out with little manly nipples. She had never seen a bare-chested man up close and personal like this.

"Okay, your turn, Gracie".

Her fingers trembling, Gracie leaned back against the counter as she unbuttoned her blouse.

"You are so beautiful, Gracie" He said.

Even more beautiful than any picture can capture, Ralph thought, as he saw the fabric fall away and reveal the rise of her luscious breasts. He wanted to nuzzle into those breasts and gobble them up, and perhaps he still would, but this was supposed to be about fudge. Not wanting to frighten her, knowing how wholly inexperienced she was, Ralph paused and asked,

"So what do you think, Gracie, should I take more off?"

Gracie felt like a kid playing that game 'I'll show you mine, you show me yours' that she must have played at some point as a youngster. She was so nervous but she really did want to see.... so she nodded her head. Ralph undid his pants and pulled them down with his boxers, allowing a very large erect dick to pop loose. It jutted in front of him quite prominently. 'That is not child's play,' Gracie thought 'That is way beyond small speculum parameters.' Gracie suddenly remembered,

"But Ralph, I'm supposed to be a virgin 'til marriage. You had better put that away."

"Gracie, how about we find another place to put it that won't touch your virginity? There are some other things on the menu. Can I order for you?"

As he spoke, he tugged playfully but intently at her petticoat and petti-pants. "Okay, Ralph. If you promise."

Ralph smiled,

"I promise."

Clothing aside, He began to spoon and pour fudge over her already delicious tits, and rub the creamy chocolate on her nipples, putting more into her mouth, and then starting to taste it back by beginning to kiss her. Gracie had never kissed before and the feel of his lips and stubble and tongue in her mouth while his fleshy rod pressed against her naked tummy, was all quite intoxicating. She was soon quite breathless. Ralph then poured some down lower, into her pubes, dripping onto her pussy. He began to feel her there and heard her gasp and moan. He gently turned her around, still rubbing her clit ever so luxuriously as he dripped some fudge down her crack. The hot fudge oozed down between and while one hand continued yummy swirls in her pussy, with the fingers of his other hand, he began to smooth some of the warm silky buttery fluid into her asshole.

"Ralph!"

Gracie exclaimed, but the momentary objection was soon subsumed in the cumulative pleasure that was already consuming every rational thought. Ralph continued his expert fingering front and back, gradually sliding more than one finger up her butt, putting as much warm fudge in a possible.

"You said you wanted it everywhere"

Ralph whispered into her ear, nuzzling her while he continued. Then at some point, he poured some extra fudge on his cock and smoothly pulled her butt cheeks apart, and with a bit of pressure and force but easily, before Gracie even knew what had happened or had a chance to even tense up in any way, he had firmly pushed his dick all the way up her ass. "Oh!" gasped Gracie, but then something amazing started to happen and her pleasure had so intensified, she began to tremble and almost lose her footing as she felt ripples and contractions and jolts of intensely good feeling undulate out and then re-converge on her privates

"Ahhhhh"

Gracie cried out as she came for the very first time. Her ass, where Ralph was already plunging his dick in and out tightly with the viscous lube of hot fudge making him almost stick and slide simultaneously, began inadvertently to clench as she came, making the pressure on Ralph's dick even more intense. In no time at all, he was cumming also, spurting a high volume of hot sticky cum up her butt. He had not cum in a long time and so had apparently been saving it up for her. He hugged her from behind, as the last little waves of orgasm subsided, and kissed her cheek.

"Did you like that, Gracie?"

Gracie was a bit speechless, but smiled and nodded. Wow. That was amazing. Gracie wondered if people really do what Ralph just did or whether he might be the only one to do such a thing. But boy, had it felt peculiarly good...

What followed was the comical predicament of their having to make it through crowded quarters to the shower while covered with fudge and with the hope that no one would see. 'At least,' thought Ralph, 'I am in charge of the camera and can destroy the pictures.'

Prudence was having a lot of enjoyment these days as well. She had started attending daily appointments with Todd in the ship medical office. About the third day, though, the law of reciprocity was starting to call to her in the worst way until she said,

"Todd, thank you so much. You make me feel so good. I only wish I could return the favor and make you feel so good as well."

Lying on her back on the exam table in a state of post orgasmic bliss, she looked awfully relaxed and receptive. Todd needed no further encouragement.

"Ah, but you can, Prudence, without any risk to your maidenhood."

So saying, Todd opened his fly and got up on the exam table and audaciously straddled Prudence's face. He put the head of his dick to her lips "Open wide, babe." Prudence's eyes were already really wide but she opened her mouth as well, and Todd slid his ample member up the roof of her mouth and back into her throat.

"Just suck, nice and easy."

Prudence began to suck as Todd slowly slid his cock in and out of her mouth languidly. Her nostrils flared and she felt all that hard flesh filling up her mouth and pushing in and out. For the first time, she smelled the uniquely male smells in that region of a man's body, like male animal nectar, wafting its pheromones up her nose, announcing roundly to her body on a cellular level that this is exactly what she has been born to mate with. She naturally put her hands on his ass and gave herself over to sucking, as he began to build momentum, thrusting more earnestly into her throat, deeper, and harder, until "Uuhhn!" Todd came, jolting a large wad of splooge into her mouth, which since she was already mid-suck, just naturally slid down her throat, which she followed with a big swallow. 'what an interesting taste,' she thought.

"Thank you, that was really good," Todd said appreciatively.

After awhile, he mused,

"You know, I don't know if the name 'Prudence' really suits you. Is that really what you want to be called? The only way to turn it into a nickname is to call you Prude and I just don't think that fits."

Prudence laughed.

"Well, when I was a little girl, I wanted to be called 'Deedee' but my parents did not think it proper and would not allow it. I still like that name. It sounds so carefree and fun to me. I am free now so if you want to call me that, that would be nice" "Deedee," Todd tried it out.

"Yes, that is much sweeter--like you. After all, it is quite a burden to have to be too practical all the time."

Deedee, as she was now called, got back to work from her lunch break, and she had only eaten splooge for lunch, truth be told.

She found Brent looking at her surprisingly tenderly. They were supposed to have a lot of routine maintenance to do but he seemed unusually reluctant to work.

"Prudence? There's something I've been meaning to ask you."

"You can call me 'Deedee' for short."

"Really? That's cute. Okay. Deedee. Would you be my girlfriend? I am really crazy about you. You are so beautiful and so smart and I just love being around you and having you with me."

Deedee was a bit stunned and was acutely aware at that moment that she still had the after taste of another man's cum in her mouth.

"I'm so sorry, Brent. I really like you and all, but I have a little thing going with Todd at the moment."

Brent picked up on this perhaps being a more frivolous arrangement than the one he was proposing.

"What do you mean, at the moment?"

Deedee did not know what to say.

"We just have a thingy going on. I don't think it's anything serious but it means I'm not quite free to be your girl. At the moment, that is, because of the thingy."

He was getting awfully close, and what if he smelled the male smells of Todd on her breath?

"I've got to go---I forgot to eat lunch. I'll be back in an hour."

"But you just came from lunch!"

Brent felt confused and frustrated. Where had he gone wrong? He decided to pay a visit to Todd. Todd was still puttering around in the medical exam room when there was a knock on the door. He opened the door only to find himself lodged against the wall with Brent's hand on his chest.

"What did you do to her? What is this thingy?" Brent demanded to know. He was flushed red with emotion and even had tears in his eyes.

"Whoa, hold on, Brent, can you back up a little and explain things to me because I want to help you out, but I am lost."

Brent took a deep breath and relaxed his grip.

"It's about Prudence, I mean Deedee. I love that girl and she said she couldn't have me as her boyfriend because of a thingy with you."

"Damn, Brent. You've got it bad. I had no idea you were so sweet on her. I mean this is serious. Well the good news is that there's no problem. I've been having a good time with Deedee but I've got a girl back home and it is only proper to let Deedee go, knowing how you've got feelings for her like this. We don't need this to come between us. We've been friends a long time, heck we've been cooped up on a submarine together for months. You're like a brother to me, man. I tell you what, I will tell you just what you need to do to win her over and make things right."

Brent had progressively relaxed as Todd soothed and reassured him. He was not going to have to fight him after all. Brent saw Todd's sincerity, and they ended up in one of those gruff but satisfying bear hugs.

Then Brent asked the key question:
"What do I do?"

"You just gotta lick her pussy, Brent. That's all I've been doing and she just took quite a liking to it. I think if you do that for her, you will win her over in no time and she will be completely over me."

"But, I've never done that before." Brent said with a little trepidation.

"Here, I'll tell you all about it and give you the best lesson ever, and then if you add all your passion and love into it, it will be great. I mean it will be more than great. It'll be perfect. Don't worry so much!"

And so it was that Todd gave Brent a condensed mini lecture with diagrams on anatomy, schooling on fail safe methods, what to look for in terms of cues and signals, and other details to boost his confidence in regards to the art of cunnilingus.

Then like a bull, Brent was again raring to go, but this time on a very different mission. Brent found Deedee as she was just coming out of the shower in a towel. He scooped her up as she came through the door and took her right back into the bathroom and sat her on the counter and locked the door.

"Brent! My goodness, what are you doing?"

But Brent had already launched his love attack and was gently swirling her pussy flesh around her clit with his tongue as Todd had recommended. He gave full vent to his feeling, with an ardor and romantic flare, far surpassing anything the more clinical medic had aspired to. When Brent tasted Deedee, it seemed like he was savoring every drop, like he must have her fluid for vital sustenance, and when he kissed and licked her clit, she felt like he really was making love to every little inch of her pussy, like he was embedding secret love letters in her pussy flesh. Brent felt extreme satisfaction as the waves of orgasm began to wrack Deedee's body and she quivered and pulsed and thrusted in his arms. He planted one lingering kiss on her pussy, and then rose to look into her eyes.

"Okay," Deedee said, as she caught her breath from all that pleasure, "Okay, I'm over the thingy and freely yours."

In his single-minded purpose, Brent had forgotten about the cameras in the bathroom. 'My gosh,' Ralph thought, as he looked over those new images of Brent going down on Deedee, 'I didn't know you had it in you!' He decided not to mention those particular photos to Brent. However tempted by ego or exuberance, at times, the guys had not been bragging and in fact had been very discrete about any special activities with the girls. There was a certain wisdom born of experience that had taught them to avoid saying anything that might inspire jealousy or be provocative in the face of close quarters for months on end. They also had a heightened appreciation for forms of voluntary privacy since the more common ones were not readily available. The women had not talked either. Each one assumed the others to be more true to their former mores and that she must be the only one having an individualized sexual revolution.

June did not make it back to a Todd medical apt. She had never figured out what to ask or say. She was also being kept very busy by Professor Deeply who seemed to be devising every possible piece of busy work he could to keep her in close proximity, especially when he was in his pajamas in bed. June knew there was no way the floor needed to be scrubbed so much, and was beginning to suspect he was looking at her rear end, but she did not feel herself in position to complain, being newly hired and such a junior member of the staff.

For his part, Liam had not figured out a legitimate way to pursue what he wanted, and in a fit of restlessness one day, bounded out of bed, his erection projecting a bit ahead of the rest of his person and quite unrestrained by loose pajamas. He pounced on June, who immediately took flight, scurrying and scrambling around the tight space. Liam pursued closely behind; attempting to tickle and grope at her. There was no room or time to open the door and so June just kept trying to stay a step ahead; that is, until Liam grabbed her blouse. Instead of getting a greater grip on the girl, as he had hoped, he by mistake wrenched the fabric and burst its buttons. As the fabric gave way, exposing June's naked breasts, it also released her most suddenly. June stumbled and grabbed at a built in bookshelf to steady herself, in the course of which she knocked down a book. More importantly, when the book fell, a particular picture toppled out. Between June's ripped blouse and the picture, Liam was suddenly sober and stock-still. June peered down to see a photo of Liam Deeply, only he was standing beside a radiant young woman in an extravagant bridal gown.

June found her words now: "Professor Deeply, you ought to be ashamed of yourself. Not only were you being rude, but also you are married and would do better to stay faithful. At least *she* was willing to have you!"

The professor did already look quite ashamed, but his chagrin deepened still further when abruptly, the door opened and in crammed Captain Dick, who had heard the scuffle and feared the cause.

"What is the meaning of this?" Liam looked down at the ground. The captain waited for no explanation. Apparently, he did not need any.

"Liam Deeply, I expect you to stay 10 feet away from June at all times, unless she voluntarily gives you express permission otherwise. She is not required ever to enter your quarters and you are no longer at liberty to give her assignments. Any infraction and our mission will be instantly aborted and I will report you for sexual harassment."

With that, he escorted June out of the room with her arms across her chest, hands covering her nipples. The captain expressed earnest concern.

"I am so sorry about all that. Are you all right? Do you need anything? Let me get you a new shirt."

June was a bit shaken but also relieved. She had sensed something untenable pending with the professor and was very glad it was now over. Additionally, she had the happy result of being freed up to spend more time with the Captain, of whom she had grown very fond. Now she finally had time to clean his small quarters. She relished it as both an honor and opportunity to learn more about him. June wanted to know everything.

In the course of careful dusting, she spotted a particularly interesting object and picked it up for closer inspection. In beautiful cobalt blue glass, it was a sculpture of men, women, and children standing against a large wave. At the bottom, inscribed in gold were words commemorating Captain Dick Smart for his fearless and dedicated efforts to save the lives of so many during the Tsunami. Without his help, many more would have died. June was so absorbed in reading the inscription that she did not notice where she was placing her other hand for support, and it turned out to be a paper hanging off a ledge, rather than the ledge itself. There was no way to stop her fall, or the beautifully solid glass piece, from slipping right from her hands and bouncing against the wall like a missile projectile only to land with a sharp crack and shatter on the floor. June cried out and burst into tears. The pressure of the day had set her up but also, this was the kind of terrible error that back home would have meant a severe scolding and probably a beating. She had been taught that things like this were unforgivable and a sign of low character. Shame and painful regret welled up like a toxic brew, filling her with self-loathing and emotional pain. Surely the captain would hate her now and fire her, and in her distress, she was convinced she deserved it.

This is how June was sobbing, when Captain Smart, having heard the crash, entered the room. He took one look at June, and immediately went down to her on the floor, encircling her in his arms, impervious to the broken glass.

"I'm so, so, so, sorry," June got out with gulps. "I know how precious that award was. I didn't mean to break it."

"Of course you didn't" Captain Smart said Kindly. "And you are right. It was precious. But there are other things even more precious."

"Like what, Captain?"

"Like being able to actually save those people. It was not the award that was so special, but what inspired it, and that can never be broken. But there is also something else that is more precious."

June was getting lulled like a child by his comforting presence and this was now like a bedtime story she would not presume to know the end of.

"Like what?"

"Like you, June. You are far more precious than a statue. Please know I would never have you suffer like this for anything."

So saying, he stroked her hair, rocked her, and eventually started humming some sea shanty with her head held close to his heart. She could feel the vibrations of his rich voice in his chest as he started to sing the words. It was a song about mermaids and fishermen finding their way.

It was after what seemed a long comforting time, in which the comfort soaked in deep, working its transformation of ancient shame into new healing. It was like the night had passed and the sun was rising again, when June raised her head and turned with her lips parted to seek the Captain's. She had never kissed before but sought his mouth from pure instinct and growing affection. Soon the kiss was melting and evolving as kisses do, deep as it was sweet, and merged so one forgot whose tongue and lips were whose.

It was not long before they were lying on the Captain's bed together, having left the glass on the floor untouched, and were just kissing and cuddling with a kind of naked abandon. Their clothes were still on, but June felt Dick had seen her very soul in all its imperfection and claimed it. Her soul had been completely naked that day, and instead of rejecting her, he had loved her so that the love penetrated her very core. Captain Dick could have taken her any way he wished that day, but for himself, he did not want to take advantage nor did he have any particular agenda in that moment beyond communion with her and so they kissed, caressed, rubbed, and hugged in a most delicious way. After a long time, at some point, June noticed a wet spot down there. She did not recognize due to inexperience that that was where the Captain had quietly ejaculated into his clothes. They fell asleep snuggled up together that way.

Meanwhile, Ralph and Gracie had been at it every chance they got. During the break between meals, before they left the kitchen, he would rub up against her from behind, hold her tight, feel her breasts and struggle to eagerly open his fly and pull her clothing aside. Their bodies had so trained together by this time, and his cock was so hard and strong to maneuver, he did not even have to use his hands anymore but could just hit the right angle to slide it right in, thickly ramming it up her butt. He would expertly make her cum every time with his fingers in front and Gracie was beginning to feel she had done this her whole life, or rather that she should have. For some reason; however, the more they fucked in this way, the more they wanted more. It was as if all Gracie's dormant horniness was getting stirred up via that cock in her ass. As for Ralph, he needed little stimulation to get him started, and now he had it in Gracie. Her mere presence was like constant foreplay.

That is probably the reason he showed up in the middle of the night in Gracie's narrow berth in the female sleeping quarters. He just had to have her and so there he was, yanking up her nighty. She was sound asleep as his member rooted for the little furrowed knot between her butt cheeks. He hoped she was still lubed up from the last time since in his eagerness, he had forgotten to bring anything. Normally in the kitchen, there was always something: whipped cream, butter. Gladly, he did not need it, and with enough focused pressure, he pushed his very hard cock easily through any resistance as always into her naturally tight spot. Gracie gasped awake as she felt that intensely sensitive point in her body yet again being pried open and plugged full. She stifled a giggle, whispering, "Ralph!" you'll wake the other girls." Looking around, he said between thrusts, "Well, June is still not back in her own bed..." then pointing at Deedee sound asleep, "And you have no idea what that girl has been up to." but when she pressed him later, he would not give details. He did not want to tell her about that until he was ready to do it to her, and he was just having too much fun with her ass right then.

Also, he did not want to screw things up somehow between her and her friends. He did not really know how their relationship worked.

The next morning, Gracie had a mind to find out what Ralph had been talking about. "Deedee, it seems like you and Brent have gotten pretty close. Are you having trouble holding onto your virginity?" Deedee brushed her off, "Of course not, Gracie. What about you? You and Ralph really have a thing going...." Deedee laughed a little, because once again she was talking about 'thingies.'

"What's funny?"

"Oh nothing."

Deedee had indeed gotten more involved with Brent and their new thing together. The last time they had seen each other, She had gotten down on her knees and undone his pants, and to his surprise, taken his whole member into her mouth, caressing him with her lips, and sucking him good and long. She was amazed because it was so different from when she had let Todd stick his dick in her mouth-- that had been out of gratitude but it had not moved her personally beyond cooperation and curiosity.

With Brent; however, Deedee figured she must have succumbed to his passion, or the contagion of it had infected her good, because she found she was otherwise inexplicably hungry for his cock. She wanted to suck on it bad. She yearned for his pleasure as she would her own, and she wanted to taste him, smell him, and drink in his juices. She wanted him to enter her everywhere, but especially any place private and sensitive. He let her suck him into oblivion. A girl had never done that to him before, and the combination of wetness, smoothness, forceful pressure, and the look of Deedee's sweet face and rosy lips spread wide around his dick, as well as her earnest intensity about her endeavor---it all took him quite by storm. In no time at all, he was thrusting uncontrollably, spending himself in jolts of jism, which she gulped down like some divine elixir. Then she planted a trail of kisses up his tummy and chest, and hugged him tightly.

Deedee suspected Gracie of something because she was so curious and asking. Why would she be so interested, if she was not, you know, interested herself? As for Gracie, she did not believe Deedee and still wanted to know what she was up to. Neither had the gumption to ask June where she had been last night.

In the end, Deedee found Gracie out first. She had snuck up to the kitchen and crept in toward the end of a meal shift. Of course, Gracie and Ralph had long since become a bit careless and casual about security. No one ever came into the kitchen. It felt like their own private world in there at this point and besides, they had been joyfully butt-fucking in there so frequently and getting away with it for awhile now. For her to bend over and him to slip it in, was so natural to them that they hardly thought anything of it now.

Anyway, as things turned out, it was quite exotic for Deedee. She had eased the door open just a crack at just the right time, and sure enough, Ralph's sizable dick was out in the open, as he was just pulling up Gracie's skirts. She had stopped wearing panties for ease of entry. He reached in front to rub her clit in that juicy way he always did, which made her tilt and lean into him in the perfect way. He lodged his cock just right, and pushed it firmly in, which made Gracie "Umpf" a little and "Ooo." Deedee did not know much about it but she could tell he was not entering her in the way or place she thought a woman got entered. She had not known this was possible, or could be pleasurable. Hence, she had some interesting questions for Brent later on.

"Brent?"

"Yes, Deedee?"

"Can a man really stick his penis up a woman's bottom?"

Brent had to think about that one.

"I'm not sure, but I suppose so." and then with a little surprise, "Why, did you want that?" Deedee had gotten strangely creamy in her nether parts watching Gracie and Ralph, but she was not about to say such a thing, and so she nodded sharply, "no." Instead, she wanted to show Brent. The next day they snuck up to the kitchen together toward the end of meal prep and as odds were good, Ralph and Gracie were indeed at it again.

Brent's jaw dropped open as he saw Gracie practically swooning with orgasm as Ralph pumped her full of his sperm, right up her ass. While they watched, Deedee reached over and felt Brent in the groin and noted how hard he was. 'Well maybe they would have to try it, after all,' she thought, although she was a wee bit scared.

Gracie too was on a sleuthing expedition. Her curiosity previously unquenched, she had looked for when Deedee seemed to be going off with Brent somewhere. She soon discovered that Todd had been allowing Deedee and Brent to use the little medical exam room when he did not have appointments and she easily got a sense of their schedule for trysts. The medical exam room was a much trickier room than the kitchen to surreptitiously peek into, but Gracie had a plan. There was a cupboard with a slit, housing a garbage pail. Gracie removed the pail and was able to squeeze in and station herself there, prior to their arrival. When they came in, she had a perfect view of the exam table. Deedee and Brent had progressed to the simultaneous oral action of 69 by this time and so Gracie watched amazed as Brent got on top of Deedee upside down, and first sticking his hefty turgid dick into her waiting parted lips, where she sucked it neatly in like she was born for this, he then dove nose down into her pussy and began licking and sucking her like an affectionate animal.

The gusto and enthusiasm of their efforts made Gracie cream in her pussy but simultaneously feel a little embarrassed somehow at the same time, as she heard all the slurpy and smacky sounds, and began to smell the sex-loaded smell of saliva mixing with sexual juices. She already felt a little overwhelmed with feeling both aroused and repulsed at the same time, when the scent intensified as Brent shot his super load straight down Deedee's throat just as her body shook with its own cataclysmic climax. Gracie of course could not leave until they were completely done and out of there. She was like a captive of all this sex. She had to stay put and continue to smell the heady smell and watch as the post-orgasmic couple turned around head to head now, their parts sticking together all damp and sticky, their lips full of the other's juices, and they began to kiss and murmur sweet nothings to each other.

By the time they left, Gracie was incredibly horny and a little perplexed. Neither Gracie nor Deedee knew quite how to broach the subject of their recent intelligence. Now that she knew what she knew, it seemed to her that Deedee would be a good person to confide in about her recent adventures. She just did not know how to begin. Gracie thought she had a safe question for Deedee, to try to bridge the gap.

"Deedee, what do you think about all those rules we learned about carnal knowledge. Now that you have been outside for awhile, I guess I mean to say, what do think about sex?"

Deedee was impressed with the breath of this big question, especially coming from Gracie who was regularly taking it up the ass. 'Did that make her a sodomite?' Deedee suddenly wondered pensively. A moment later; however, she felt she had her answer.

"You know what I think, Gracie, I think if God just wanted us to make sure we reproduced and that was all, He would have made reproduction like the urge to go to the bathroom. It would be irresistible but otherwise unremarkable. There are other ways to make the necessary expedient. Instead, though, God gave us all these parts that can impart extreme pleasure. Perhaps it is to bring us together, solidify our bonds, but I also think it is simply another miraculous wonder and gift in life. In short, I don't think He would have made it all quite so much fun, if he did not expect us to enjoy it."

As for June, she had perhaps not come to quite so radical a conclusion about the nature of sex as a Divine gift, but she was beginning to have compelling desires to give greater expression to her rather profound feelings for Captain Dick Smart. Only recently, they had again been in his little study, and he had taken her hand like she was a princess and whirled her around unexpectedly. He had then gone down on one knee, and said, (as dashing as could be), "June, will you marry me?" June, like a gushing schoolgirl had not hesitated for a second "Yes, oh yes!" and Dick had promptly pulled her down to the floor where they had kissed sumptuously for perhaps an aeon or two. During these protracted kissing sessions, they had begun to shed more and more clothing over time. It was all too confining and they longed to be closer, to have fewer interceding barriers between them.

The next time after the proposal, when they were engaged in more ways than one, they had ended up with no clothing on at all, jointly shedding such outworn encumbrances like snakes wriggling toward new lives together. They were reborn fully naked. Dick's nice thick dick was hard and fleshy against June's skin. She had never seen a phallus in all its erect glory before and it sure looked large and imposing, like it had a mind of its own, and yet Dick seemed to be keeping it under wraps, tightly lodged in the warmth of June's soft tummy right under her belly button, only undulating and pressing at times as he was moved. Dick's hands were caressing and fondling June's breasts in delicious ways, and running all over her body with soothing strokes, like painting her and infusing her with even more love than she already felt. June was clinging to him. At one point, she pulled herself up a little and parted her legs.

"Take me, Dick, I'm ready. I'm yours."

Dick smiled into her eyes,

"Are you sure, dear?"

She nodded, wide eyed with a little trepidation but much open fullness of desire. The soft little flower of her virgin pussy flesh was already full of cream, but it would be a very tight squeeze. Dick shifted slightly, positioning the head of his cock at the tender opening of her pussy, He rubbed the head of his dick gently on her clit and pussy lips, sliding it up and down, spreading the cream around, in a way that June could feel everywhere in trills of pleasure pulsing through her body. Then he gently pulled her pussy lips apart with one hand, and with the other holding his rod at first, began to plunge his big cock pointedly into that juicy tight spot. He hit the initial barrier of her hymen, but with another push, June cried out as he burst right through.

All his restraint seemed to have been exhausted at this point because he was soon fucking her hard and in earnest, pent up desire propelling his motions at high speed. June held on for dear life as she felt herself stretched open by her beloved as he pounded her depths, making her tits jiggle, and a hard core Morris code that she belonged to him being knocked into every cell of her body. Dick began to kiss June deep tongue throaty kisses as he thumped her, taking her breath away, and then all of a sudden, he held her hips firmly in place as he jolted a series of tighter thrusts. He shot his wad, which was copious, dense, and gooey from the long wait for her, hard up her cunt. The sperm laden semen pooled stickily inside her, and later she would discover, it was soon already giving fruit in her womb.

More proposals were soon under way. Ralph and Gracie were in the kitchen and he was lodged firmly up her tight ass, where he of course liked to be as much as possible. It was just Ralph to think that was a good time to ask her. "Gracie," He whispered in her ear as he slowly pumped in and out, penetrating her deeply,

"I want you with me forever. Will you marry me?"

"Yes, Ralph, yes," she replied, in between moans.

As for Brent and Deedee, they had been in the engine room. Deedee already knew how Brent felt and what a steadfast reliable type he was. She also knew that after that first conversation they had had about being boyfriend and girlfriend, he might be more cautious this time about timing. To save him the worry, Deedee sidled up to him in the hot engine room and said,

"Brent Strong, if you ask me, I will say yes."

Brent lit up like a light bulb, scooped her up in his strong arms and said,

"Deedee, will you be my wife?" and Deedee said as promised, "Yes!"

With so many weddings to occur and a desire for minimal delay, Captain Dick Smart arranged for the three couples to head for dry land. He located a sweet tropical island where the local pastor was willing to do the ceremonial honors. Liam and Todd would kindly hold down the fort on the submarine. The couples would all supply each other's best men and bridesmaids.

The hot sand on their feet, warm sunshine, and view of the sky were stunning and marvelous sensations after being so long undersea. The couples said their vows and then feasted their fill on mangoes, barbecue, and coconut milk. They watched the sunset and then leisurely retired to palm huts on the beach. There, the respective couples lay together on sweet smelling straw mats, and surrounded by the sound of ocean waves beating on the sand, they engaged in rapturous consummation.

Harry the octopus was never sighted again.

THE HOUSE IN THE THICKET (3)****
(Or, Miranda's Cherry for a Faery King)

  Miranda had gone to stay with her uncle after a particularly unpleasant altercation with her parents. She really had not meant to come home so late. But, she was having so much fun. Sam had started to kiss her for the first time. It was such a luxurious kiss, and then he had begun to feel her up. She had never let a boy get that far before but he was so cute and urgent about it. His breath was all hot and kind of panting and for the first time she had felt herself feeling a lot the same way. He had also been really sweet to her all evening. "Miranda, you are just the prettiest girl I have ever seen." "Wow, how can you be so smart, too?"

  They had gone to the fair and managed to get dizzy on the Ferris wheel. The ride was pretty slow, but apparently they were not. Miranda had thought she might faint from a kind of breathless rapture, swinging and rotating under the stars with Sam. They were thinking no one could see them very well up there in their little Ferris wheel compartment and that surely everyone would be too busy themselves having fun to notice even if they could. He had leaned forward and drawing her close, began fervently to kiss her, pressing her lips with his, then sliding his tongue through them into the warm sensuousness of her mouth. Miranda was at once surprised and taken with it. She went with it with a kind of wonder. He tasted male, rough, and sweet all at once. Then, his hands started to slide up her skirt and find their way to her legs above her garter bands and also her breasts, nipples erect through her pointy bra.

  Miranda tried a half-hearted protest for good form, but he swept her quite off of the attempt with more and more of the same. The intensity heightened as the potency of his desire combined with the new awakening of her own. Her body inexorably responded to him. They were so engrossed at that point, that it was with some surprise they found themselves landed on the ground with light shining in their eyes. A little crowd of shocked onlookers was staring at them; watching the show. Sam and Miranda stayed stock still,

---

* (The House in the Thicket) Another fantasy Fairy Tale, some moments of non or dubious consent, tentacle sex, barely legal

helpless for a moment until the ride released them. Sam waited for that click, then flipped the lid off their gondola and scrambled out, pulling Miranda along with him as he ran.

They ran until they were both panting breathless and having left the fair, found themselves now quite alone in a field. The grass smelled fragrant of warm clover and they were surrounded by chirping crickets.

"They are calling for their mates,"

Sam said slyly as he picked Miranda up like a bride about to cross the threshold, and then kissed her some more as he carried her. He placed her down on a bed of clover and wildflowers, still pretty even with the petals all folded up into buds for the night. Flat on her back now and so alone with Sam, Miranda realized at once that things were getting serious. She could tell this was headed way beyond first base.

"Sam, I think we should probably be getting back. Don't you think it's kinda late?"

But she did not sound very convincing, even to herself. She just felt so good and was having so much fun. Why should fun ever end? There was a kind of rush going through her whole body. Her senses were vibrantly alive to the star studded sky, the soft grass beneath her, and Sam's passionate pursuing of her. She had never experienced this kind of a thrill. Sam lay beside her and with his head propped on one hand, began to slide the other one down the top of her dress, this time under the bra. Miranda could not believe she was allowing him to feel her there, but she was curious and could not pull herself away. It kind of tickled while at the same time feeling like the best massage ever. Sam resumed kissing her as he gently squeezed her breasts and nipples and then slid his hand down lower, under the bottom of her dress, again easing it up, caressing as he went.

When she suddenly felt his fingers on her panties, though, it was like a lightening bolt went through Miranda. She leaped up and began to run from him, acutely titillated and a little scared at the same time. Was she teasing him? Did she want him to chase her or was she trying to elude him? It could have been both or neither and it made no sense at all, but there she was running in the dark, giggling almost hysterically as she went. Sam's desire had reached a kind of fevered pitch at this point, and he was no longer thinking with his brain. It was the most natural thing in the world. He gave chase, running after the beautiful damsel. He had claimed her and she was his, like a lion marks a gazelle. Even with her lead, Sam caught up to her in no time, and tackled her easily from behind, knocking her down onto her stomach on the soft ground. He lay on top of her, uncontrollably thrusting as he unbuttoned and pulled his pants open, eagerly felt her breasts from the sides and underneath, in long strokes down her body. Then, he could hold off no longer and roughly pulled up her dress and yanked down her panties, Miranda murmured some unintelligible protestations, but he hardly even heard. He was so excited, all he could think was how he wanted to plunge his dick into her flesh. Just as he was pushing her legs apart and preparing to finally enter her from behind, he lost control and in a shuddering orgasm, came all over her instead, shooting spurts of creamy semen all over her buttocks and thighs.

A bit embarrassed, Sam came to his senses as if out of a dream, and took a handkerchief out of his pocket and began frantically trying to clean her up. Miranda did not wait for him to finish; however, being back to her more normal frame of mind herself. She sat up and flipped around.

"What did you do?" She asked Sam. Not waiting for an answer, Miranda hurriedly pulled up her panties and down her dress and smelled for the first time the scent of fresh semen. It seemed to be everywhere. Trying otherwise to straighten herself, she pulled grass from her hair and then tried to smooth the teased up mess with her fingers, but since she had gotten Sam's splooge all over her hands from pulling up her panties, she only managed to transfer the stickiness to her hair. Sam took one contrite look at her and said,

"You're right. We ought to be going. It's late."

It turned out that it was late; really late. This was a fact only made more evident when Miranda got home all disheveled from the fair and her embarrassed date did not even bother to walk her in the door, but stayed in the car outside just long enough to make sure she got in. Her parents were not pleased. Mom prodded her with:

"What about your reputation, Miranda?"

Whereas her father stayed more in the category of:

"Have you lost your mind?"

Miranda had run screaming to her bedroom and slammed the door.

"I'm 18 years old. I'm an adult. I shouldn't have to deal with this," she sobbed into her pillow.

When she calmed down, in the peaceful atmosphere of a welcome shower, she was able to remember how much her parents cared about her and think, well, that she had been acting a little risky that night. What if *it* had happened and she had gotten pregnant? She was not so naive as to assume Sam was prepared to marry her at this stage in their relationship. He had not even gotten her a friendship ring yet. 'Really, Miranda, you've got to get yourself together. You would think that you wanted him to do it, the way you behaved.' Well maybe she did, she thought.

She was now feeling somewhat torn and confused by this inner acknowledgement that she had wanted a man to enter her and that she was thereby very vulnerable to exactly her parents worst fears; that she would prematurely lose her virginity. She consequently made no argument, when they presented to her their plan for her salvation. They would send her way out to the woods in the middle of nowhere to live with her uncle Tony. This was the summer time and so there was no school to miss or worry about. The biggest risk out there would be boredom. Or, so she thought.

Miranda packed every thing she could think of to entertain herself with. Her books, violin, sewing machine and a host of unfinished projects, all made their way into her bulging luggage. 'Two months is a long time,' she sighed to herself. If she wrote to him constantly, would Sam stay true? Miranda, reflecting that his urgent need for her flesh may not have been wholly personal, could easily imagine him falling for another girl; especially if she were yielding and gave him what he had been trying so hard to get at the Fair. Just thinking about it made Miranda already angry in jealous anticipation. Off she went, then, in a bit of an apprehensive huff.

Uncle Tony's shack of a house was dark and shady, being in the middle of a thicket. He had tried to compensate for this by making his own oddly shaped windows everywhere, in a bid for sunshine. In fact, he had made a multitude of windows, and clearly not according to any regular specifications. Often, they presented with all manner of latches so that they could be easily opened; even strangely, from the outside. They were in various shapes and sizes, including round portholes like you see on ships and prism shaped triangles with divided lights.

"You've got to let the light in," her uncle had told Miranda generally. "Plus, that way you can see out, and they can see in."

"Who is 'they'?" Miranda had asked, but her uncle pretended he had not heard her. The more she thought about it in terms of actually living there, the more the situation seemed a bit odd. There were so many windows and no curtains, so there was no way to block the view of anyone peering in from the forest. This was true even in the bathroom. When Miranda asked Uncle Tony,

"But what about privacy?"

He had responded wryly,

"Who do you think will come by and see? We are in the middle of a thicket."

This was true, but completely at odds with his comment about *they*. At night, in the light of oil lamps, she could see nothing outside; only the glimmering reflections of the inside on the glass. Nonetheless, the environment seemed so cozy and safe; she decided to pay it no mind. She set about settling in, took her time getting undressed out of her underthings and into her nightgown. Miranda was quite pleased to find the bedding fluffy, warm, and comfortable and the room otherwise so suitable to her needs. Uncle had made a nice warm fire for her in her fireplace and the embers were dying down as she climbed into bed to go to sleep.

In her dreams, she heard the most amazing whispering. It was almost like a concert choir of whispering with so many voices in varied pitch. Additionally, it seemed to be all about her and there was drama to it, albeit in an archaic, somewhat stilted tone.

"Well she looks young and pretty enough but is she a virgin?"

"Of course she is. I can smell all her untapped newness."

"Yes. I smell that too. Her maidenhood is intact, but ripe for the plucking. She must have already awakened to wanting it…"

"Can you smell if she is fertile? Of course we must wait anyway for the full moon." There was a chuckle and then, "That is when *she* will be ready to be made full also."

When Miranda awoke, she chided herself. 'My girl, you have become obsessed with your own virginity. You have got to focus on something else or you are going to drive yourself nuts out here in this thicket.'

So saying, she got to work trying to keep herself busy. She helped her uncle by cooking and cleaning, set to work on her sewing, and practiced her violin daily. Uncle Tony was touched by her good will and impressed with her industry. He accordingly wrote complimentary letters to her folks back home. Miranda wrote also, making sure to write regularly to her parents, even if she had little to say. Mostly though, she wrote to Sam, to whom she always had a lot to say. She wrote things like: 'Did he know how much she missed him?' 'Was he keeping out of trouble?' Writing was crucial because Uncle Tony did not even have a telephone. It was a really rustic place.

Her period came a couple days after she arrived and she had to use fabric pinned to her garter belt, the old way. She could not help but be a bit fussy, having terrific cramps this time around. That night, the whispering dream came again but this time, it was even stranger.

"Her womb is readying itself. You need to take a sample of the blood to give to him. You know he will want it; the fresher, the better."

When she awoke in the morning, she felt disoriented and confused to find her nighttime pad missing and everything a mess. This happenstance so matched the communications in her dream, that she was instantly convinced it had been stolen. 'But who would steal a menstrual pad?' she asked herself in perplexed irritation, as she scrubbed the bloody sheets.

As the nights went on, Miranda began to feel like she was not actually getting much sleep at all. There was so much of a whisper fest going on all the time, and she wanted to know what they were saying. It seemed important. 'I guess we always want to know everything when it is about us,' she thought. Meanwhile, she began to develop dark circles under her eyes.

Miranda confided to her uncle that she had been having some very strange dreams, but did not give the details. Uncle Tony said he thought he could help. He grew interesting greens and herbs in a little garden, in the one patch of sunshine to be found in the thicket. He made her a strong tea of some of them for her to drink at bedtime. He said it would soothe her dreams and deepen her sleep. The concoction tasted like pure freshly mowed grass, licorice, and some slightly bitter, pungent taste that went up to the top of her nose and hung there.

That night was distinctly different. She could still hear all the whispering, but she was somehow in a much deeper sleep. She hardly moved all night, so heavy and relaxed was her body and she awoke thankfully feeling well rested. 'What had they been talking about last night?' She quizzed herself in the morning. 'Oh yah, anticipation of the full moon and wanting to know the texture of my secretions.' 'Texture of my secretions?!' Miranda, still thinking these dreams were a mere product of her overactive imagination, was just very glad no one else knew about all this.

Miranda had not gotten much exercise lately and had yet to go explore the grounds. She elected one day to go for a walk in the day time. She had not anticipated; however, how easy it would be to get lost. Soon, she had no idea which way to go. Walking here and there, she began to think she had only gone in circles. She became progressively more frantic and frightened as the shadows lengthened and the sunshine filtering into the forest became the dim gold of the magic hour.

Knowing how soon it would be getting dark, Miranda's eyes started to tear up in frustration and anxiety. She decided to stop and take some deep breaths. Perhaps she could think her way out of this, if she could just calm down. To that end, she leaned against a tree to rest for a moment.

At first, the tree seemed to be holding her in support. 'Oh that is so nice.' Miranda thought. Within a couple minutes of closing her eyes, taking some deep breaths, and just trying to clear her mind, she heard a little rustling noise. Looking down, she saw a multitude of vines had appeared. She had only a split second to register on them before they had started to rapidly wind their way around and around her legs, budding and sprouting more vines here and there. At first Miranda struggled to free herself, but it became obvious that these vines had the prehensile strength of steel. Nothing she could do, could even begin to budge a single sprout. The vines continued their climb, wrinkling and messing up her blouse and skirt. Her slip got snagged and pulled up just as she felt a garter band pop open. Noticing how sticky she felt, she realized that the plant was oozing a kind of sweet smelling sap. "This is a very busy plant!" Miranda exclaimed to herself. The vines were toppling over themselves and weighing down her underwear and even between her legs. Miranda thought for a moment how ridiculous it would be to be all the way out in the middle of nowhere for safe keeping, only to find herself deflowered by a plant. The plant; however, did not seem especially interested in her female parts. With all this constant motion of growing and winding and budding, Miranda soon found herself all bound up, spread eagled and held very tight.

Pale, tuber-like roots began appearing and also began to ease their way up. Within minutes, she felt one pressing against her buttocks, "Oh, no!" she shuddered, clenching her gluteus muscles hard. The tuber root stayed close but seemed to pause, which gave her some relief. Continuing to keep her ass clamped shut, she began to concentrate on the magnificent display unfolding right before her face. Marvelous blooms of enormous size were unfurling layers of delicate and extravagantly colored petals before her very eyes. They were like roses and tiger lilies and tulips of unearthly beauty, each larger and more ecstatically constructed than the first, vying with each other to be situated close, almost snuggling up to her cheeks.

"You have just undone yourself!" Miranda exclaimed, "I am just so impressed."

The fragrance was similarly amazing. It was so sweet, yet so fresh, and somehow stirring. Miranda felt touched and tenderized somehow, moved by the beauty of the flowers; so much so that she was well off her guard, (though still keeping her buttocks tight). The flowers began to tremble and produce at rapid speed a heavy load of pollen, like little hills of sparkling fluffy bright orange dust. She watched, fascinated as all of a sudden, it all went up in a puff right into Miranda's nose and with a spasmodic sneeze, "AaaaChoooo!", she gave way. Of course this resulted in a momentary involuntarily release of her buttocks that was just enough for "Umph!" as the sap covered tuber root jammed its way between her cheeks and into the tight squeeze of her butt. It slipped in so fast, there was hardly time for it to hurt, and now in quite a ways, the sap seemed to sooth her tissues. She could hardly admit it, even to herself but it began to even feel kind of good in an entirely rare kind of way. She got goose bumps and moaned a little. The plant seemed to be edging up very slowly now and she could just feel the titillating pressure in her bottom with a kind of tickling at the top.

It was in this strange state of affairs, tied up with her nose in a bunch of beautiful flowers, coated in sap and pollen and with a fat tuber lodged up her ass, that some particularly buoyant beings came floating across her field of vision. They were all a shimmer in gold, violet, pink, and green light. They flitted in front of her on gossamer wings. Somehow they knew her name.

"Hello, Miranda. Oh, I see you've met Irmaguard. Don't worry, she will not harm you. She can just be a little aggressive seeking the nutrients she needs and she loves human manure. The only thing is, she would probably really like to keep you as a pet for her own pleasant source."

Their voices sounded similar to the whisperings in her dreams.

"We *could* free you. Do you wish to go back to the window house?" They asked.

Miranda nodded as much as the vines would permit.

"Then you have only to promise you will let us and our friends visit you. We have some business to attend to in your regard."

They were so sparkly and pretty, and seemed kindly enough. Anyway, what other choice did she have? To be continually sodomized and kept by a plant? Miranda agreed and the shimmering bunch gave a special cue to Irmaguard. As if at once, the root slid easily out of her butt and the vines unwound. Released, she tumbled to the ground. The faeries, as they must surely be, proceeded to float on ahead, gently showing her the way back to the cabin.

Miranda arrived home sticky and stained with sap and pollen, to find a very worried uncle.

"You should really stay closer to home, Miranda. There's some strange things out in those woods."

"You are so right, Uncle. I just got attacked by a plant," said Miranda, unconsciously stroking her bottom, (a little sore now from the stretch of forced entry). Uncle Tony did not bat an eye and instead gave her a little tube of balm for her wounds.

"I wonder if he has any idea where I am going to put that." thought Miranda. After she drank the special green hot toddy he gave her, she went to her room. She pulled down her panties and unscrewed the tube, parting her butt cheeks with one hand, she gingerly began to smooth the warm paste onto her butt hole with the other. It actually felt really good and so her fingers lingered a bit longer than necessary. Miranda blushed as It crossed her mind: 'Goodness--I wonder if the faeries are watching me now?' She quickly changed into her nightwear and got to bed.

That night, true to their request, the faeries did come to visit. Miranda could barely move but was aware of all they did, and now she knew it was not at all a dream. There were just two of them. As they flew about the room, Miranda wondered how they could have gotten in, but then remembered the latches. In a flutter of wings, the faeries pulled back her covers, and unbuttoned her flannel nightgown so they could see the length of her body in the glow of their light. They looked carefully at every inch. Examining her breasts, they noted that her nipples were inverted. The faeries expertly manipulated the little dimples and teased her nipples out, then seemed reassured. Gently parting her legs, they bent down and looked closely at her pussy.

"Look, Margot, it's like a little flower bud."

They spread her tender pussy lips with their tiny fingers, toying at them and then pulling the soft flesh up to expose her clit. If she could have moved, Miranda would have squirmed a bit with pleasure and surprise. As it was she began lightly to tremble. All the sensations were so new. The faeries seemed to sense the affect they were having on her and in a flutter of excitement, the talkative one exclaimed:

"Oh this *is* fun, Margot. She's such a pretty one. He's going to be so happy."

The more reserved one who apparently must have been Margot, plunged her fingers deeper into the cleft of Miranda's pussy, eliciting a gasp, and pulled out a little sample of cream. She then snapped open a little velvet lined gold box, and wiped the virginal jelly onto the velvet, and snapped it shut. She smelled her fingers as if savoring them and smiled at the other faery.

"Yes, She will do quite nicely. He will be pleased."

They covered Miranda up and said in chorus, "Sleep well, dear one," as they floated away.

The next day, Miranda was almost beside herself with anticipation and nerves. What was going to happen to her? What were they going to do to her? The full moon was going to be here very soon. To add to her confusion, she seemed to feel tremors of strange sensations and yearnings in her privates at times. That was something that had never happened to her before. She had been in such a fog from all of it, that she realized she had even forgotten to write Sam. As it turned out, when she sat down to finally get to work, there waiting for her on her writing table was a letter from Sam. Eagerly, also knowing she could use the distraction, she tore open the envelope with a letter opener. This is what she saw:

Dear Miranda,

I'm sorry to tell you this way, but I'm calling things quit between us because I am not worthy of you and maybe I am not good at waiting. I may have gotten Suzy pregnant and, well, I'm with her now. It's not your fault. You were a nice girl. I am just not good at long distance. I hope you find the kind of guy who can be true to you. I hope there's no hard feelings between us and we can still be friends. Let me know when you're in town. Maybe we can even go to the fair again (ha, ha). Anyway, I hope there's no hard feelings.

Take Care of yourself out there. Don't do anything stupid.
--Sam

Miranda cried and sobbed. She had never been dumped before either. So many firsts! How dare he break up with her before she could break up with him. No hard feelings? What did he mean, look him up when she is in town? Indignation and hurt battled for her full attention. Uncle Tony overheard and came and tried to comfort her. She cried on his shoulder for a while. He listened sympathetically and gave no advice. He knew with breakups, you just have to feel the raw edges of the open wound before it can begin to heal.

Miranda was utterly exhausted and indeed, quite effectively distracted from her former anxieties. She was in fact so preoccupied, that she forgot to drink her now customary bedtime green brew, which which Uncle Tony now always left on the counter for her as part of their bedtime ritual. As soon as she hit the pillow, she fell promptly asleep but lightly and fitfully. Perhaps it was all the light streaming through the un-curtained windows. That night happened to be the full moon. Moonlight shone through the windows with the intensity of blue tinged strobe lights, making her skin glow. Hosts of exotic moths filled the room having entered through the unlatched windows as if the moon could be found inside the room.

Later in the night, Miranda woke to find hundreds of faeries crowded around her bed. Some were floating above her and others were clustered on her bed, using her arms like benches. Miranda was startled to see; however, that even more importantly, there was a special one among them. This one was massive; much larger than a man. He looked otherworldly. His expansive reddish and blue wings, had veins in them that seemed to connect to the veins in his bulging muscles. His eyes did not look at all human, but they were beautiful, like floating galaxies. She saw with a shock that his lower region was naked, and standing out like an impressive other limb, was a substantial member, bulging tumescent and shrouded in skin, of a greenish purple hue with drips of a greenish fluid oozing out the top. Miranda could smell the ripe smell of it, quite different from that human substance that had gotten in her hair. This was more pungent and striking, but also compelling and kind of addictive. She periodically sniffed for it to make sure she could still smell it. The scent seemed to be having some other affect on her, because her fear was melting away and she was instead starting to feel inviting and hospitable.

"She's awake and can move this time," the faeries noted. They still treated her like she was asleep; however; fussing over her and pulling down her covers, unbuttoning her nighty, and then proudly showing her to their king. He took it all in, but mostly stared deep into her eyes, which were now open wide in wonder. The faery king's eyes were like luminous cosmic spirals that seemed to pull her in deep, while meanwhile his member continued to ooze its fragrant nectar in anticipation of her. Miranda felt somewhat transfixed as if she were in an alternate universe where the meaning of life was about going with the faery program. Get with the program! It just seemed so exciting. It had all come to this. He was there for *her*. Really, what else could there be but Him filling her body, mind, and senses? Miranda felt like he could see her within and without. He nodded, and seemed to be sending her flavorful and heavy-laden messages. They dropped into her consciousness like a cornucopia of sensations and were very much in earnest, full of trees and light and growing things. She felt them like delectable tastes of a new life and how things could be. After giving her a moment to digest it all, he reached down and caressed her from her face, lips, down her tummy.

Suddenly a complete hush fell over the room as even the beating wings of the faeries stilled. The majestic creature spoke in penetrating words:

"Now is the time, Miranda. You must choose. Go back to your ordinary life or..." and he licked his lips;

"You must give yourself entirely to me, the king of the faeries. I await your word."

It was so momentous but she, Miranda was being asked her own mind and heart. In that moment; however, she found she already knew and cried out "Yes, yes!" The room burst into relieved giggles and then became quite serious again attuned with the mood of the king.

Pulling back the foreskin from his rod, he knelt his massive frame and to Miranda's surprise, brushed the hot swollen glands between her lips, dripping the greenish pre-cum into her mouth. Miranda gasped as she swallowed and it hit her like a drug, in itself giving her pleasure, and adding to the already building feelings inside her. He gestured to the faeries and they drew up Miranda's legs, spreading her wide open. He lay between her soft thighs, his large member just nestled against her vulva for now, his wings spread like a canopy over them. He smelled her with his tongue and then slid it between her lips, sensing every part of her.

"What is your name?" Miranda tried to ask with his tongue in her mouth. He understood even though the question was unintelligible. "Dragonfly," he answered, almost shyly.

"What are you going to do to me?" She thought she knew but she just had to ask.

"Impregnate you and make you my Faery Queen" ('Well it was nice to know it was so straightforward,' Miranda thought)

"But why me, why a human?"

"Every 100 years, we need a human maiden to enhance our bloodline and we have been watching you... Now shhh."

So saying, he began to rub against her with his member, gently, in just the best way for her inexperienced clit; as if she had even known what it was. All she knew was that it felt really good. He took his time, while the faeries flittered around in anticipatory excitement. A couple of faeries had gotten underneath her somehow, and she could hear one of them saying

"I know she likes it, Margot. Please let me do it."

"Oh, alright, Lila, you can do it."

Miranda felt a little tickle at her butt hole and then the now familiar feeling as a moist something was crammed through the little furrowed opening and up her ass, but now even more intense, it was being pushed in and out. She had no idea what Lila had put up her butt but it felt really good and the fullness, well lubricated pressure, and friction working her butt, combined with the arousing presence of Dragonfly and all he was doing served to propel Miranda into an acute state far beyond anything she had ever experienced. Miranda began to moan uncontrollably, kissing Dragonfly's chest, biting her lip. Dragonfly just kept, luxuriously rubbing on Miranda, tenderly stroking her breasts, kissing her, and periodically taking some pre-cum with his fingers, and slipping it between her lips which made her gasp every time as that smell and taste hit her full force, taking things up yet another notch and making her want to yield to him, give everything to him, in an almost desperate way. He rubbed and rubbed against her pussy and clit while the faeries fucked her in the tail until she could not hold back from whatever it was any longer and waves of sensation rocked through Miranda. She was jolting and contracting and feeling the most amazing electric pulses of pleasure through every cell in her body. The faeries withdrew from her bottom and smiled proudly at each other.

"I told you, she liked it," said Lila.

Dragonfly waited for the aftershocks to subside and knowing how very wet and relaxed Miranda was at this juncture, he placed the big head of his hefty cock, so thick, hard, and fleshy, at the best angle for optimal leverage, and with one slow thrust, pushed it forcibly into the tender flesh and tight virginal opening of her maidenhead, lodging it deeply all the way into her pussy. Miranda cried out a little, as she felt herself stretched and pulled apart but then there was a delicious feeling as he proceeded to slide more slowly in and out. Expertly, he took his time and Dragonfly actually turned colors with his own pleasure as he penetrated her so fully with each thrust. Gradually he built up momentum, harder and faster, until he was pounding her such that her tits were jiggling. She was breathless, ready to pass out, when suddenly, he squeezed her and holding her hips, thrust even harder in fast succession until she felt him convulse in waves. Her insides flooded with his warm pungent seed. He stayed inside her and even dozed off that way, his full weight on her body and his now flaccid member still large and snuggled up inside her. Shortly before daybreak, the faeries woke their king, and he reluctantly parted from Miranda. "We will come back for you, when you begin to show. Until then, act as if all is normal while we make the necessary arrangements." Miranda heard these words but soon fell back asleep.

When Miranda awoke, there could be no doubt as to the reality of what had transpired in the night. Right there in evidence on her inner thigh, she could see both the blood from her burst cherry and the green jism from Dragonfly, which she could not help but taste again to confirm that compelling spark. Whew, yah! That stuff was powerful. Also amazingly, she already had her first bout of morning sickness.

Uncle Tony seemed to know just what to do for her, without being asked, and gave her a nutritional concoction from his garden which made her feel much better. She made an effort to return to her normal routine but was understandably a little distracted. There was a pressure in her womb, and when she felt her tummy, it seemed to be hardening and filling up from the bottom. Her breasts were swollen and her nipples were now poking out, the areolas had deepened in color. It all seemed to be happening very quickly. She had thought she would have a few months to show, but she was bursting out of her clothes in no time at all. Additionally, every cell in her body seemed excited about what was happening. Her hair grew unusually fast and thick, her cheeks became very rosy. She was hungry all the time, especially for all the things in Uncle Tony's garden.

One day, she received a letter from her parents that they were so glad she had elected to marry such an important personage and that they understood, given the demands of travel and faraway location, that visiting would be difficult. They were just so relieved she had ended up well taken care of and respectable after all and they sent their blessings. They also understood, given the inconsistencies with post in that part of the world, that she might write far less frequently, when she was living in India. They did not mind as long as they knew all was well and they had been reassured by the royal navy that no news was good news. India? Miranda thought in wonder. My goodness, *"they"* were indeed making preparations.

Soon, there was no hiding her burgeoning bulge at all, and she became very excited about what was to come. Sure enough, the faeries came with their beautiful colored glow again to her in the night. Dragonfly first kissed her lips and then her belly with pleasure written all over his face and spinning in the galaxies of his eyes. Then, A veritable swarm of faeries bundled her up in her bedding and carted her off on their wings into the forest with Dragonfly leading the way.

****

Miranda found her new life much to her liking. Soon it became difficult to move around much due to what the faeries told her were a very healthy set of twins. Her ease was assured thanks to hosts of faeries assigned especially to support, assist, and attend her. Their home was an epic ancient tree, still alive but hollow on the inside. This earthy living space was warm inside and surprisingly homey, with multiple levels reachable via trained vine and root bridges, furniture padded with loads of very soft moss.

Dragonfly visited her frequently, fussing over her in his way. He made sure the faeries took proper care to massage balms into her nipples, the now taut skin of her belly, and even the soft tissues of her pussy opening, to ready her for birth. Miranda had little to do or worry about, her purpose being now fully to grow the babies inside of her. The faeries, not only fed, pampered, and massaged her, but they tried to teach and entertain her as well. They would even compete with each other to make her cum and so she had many more orgasms after that first. Dragonfly continued to have sex with Miranda also during this period, saying it would still be good for her and it was very good for him, but he was exceedingly gentle with her, reveling in her heavy swollen bosom and belly and taking her from the side or behind. At other times, he would have her suck him, teaching her to swallow every drop of his inebriating cum.

One morning, she felt what at first felt like strong menstrual cramps but then they intensified. The faeries, seeing the expression on her face, ran and got Dragonfly. They got Miranda to go on her hands and knees in front of him, and Dragonfly eased his substantial member between her lips, supporting her head with his hands. Amid contractions, the faeries flitted around and massaged her all over, including rubbing sensuous jelly into her pussy, Miranda had sensory confusion as on the one hand she was going through rhythmic painful contractions that felt like she was going to split right open and on the other, she had Dragonfly's member deep in her throat to suck on and pleasurable sensations from the administrations of the faeries. Just as the pain was starting to take over; however, Dragonfly thrust hard into her mouth and spurted a hefty wad of his green gooey cum down her throat. As soon as she had swallowed it down in full, the pain disappeared, leaving only some residual pressure.

Soon thereafter, she felt a strong urge to bear down and the faeries told her excitedly that they could see the baby crowning. They chanted at her to push. Still on her hands and knees, she began to push, and felt the first wonder slide in a ripple and on the second push, come all the way through. The faeries caught the baby tenderly as Miranda was already pushing the second one out. Dragonfly eased Miranda onto his lap so he was kind of spooning her sitting, with her knees up. The faeries put the cooing babies to her breasts, where they hungrily rooted for her nipples. She felt a clamping down, hard contraction as the afterbirth slid out. Soon, the faeries cut the umbilical chords and neatly picked the after births up and carried them away, reporting all was well.

Miranda could feel the powerful pull of suction on her nipples even in her womb as she gazed on the delightful sight of these sweet cherubs suckling. Their eyes were closed and they were covered with the sweet newborn cream babies are born coated with. "Oh, my! These little miracles came out of me?" She took it all in; The little hands twirling and eyelashes fluttering, the feel of their breath on her skin, their sweet smell, like only newborns smell. Cradling them to her, she saw also that they had their very own faery wings, all tucked up against them and still a bit moist.

Miranda asked about Uncle Tony, to whom she had come to feel close. She wanted him to see the babies. To her relief, Dragonfly said that would be no problem at all. It turned out that Uncle Tony had a friendship with the faeries. They had helped each other over the years and they were always welcome at each other's homes. That was why his windows had latches on the outside as well. That is also how he had come to know so much herbal lore. Uncle Tony had suspected the faeries had their eyes on Miranda, but he saw no harm in it and so had kept his speculations to himself.

Uncle Tony brought her, her violin when he came to visit and was delighted to see the brand new babies and that Miranda was well and happy in her new life. The babies grew quickly and were beautifully taken care of with the same quality of attention bestowed upon Miranda. As soon as they were weaned, and she was again ripe with fertility, Dragonfly got her promptly pregnant again, keeping her quite full with twins for many moons to come in the magic of the thicket.

BRAD & THE SEXTIFICENT GENIE (2)***

(or Strange Cure for a Dead Bedroom)
Dedicated to any horny married folk who have ever found themselves in a sex-less situation...

Back when they were just dating, it had been awesome. They would have sex so frequently. Anytime they were together, she would be willing and able. She went along with his ideas. She was unattached to missionary, so they could do it with her on top or doggy style. Goodness! She would even give him a blowjob here and there. Although she never had an orgasm, she always reassured him it did not matter and seemed to thoroughly enjoy their activities.

After they had been married a little over a year; however, everything changed. The pliable, playful, and sexually receptive "Samantha," from their dating days, became the more serious, somber, and subdued "Samantha" he found himself married to. First, it was "Later, honey, I'm tired" and of course, "I have a headache." But then, as the days turned into weeks, Brad finally confronted her. She responded with, "You're too big and you make me sore," "It's kind of gross," and "I really don't have time for that any more." She did not think the subject worthy of discussion and acted as if he were a sex crazed animal if he dared bring it up.

To make matters worse, he could not even relieve some tension on his own. The problem was that he had not figured out how to get himself off solo without some kind of visual stimulus to supplement his hands. Meanwhile, his wife hated porn. She was perpetually on the warpath against his sources. After enduring her tantrums and demands for him to quit what she termed his "Sex addiction," he had developed an erection deflating level of anxiety about the whole thing. He remembered well what happened the last time he tried to look at some eye candy or jack off. He had ended up feeling like a worried wet noodle. There had been absolutely no way to just relax and enjoy it.

---

* (Brad) contains a strange kind of no-harm dubious consent due to a spell. There is also a fleeting moment of his being molested by a genie

By the time his wife took off to go visit her ailing mother for a few weeks, he guessed he had neither had sex nor an orgasm by other means in over a month. He felt the dearth of sex affecting his spirits and self-esteem to such an extent that this very fit 45 year old was starting to feel like a crotchety old man.

Brad had tried to cope by upping his exercise routine and throwing himself into cleaning the attic. It was so hot up there. He usually ended up shirtless in just his boxers and jean shorts. He had gotten an awful lot done. Now he was down to deep attic where the crannies and lower layers of junk had not seen the light in decades at least.

Brad leaned over while he wiped off some sweat and squinted into an unlit corner. He spied what seemed like an antique bottle. It was bulbous and deep green. There were raised areas of writing on the glass, but it was so well coated in dust, it was impossible to read. Brad naturally took his hand, already dirty anyway, and rubbed some of the dust off the inscription. Suddenly, a big swoosh almost made him drop the bottle, and there was a whirlwind of this heady dust which lit the whole place up with blue green light. Brad began to get his bearings, only to witness the sight of a smallish voluptuous personage in sparkly satin green garb. She had a remarkable cleavage, held well aloft by her gown over an extreme hourglass figure. As he looked admiringly over all this bounty on someone so miniature, he noticed that she was not actually quite on the ground, but a little above it.

"I guess you're wondering what in daisies I am. Well you must be behind on your storybook reading then. I... am a genie!"

This latter, she said with a little flourish and spin. Brad was speechless and he only noticed much later that his mouth had been hanging open for some time.

"You have freed me from the bottle! Thank heavens. It was a dreadful long time this time and I have people to visit and shopping to do. Yes, as I was saying, you have freed me from the bottle and you get to make a wish." Brad gasped. Was this real?

"On second thought, Mister, you do not even have to tell me your wishes because I can see exactly what you need written all over your face. Tut, tut, tut---married and this neglected!"

With that, she flounced down towards his jean shorts and promptly unbuttoned his fly. Within seconds, she had his dick out and it was already standing at attention like a soldier. In a flurry of green sparkle and only a matter of seconds, she had her big soft lipped smile wrapped around his cock and had gently slid his tumescent rod deep into the warm recesses of her mouth. It felt so warm, silky, and smooth as she massaged him sweetly with her tongue and began to suck in an undulating pressure kind of way.

Brad was not normally a blowjob kind of guy but he had never experienced one like this before. It felt so good; he could not even manage to think anything at all except how good it felt. He had no chance to wonder about who in the world this really was and how she had come to truly be doing what she was doing when he had just been up in the attic. It was like she was not only sucking on his member, but on all the pent up sexual frustration and desire that was focused there and the pressure of underlying need was serving only to intensify his pleasure. Her warmth, motion, and soft silken slickness combined with just the right kind of friction. The sensations began to mount and all at once, he was convulsing and gushing, his frame wracked by one of the most delicious orgasms he had had in a very long time.

The genie gave his dick a parting gentle suck, sweetly kissing it on the head, and then licked her lips.

"A little better now, my dear?"

Brad nodded, 'yes.' He actually felt a lot better. All his senses felt crisp, his mind clear. He actually felt like the man he aspired to be: serene, calm, confident, and capable. 'Wow!' He thought, 'well, I guess it's over. That must have used up my wish.'

"No, my dear," she said, reading his mind. "That was only the first one. You still have two more."

Brad wondered if he would get any active say in this one or whether she would read his mind again.

"It's pretty obvious that you need more sex, Brad."

Yep, she had read his mind.

"It is beyond a genie's power to meddle in domestic issues between a married couple, but I can grant a couple of wishes which together will provide all the supplementation you need to weather recent turbulence until conditions can be resolved. And by the way, dear, one way or another it will be resolved. Everything gets either better or worse. Nothing and I mean nothing stays the same!"

It was difficult for Brad to concentrate during this little talk. It may have been the fact that the Genie had a strange wiggling luminescent green and purple worm that was crawling over her shoulders and then from one hand to the next as she spoke. It may have been that he was also just so excited. What was she going to do?

She was still down there near his dick. Suddenly, she embraced him with his cock against her face and her arms wrapped around him. Brad could feel her breath on his dick as she began to whisper to it. Then he felt his butt cheeks being pulled a little apart.

'Wait! Not the butt! Even genies had no business anywhere near there as far as he was concerned....' But right as he was about to muster a verbal objection, he felt a slithering sliding up his ass. 'Was that the worm?' He wondered in dismay. It seemed a bit late to say anything now. He could still feel it too. It was wiggling and gliding up there, and, oh my goodness that was just not right. Uh oh, what was worse is that it felt embarrassingly good, so good he had sprouted a brand new erection.

Change duly noted, the genie happily repeated her first performance and sucked his dick promptly into her mouth, holding it with her lush red lips. He again had an amazing climax and shot his wad, which she enthusiastically swallowed down.

Afterward, she said,

"Well, Brad (I believe that's your name, isn't it?) you have given me a nice little genie meal. Let me tell you a touch about your wishes and if you have questions later, you can seek me out.

Wish #1 is that any female, besides your wife, that you wish to have, will willingly spread herself for you. Just to clarify, if you have interest, she will be available to you.

Wish #2 is that nothing you do with these women as a result will be or have any kind of consequence whatsoever."

Brad was trying to understand,

"Wait, no STDs or pregnancy?"

"Nope."

"My wife won't find out and be hurt?"

"Nope."

"They won't want more later or expect something I can't give or treat me differently?"

"Nope, nope, and nope!"

"Wow..."

And with that, she was gone. Brad was left to ponder what had gone up his butt, how he had come to see a Genie in the first place, and what these newfound wishes would portend if they were really real at all. Perhaps he had just had a heat spell up in the attic. He *was* very sweaty and felt a little faint. He could not believe nothing had happened; however, because he felt so tremendously relieved and free of the strain of acute horniness he had labored under for so long. It was just gone. He felt so vibrantly and vitally male and almost carefree, like a burden was off his back. Or maybe 'balls' would be more accurate. A burden off his balls! Brad chuckled to himself.

Brad went downstairs and took a very refreshing shower. He looked out the bathroom window as he was putting on deodorant and shaving, and saw that the next door college coed was home on break. She was in her parent's backyard in little tiny shorts and a similarly small tank top, with no bra and her nipples showing through the thin cotton. Her hair was in fetching disarray as she did some gardening to help out her folks. Brad could almost smell the sweet smell of her. He thought she shined with her own light in the sunlight, surrounded by flowers.

Brad knew he was interested and decided to test out these special new powers he supposedly had. He went downstairs to the sliding glass doors that opened into his backyard that adjoined the neighbors. As he saw her again, he remembered her name. It was Trissa. He went toward the fence. Trissa, as soon as she caught sight of him, came bounding towards him. "Oh, Mr. Dodger, how are you?" They were such normal words, but less usual was what she was doing as she said them. Trissa had slipped her tank top over her head so her tits were jiggling freely, while just as quickly trying to undo and wriggle out of her shorts.

"Good, thank you, Trissa, but I'm sorry, I have to go..." And Brad ran away. He dashed for the sliding glass doors, slid them open, got inside and locked them.

'What in the heck am I doing? Am I really going to be unfaithful to my wife?' Brad had never really thought much about it. He had been faithful throughout his marriage but had never had sex flung at him like this on a silver platter. Of course he had no religious or strong moral compass that told him yes this and no that. He did not live by a lot of rules. If you had asked him why it was best not to cheat, he would have cited the consequences. It would hurt feelings, cause long term scars, and be a source of shame and complication for years to come. Those would have been the kinds of reasons that in his mind contraindicated affairs. But what if what the genie said were true? What if there really were no consequences? Clearly wish # 1 was true. Trissa had never even remotely noticed him before. Wouldn't it follow then that wish #2, of there being no consequences, would be also be true?

By this point in his thinking, Brad now started heartily to regret having run from Trissa. She must think him a jerk and here he had dashed his chances for that delightful girl! He could feel that his balls were sad about it too. Brad was beating himself up and having a bit of a field day at it, when he decided to go and take a peek and see if she was still in the garden. He could not see her at first through the glass, so he opened the sliding glass doors and walked out back again and saw that she was sunbathing nude on her tummy on a towel. Brad fell into full gear admiring the roundness of her ass, and the feminine lines of her back so nicely tapering in at the waist. As if she felt his interest on her back, she turned onto her side and beckoned him with her finger. Brad climbed the fence again and came to her. He sat down; having trouble looking at anything except her breasts. They were so pretty with their nipples and everything.

"Oh hi, Mr. Dodger. Nice to see you."

She acted like this was the first time that day. 'Oh right,' thought Brad. 'No consequences means I can't really use up my chances either. It will always be like the first time...' She looked so beautifully fresh and kissable. Because he now knew he could do just that, he leaned over to kiss her. In the luxurious process, he somehow ended up rolling right on top of her. They kissed a long, deep succulent kiss, all the while he was running his fingers through her hair, over her breasts and feeling her soft nipples, touching her side and stomach, reaching down a little further to ever so gently caress her pussy until he felt it get creamily wet under his care.

He unzipped his fly and pulled off his own shorts with a sudden burst of urgency. He felt how immensely hard he was. My goodness, this rod could move trucks! Trissa was panting and trembling slightly, already very aroused and ready for him, when he parted her pussy lips, and began to shove his big cock through the warm squeeze of her entrance. He pushed firmly to get all the way in. The cream helped, but she was still pretty tight. Once fully in, he lingered a moment, enjoying the snug fit. He had the feeling of being fully at home; having a precious part of himself happily embedded in yummy female flesh, after so long. It was so cozy, warm, and moist in the best way.

He began slowly easing all the way out. They could both feel all that juicy friction, as he went out and then doubly so as he slid all the way back in. He thumped her a little on the inside upon arrival, to let her know he had arrived. Also because it just felt so good entering her like that and getting to the bottom of her.

Trissa arched and moved her hips up to meet him, starting to moan. Then she even started to make louder sounds of different degrees of ecstasy in response to the nuances of his thrusts. He began to worry as she waxed louder, but then he remembered 'Wait…no consequences!' and so let her scream all she wanted as he thumped and thrusted harder and harder. "Oh, oh, OOOOOOOH!" "Uhuhuhnnn"

She began to gasp on the in breaths, and he could feel how somehow, as it sometimes does, the penetration had even deepened and gotten still juicier, the pressure had shifted and become still more intense. He gripped her ass as he began to have his own chills running up his spine and feel his testes clench up close, and it was like his cock was still harder and felt so good along every inch of it. He felt like his cock was actually his body, or maybe it was that his whole body felt like his cock, like it was getting thoroughly and luxuriously massaged by Trissa's pussy. Soon, he was moaning uncontrollably himself. Intensity of pleasure miraculously cranked up yet another notch and he started thrusting in little jolts. Electric pleasure pulses consolidated and propelled him inexorably to climax until in one major gush, he had shot a hot load of cum into Trissa's pussy.

"Damn that was good. Thank you, Trissa."

Trissa smiled,

"Totally, Mr. Dodger."

Remembering that it would always be like the first time, he did not bother to tell Trissa to call him "Brad." He just smiled back at her, gave her a parting kiss, and got his clothes back on. Trissa rolled back over to finish her sunbathing, and he saw a little of his cum dribbling out onto the towel, but even as it landed, it seemed to evaporate in the sunlight. Trissa waved a little "toodle-do" to him and he hopped back over the fence and went back into his own house.

Brad decided to go run some errands. He had not been to the Trader Phil's grocery store in awhile and wanted to pick up some good grub for his bachelor-like days 'till the wife came home. Pizza would be nice. Of course, they had a host of other gourmet delectables at that store that required little cooking and would be nice for entertaining in a pinch, in case he wanted to have some friends over. While he was in the pasta aisle, Brad was amazed to find himself getting another erection. Wasn't this like the third in one day? Had that worm up his ass included an elixir of youth as well or was he just super excited about his new lifestyle? Or perhaps, he thought, it was the sight of this really cute chick he had just seen. She was around his age, and had a really hot walk. It was the walk of a woman who digs her own body and knows her own pussy. He could tell she would be really good in bed.

Bed is not; however, where they ended up. Trader Phil's has single occupancy bathrooms that are generally very clean and kind of homey and before he knew it, they were already in there together. "What's your name?" She asked with a certain charm, as she reached behind and unhooked her bra. "Brad. It's Brad." He said a little breathless. "What's yours?" "Amelia." He wanted to grab this woman and take her from behind and as if she read his mind, she just turned right around and gracefully began to pull down her pants and panties and bend over. He could see her plump, juicy vulva poking out from the back. He could even see a little of her pussy juice already on the lips. She braced herself on the handicapped grab bar as he took hold of her hips and without further adieu, began to slowly thrust his dick between those fat lips and way up deep into her privates, aiming for the center of her being. Oh it felt good. Could he ever get tired of this? He alternately felt her ass and tits as he thrust in and out.

    At some point, he pulled her up to standing so he was still inside her but hugging her tight from behind. He felt her whole body so close against him, nuzzled in her ear, and clasped her tits, as he continued to pump in and out. Having a feeling this strong, dancer like girl was probably pretty flexible, he helped her bend one of her legs to bring it across his chest and slowly turn her to face him, so her whole body was pivoting around and still staying well penetrated by his dick. He then picked her neatly up and propped her on the edge of the sink and began to pound her more in earnest. He must have been hitting her g-spot really good in this position because she began to show signs of heightened pleasure, and with a little touching of her clit, came very suddenly, her pelvis moving of its own accord and paroxysms of delight shuddering through her. That was it for Brad--he came as if for the first time that day, with a wave of ecstasy so intense, he gripped her hard as he almost reeled with it. "oomph!" he moaned, as he ejaculated another heavy load of steamy semen, this time, into the body of Amelia.

    Brad kissed and thanked Amelia, and went out of the bathroom first, peering out a little nervously first to see if there was a line. Thankfully, there wasn't and so he went back to shopping. Brad was a little distracted contemplating his recent good fortune but did manage to get through the rest of the items on his list. When he later saw Amelia in the check out line, it was like they had never met.... 'It is a little odd,' he thought 'But well worth it.....'

    Brad slept especially good that night; better than he had in years. He felt like a lot of accumulated psychic gunk had gotten cleared out. It was like all that ejaculating had gotten out years worth of impurities that had been clogging the system. He awoke energized and refreshed before his alarm went off for work. He hopped out of bed and got ready, ate a high protein breakfast full of high density nutrition (he thought he better with all this sperm output he was doing these days) and headed off to work.

Brad worked as an information technology man for the government. He strolled briskly in to his tiny office on the corner of the building and dropped his belongings. With a smile, it suddenly dawned on Brad that work was going to be a bit more exciting now. 'No consequences,' he thought. 'I mean I can have anyone that interests me at work and it is not sexual harassment and it is like pleasure guaranteed.' Of course, Brad thought the "no consequences" rule likely did not apply to behavior outside of sexual activity. He assumed that if he was a jerk, like attempting to brag or treat a girl differently as a result of his carnal knowledge, he would certainly get what he had coming to him; especially since everyone would deny that anything had happened and there would be no proof to the contrary. 'Well, thank goodness I am not a jerk,' Brad thought. He realized; however, that what would be fun and likely covered, would be getting to do all those sexual activities his wife would have never consented to. Of course, he did not have that long a list...but there were a couple things.

Brad continued his musings as he walked into the hallway to go get a cup of coffee. "Good morning, Brad." Two members of the clerical staff, Pamela and Jenny were in the staff room. They were of the type that still liked to dress up on a regular basis. Their style was of the ultra feminine and kittenish variety, and so they were in high heals with long painted nails. Pamela was wearing a shortish floral dress with stockings and Jenny had a little suit dress with brass buttons and a touch of lace and cleavage. "Good morning, Pamela, Jenny" He nodded admiringly to each, poured himself a cup, and then headed back to his office with his coffee.

He was not all together surprised when there was a knock on his door. "Hello, Brad, may we come in?" There they were. Brad had never been with two women before and was not sure where to begin, but there was only ease as Pamela came over to him and touched his hair and snuggled up to him on the side and then Jenny took the other. He did have a small love seat in his office for cat naps and so they turned as a unit and sat down together. As Pamela sat down, her dress rode up, and Brad could see that she had thigh high stockings on so the skin of her legs was showing at the top. Pamela began pulling at his pants while Jenny ran fingers up his chest and shirt, and began kissing him.

He was so involved in what turned out to be very luscious kissing, he was surprised with a jolt to find his cock out in the air one moment and then warmly enveloped in the next. Pamela had taken it in her mouth and was kissing and sucking it and then sliding it out more and kissing it again. She seemed to have other designs on it; however, because she climbed onto his lap as if she were just going to sit but instead, holding her G-string aside, had sat right down on his cock in the perfect way so it went straight into her pussy in one fell swoop. She moved up and down as Jenny continued to caress and kiss him, and he felt her tits. Pamela then leaned forward so her hands were on the ground in front of the low lying love seat. She let his very wet cock come almost all the way out, and then scooted back so his dick went full on back in again. Brad felt like following Pamela to the carpet and so was on her from behind as she went onto her hands and knees. Jenny's soft body felt so sweet along his back as she in turn took to spooning him from behind.

There was something he had always wanted to try and it seemed no harm to attempt it now, so while his cock was so hard and already so wet and well lubed from Pamela's pussy, he reached to spread her butt cheeks a little with one hand. Jenny kindly took this over for him, and put both hands on Pamela's ass to pull her cheeks apart for him. Pamela held very still, fully submitting, while Brad attempted to poke the head of his dick into her tight butt hole. 'My goodness,' Brad thought, as he felt like he was trying to burrow with his dick 'It is as if there is actually no hole there at all!' As he explored, however, he found that what worked was to very gently but persistently press to make way. Then, there was a melting and softening, and slowly a little opening. If he held firm, he could maintain his gain. In this way, with patience, he gradually entered fully into her ass, until he was in up to the hilt. There were spirals of warm tight tender squeeze encircling his dick now and he was completely absorbed in the feeling.

He reached around and fondled Pamela's breasts as he slowly thrust in and out, then felt down lower to her pussy, and felt her tremble as he found the soft nub of her clit and began to caress it. It did not take long for Brad to get swept up as the building intensity took hold and begin pumping harder and harder until he cried out in a cascade of bliss. He squirted and gushed a mini fountain of jism up

Pamela's ass. Then they all lay together for a moment as a triple sandwich. Moments later, they all got themselves put back together and sure enough got back to work as if nothing had happened. Brad did not have to fret about how the interlude had gone because it would not be remembered any way.

In fact, that was one of the things that was starting to bother him a little. Now, when he had so many special adventures, he strangely had no one to share them with. He had never known how much a shared and cumulative memory of experience had meant to him. Here he had such grand access to an unlimited number of one night stands, even with the same people, but he was beginning to miss having a story in common. There was no joining of personal knowledge that grows over time. In short, in the midst of all this intimate access, he was starting to feel the lack of a different kind of intimacy.

Brad went and delivered a paper to the clerical office, and handed it to Pamela, and found himself thinking 'I was just penetrating your ass a few minutes ago. Can't you still feel my cock rammed up you? Don't you know me that way now? Let's at least laugh about it secretly...' but he was back to being a courteously but distantly regarded co-worker; attractive, possibly, but not someone Pamela would date. She did not date anyone from work or who was married. Brad consequently had two counts against him. As if he would date any way. What was he thinking?

Brad's wife, Samantha, came home that evening.

"It was an exhausting trip. You know how mother is and she is not getting less cranky with being ill. So what were you up to while I was gone? Did you miss me?"

"I tried to get a lot of work done in the attic, dear." That at least was true.

They slid back into their normal routine together; only something was different. Brad did not make any moves on Samantha. Why bother just to get rebuffed now that his sexual needs were so well and easily tended with no risk to his ego or feelings? Samantha would have expected after a long trip away that he would be after her for sex.

Not that she was in the mood. She was never much in the mood. But, she was especially not in the mood now; just home from a grueling trip. She could hardly entertain the idea of having to get naked ('I'm sure I've gained weight with all the stress!') and spread her legs for her husband to stick his wiener up her privates. Well, it was about as appealing to her as allowing someone to stick a baby sausage up her nose. She just had no feeling for the thing and it seemed like such an unnecessary hassle.

Nonetheless, it took awhile but it did start to eat at her that *he* did not seem interested. 'Didn't he still think she was attractive?' 'What if he never wanted her and they never had sex again? Wasn't that a bad sign for a marriage?' 'Why didn't he want any suddenly after all this time. Was he getting it elsewhere?' And yet, she could find no evidence of an affair either otherwise in his behavior or by any other sign. To make things even more complex for Samantha, Brad was looking particularly attractive. He had a sparkle in his eyes and a bounce to his step like he had in the early days of their relationship. He looked like the world was his oyster and he could have whatever he wanted in life. He looked so capable, confident, and well...yes, he looked sexy. That was the best word for it--*sexy*, Samantha realized with a start.

Samantha complained to her friends about the situation. They were out together at a cafe. Tabitha was like,

"Well what did you expect? You told me yourself, you said 'no' more often than 'yes'."

Sandra was even more blunt,

"Your pussy is going to close up."

"What!" exclaimed Samantha.

"Yah, they call it adhesions. Basically, with no action, your body seals up your pocket. At our age, it is use it or loose it, girls."

Tabitha nodded in agreement and then rubbed it on thicker,

"I don't think many marriages ultimately survive no sex. It is like a primal glue that helps couples stick together. Otherwise you end up like roommates. Only, I ask you, if you were choosing a room mate, would you ever have chosen your husband?"

"No. I would have chosen one of you."

"Well, let me know when you need to move in."

Samantha was a bit shaken after her outing with her friends and for the first time in ages, stuck her finger up her pussy just to make sure everything down there was still okay. It actually felt really good. For the first time in over a decade, she played with herself a little and felt some sensations of pleasure rear their sleepy heads and make her tingle and tickle in long ignored private places.

Samantha called her friend Tabitha,

"But what should I do? Should I dress up in lingerie for him and seduce him?"

She knew Tabitha would tell her the truth.

"Sure, Sam, that would be great. But, only if you are prepared to start really having sex and stop rejecting him. Men can be like elephants and have a long memory. You may need to just assume you have used up all your no's to sex for the duration and follow the advice from the Koran that you will do it even if he asks you to on a camel."

"I think the First Testament had something like that too."

"I bet it did. They did not make all those rules about where folks could not do it, only to set folks up to also not get it in all the "'right' places."

"That's an interesting theory, Tabitha."

Samantha was not sure she was prepared to say a big or frequent "yes." She was long in the habit of not putting time or energy into something that seemed so messy and indulgent, maybe even somehow degrading. She had never come to terms with the whole idea of being penetrated or being valued for her sexual parts. Perhaps, this was because she had never valued them or fully owned them herself. When she looked into it on the web; however, the views mirrored that of her friends. Even low libido folk get health and relationship benefits from being sexually active.

Samantha began to have trouble sleeping. All the focus on the sex she was not having, also meant she was thinking a lot about sex. This led to her having all kinds of interesting intrusive thoughts on the subject. She began to notice men's bulges, and when she had an answering twinge in her pussy, or when she got wet at a thought. With no engagement from Brad, she could not blame him. She began to have to reckon with her own sexual nature; even that she had one. Soon, she found herself to be uncomfortably the horny one, and with no good outlet. This in turn gave her a certain feeling of vulnerability. She began to experience a newfound compassion arising for Brad, that he had had such unmet needs; that he had been so yearning and unrequited in his affections for so long.

Her friend Tabitha, in a well meaning way, had encouraged Samantha to delve into all this more deeply to find the hidden gift and heal herself. Tabitha suspected it would all be solved with time and effort. "Girl, you just need to get in touch with your own sexuality." She had even bought her a gift certificate for "Good Vibrations" a sex positive store with an ample supply of women oriented high quality sex toys and paraphernalia. At first it was difficult for Samantha to even look at the website without blushing or feeling like she was doing something illicit and must be in the wrong place. But, she was never one to waste a gift certificate. When her very modest but highly rated magic wand vibrator arrived in the mail in nondescript packaging, she opened it in private. She was touched to see the slogan on the invoice:

"Pleasure is your birthright!"

Was it indeed? That night, she used the thing, had a great orgasm like she had not had in many years, if ever, and finally got some sleep.

Still, something was definitely missing. It was like an itch she could not scratch, a puzzle with all the pieces except the one piece that would make the picture make sense. 'How can you just develop a need?' She wondered. 'It was never an issue before.' In truth, it always was. It had just formerly been in Brad's lap and now it was squarely (or roundly) in hers. A genie had indirectly put it there.

Brad barely noticed Samantha's crisis as he tried not to focus on her too much beyond what seemed pleasant and constructive. They had not been intimate friends in so long, it was easy to play the part in terms of the mundane day-to-day to see that bills were paid, groceries bought, meals cooked. He went to work and kept on keeping on. Whenever he wanted sex, there was an attractive woman nearby ready to gratify him in any way he desired.

That was why he was extremely surprised to come home from work one day to find Samantha in a little camisole top and nothing else. She seemed to be waiting to see if he would open his arms, which of course he did. She rushed to him, hugged him, and whispered in his ear,

"Please, Brad. I'm sorry. I love you. I need you. You can have me. You can have me any time you want."

The truth was, he wanted her now. He wanted her with the same ancient passion from when they had first come together. The need for her had only gone deep underground to protect itself. He picked her up, and placed her on the sofa. He kissed her deeply, slowly and very sweetly, both their cheeks moist now with tears. He touched her breasts gently, felt her tummy, held her in his arms, stroking her back through the silky camisole. He reached down and undid his fly, letting himself out, and gently parted her legs, feeling her pussy and how it was already wet for him. He could not remember when it had been like this. He put his finger into that moisture, and stroked the cream up her pussy lips and to the hood of her clit, coating all her soft tissues with her own juices, and heard her moan and sigh. He looked at her pretty face, so open to him. Her lips were parted, expectant. With his member in one hand, he stroked the head on her pussy before beginning to plunge it into her tender opening, through the flower of her pussy lips clinging to him, stretching open a sweet little hole that had not been entered in a very long time. "Ooohh," She cried out. It was not just her pussy being stretched. There was a new part in Samantha's consciousness being opened. Looking into Samantha's eyes, it felt like the first time for both of them. Samantha knew now, as she returned Brad's gaze fully and as he penetrated her so deeply, that she needed this. This was part of what she was created for and he was marking her into a new era. "This," they both thought, "Changes everything...."

*****

So what of Brad's special powers and the Genie? Brad got to keep them but with his needs being now more fully met by his wife, he naturally did not signal interest in others as much and also learned that he could easily decline genie-generated opportunities. Brad kept the special green bottle carefully packed away in a treasure chest in the attic as a comfort but did not again call on the Genie for many many years, or until he was in his 90's. Ah, but that is another story.

232

Made in the USA
Coppell, TX
17 January 2026

65813218R10128